MIKHAIL: A ROYAL DRAGON ROMANCE

Brothers of Ash and Fire Book Two

LAUREN SMITH

1

Sleeping on a dragon's hoard with greedy, dragonish thoughts in his heart, he had become a dragon himself.
—C. S. Lewis, *The Voyage of the Dawn Treader*

England, September 1559

The halls of Hampton Court Palace were quiet so close to midnight. There was no sound of laughter from the courtiers, not even the hushed murmurs of gentlemen luring young maids into dark corners for secret kisses. The tapestries lining the stone walls rippled faintly with the breeze that slipped in through half-open windows.

Mikhail Barinov adjusted his black-and-gold doublet as he walked in light, quiet steps toward a bedchamber door.

He ignored the prickle of unease he felt at the silence cloaking him as he saw a guard ahead. The man was posted outside the door, his hand resting on the pommel of a lethal-looking blade that Mikhail wasn't the least bit afraid of. He was, after all, not human. He was a dragon shifter, and there had been no human yet who had been able to do him harm.

"Halt!" the guard growled. Mikhail was close enough to see the whites of the other man's eyes in the flickering light of the wall sconces.

He raised his hands, showing his empty palms before he offered a slight courtly bow. "My name is Mikhail Barinov. Her Majesty requested my presence." When the guard relaxed, Mikhail removed a small bit of parchment from his doublet and handed it to the man.

The guard scowled as he stared at it. The odds that the man could even read were small, not that he would admit such a thing. But the royal seal of Queen Elizabeth was visible on the paper, and the guard recognized it at once.

"Wait here." The guard rapped his knuckles on the door behind him, then disappeared into the queen's antechamber. A minute later he reappeared, flustered as he pushed the heavy oak door wide, allowing Mikhail to enter. He nodded at the guard and stepped into the antechamber.

A soft voice rose from a chair beside the fire. "Well now. I was worried you might not come." The woman leaned forward in her chair, allowing the light and shadows of the flames to dance upon her. Her long reddish-gold hair was unbound and cascaded over her shoulders in ripples of fire.

Mikhail swallowed hard as a bolt of desire shot through him. Queen Elizabeth, the newly anointed monarch, wasn't a traditional beauty with delicate elfin features. Rather, there was a cunning curve to her lips and a keen sharpness to her eyes that warned a man she was not some wilting flower, but his equal. He found it enticing.

"I would not refuse my queen's summons," Mikhail said as he drew closer.

"Am I your queen?" As she rose from her chair, he caught a glimpse of her gown. The orange satin overskirt and the gold-and-silver embroidered bodice presented a tempting view of her breasts. She wore no ruffles or stiff collars tonight. She looked more like the twenty-five-year-old woman who had unexpectedly learned she was to become queen and not the cold, disciplined monarch she'd become.

"You are my queen," Mikhail replied, his voice turning husky. The scent of her body lulled his inner dragon into a heady state of submission. He wanted to growl in pleasure and rub himself against her. She was untouched, the virgin queen, and Mikhail knew that was a dangerous thing to be around. A dragon was drawn to maidens; the purity in them was as bewitching as an uncut gemstone. Their scent alone could drive a dragon to sweet madness.

"Don't you owe your loyalty to Ivan? Would you forsake your czar for me?" Elizabeth trailed pale, delicate fingers along the back of her chair, a coy smile upon her lips.

"The Barinov family makes alliances with whomever we please," Mikhail said. He had traveled a long way from his home in Russia to come to the English court to arrange for a treaty with a clan of English dragons. He'd thought he would long for Russia, but in fact he did not miss his homeland. Not when he looked at this woman. England felt right, and Elizabeth... She was his true mate. And when a dragon mated, it was forever.

True mates were sacred, and from the moment he'd seen her, he'd known she was his, the one destiny had chosen for him. There could be no other. He'd answered her summons tonight to tell her what he really was and to offer her his heart and his love. He didn't care that mating her would shorten his life immeasurably—all that mattered was being with her.

"Yes. The Barinov family. I was so curious when you arrived at court. The rumors I've heard are quite...interesting." She came closer and reached up to brush the backs of her fingers along his jaw. His skin burned at her touch. Once they kissed, he would begin to bond with her so strongly that it could never be undone. His heart and hers would unite in a way that human lovers could only ever dream about.

"Rumors?" he replied, his eyes half-closed as he

enjoyed her sensual caress. It made his inner dragon growl in pleasure.

"Hmmm... They say that you have an ink marking on your back, a mighty dragon that is said to move." Her brown eyes were cool and impassive, but a hint of a smile lingered on her lips.

That sense of unease returned as he studied Elizabeth closely. His tattoo was the beast's outward form when he was human. How could she know about that?

"I..." He hesitated. Was now the time to confess it all?

She ran a fingertip down his doublet to his stomach, making his abs quiver and tense. "Show me, Mikhail. Please your queen." He'd wanted to show his true self to her for so long, and now the time had come. His heart raced as he accepted this moment, this unveiling of the truth to his intended mate.

He'd spent the last year in England and the last six months falling in love with England's virgin queen. At last, he could show her his world. Watching her through hooded eyes, he slowly removed his doublet by unlacing the leather points and letting it drop. Then he removed his shirt, allowing Elizabeth to gaze at his bare chest.

Her dark eyes surveyed him with a possessive gleam, one he recognized all too well. He'd come to England on a quest for a fortune in jewels to take home to Russia. The moment he had collected his hoard, he had clutched a handful of gemstones in his hand for hours, watching them glint and sparkle in the firelight. Elizabeth was looking at him now as though he were a precious gem that she held in the palm of her hand.

"How beautiful you are." She traced a pattern over his biceps before walking around to examine his back. The silk of her skirts whispered on the rug.

The gasp she gave made his muscles twitch. He could feel his dragon stirring inside, longing to reveal itself.

"It moves?" The queen's voice was full of awe, and he smiled at the touch of her fingers between his shoulder blades. "Is it sorcery?" she asked in a whisper, almost too quiet for him to hear.

"Sorcery? No, it is something far more ancient, Your Majesty." Now was the time to tell her what he really was and to ask her to join him in mating. His heart skittered in his chest, and he nearly laughed. He, an almost two-thousand-year-old dragon, was nervous.

"Ancient?" She circled back around to face him, and her cheeks glowed with a soft pink blush. Her breasts rose and fell as she breathed faster.

"Yes. I wish to tell you what I am." He should not be nervous or frightened, but he was. What if she wanted him no longer? After six months of secret courting, he could not stand the thought of being turned away, not when his dragon had decided she was worthy.

"What you are..." she said, echoing the words. "My dear Lord Barinov, I believe we should have a drink before we discuss our dark secrets."

"A drink?" He watched in surprise as she brought him a goblet and took one of her own.

"'Tis mulled wine. I believe you'll find it to your liking." She took a sip of her glass, and he did the same. The wine was sweet with spices on his tongue, and he drank it greedily.

"You are what we believed long dead, aren't you?" she asked.

Mikhail took another sip of his wine, wondering how best to answer.

"I am a dragon shifter. I have lived upon this earth for more than a thousand years. I am fully man and fully beast." He waited, watching, hoping his announcement wouldn't scare her.

"Two beings in one divine body." She ran her hand over his chest again, a coy smile on her lips. "The church would have you burned at the stake if they were to discover such heresy."

Mikhail chuckled. "I do not fear fire. It obeys my will." He raised his hand and gestured to the nearest candle on the table closest to them. The flame winked out.

Elizabeth's eyes widened. "Such power…"

"And it is yours, my queen. As my mate, you would have the might of my people at your disposal." He held his breath, afraid to tell her that if she became his mate, it would shorten his lifespan, but love was worth that sort of sacrifice.

"Is it true that dragons hoard jewels?" she asked

suddenly, mischief glinting her eyes. She was breathing faster now, her breasts pressing tight against her corset, making it hard for him to think of anything but taking her to bed. He gulped down more wine, pleased that he was winning her over so easily.

"We love all things that glint and shine, my queen, whether they be jewels or the eyes of a pretty woman." He grinned at her, feeling strangely relaxed and confident.

She set her glass down and then moved to the doorway that led to her bedchamber. She leaned against the doorjamb, her gown trailing behind her, the tiny diamonds on her sleeves winking at him.

"I believe we should find a much more suitable place to whisper our secrets." And then she vanished into the darkness. Mikhail followed, his steps a tad heavy and his preternatural senses strangely dulled. By the time he reached the large canopy bed, he felt weak as a drakeling. Was this how it felt to claim one's mate? To feel weak and giddy like a mortal man drunk on mead?

"Mikhail," Elizabeth crooned as he collapsed onto the bed, his brain fuzzy. She leaned over him, and the distant candles from the table by the bed lit her face.

"My queen," he sighed dreamily, wishing that he could lift his arms to pull her down for a kiss. Why was he so tired? It wasn't like him.

"Where is your hoard of jewels, my love? I wish for you to share them with me."

"Secret. Safe," he said, his voice slurring a little.

She feathered her lips over his, and he thought he would die with how wonderful it felt. "Tell me." She tortured him with her sweetness. He wished he had the strength to grab her and pull her beneath him, but he could barely move.

"Mikhail, you must tell me where the jewels are, the ones you are taking from the Belishaw family."

He frowned, confused. "You know about the Belishaws?"

"I am the queen. It is my duty to know everything," she said, her voice slightly cold. "Those jewels were my father's, not theirs, yet they took them from him." She dug her nails into his shoulders. "Now, *tell me!*" Her tone was more insistent, and he found he couldn't fight anymore.

A distant flash of alarm came too late for him because he was already speaking.

"Buried beneath a copse of trees close to St. Giles in the Fields." His head fell back onto the feather tick mattress, and he could feel his body betraying him with its weakness.

"Thank you, my love. You have given me a dragon's hoard of jewels. Sleep now, because when you wake, I fear you shall be most angry with me." Elizabeth pressed her lips to his, and the kiss was bittersweet.

"But...you are my true mate. Why would you betray me?"

"True mate?" she scoffed. "As if I could ever love one such as you."

His eyes widened.

"You think I didn't know what you *really* are?" she said with a laugh. "I have been warned about you, *love*. My royal advisor discovered what you were long ago. My father left warnings about your kind when he was still alive. You would seduce me, plunder my country's riches, and leave me with nothing as you returned to your home. You *disgust* me."

"No, I would... never..."

"The drink I gave you? A gift, from my most trusted magician. He spent months learning all he could about your kind. Formidable as you are, you are not invulnerable. He learned of a way to make you weak, make you human, just like the rest of us."

"Human?" He choked on the word, fear tearing through him.

"Yes, human. You even say the word with contempt. Do not worry, it will not last forever, but long enough for me to take back what is rightfully mine and to punish you properly."

"No. Please. You cannot...betray me, I am... I am your mate."

"Mate? I would never mate with an unholy beast whose existence is built upon lies and greed." She slid off the bed, leaving him lying helpless in the shadows of her bedchamber. "Oaths hold no power over you. How could anyone love such a serpent?"

"That's...that's not..."

But he could say no more. Words abandoned him. She was stealing the jewels, the ones he was supposed to take home. He was a fool. He had failed in his duty. And even if he escaped this fate, he would be exiled for this. The dark rush of thoughts consumed him as he slipped deeper and deeper into unconsciousness.

MIKHAIL JERKED AWAKE, THE MEMORY FROM HALF A millennium ago still lingering in his mind, the taste of Elizabeth's kiss still on his lips and her mocking smile still burned into his memory. But it wasn't 1559 anymore. Half a millennium had passed between that fateful kiss and the solitary life he led in Cornwall now.

He sat up, eyes adjusting to the lack of moonlight, his thoughts still back at the moment his life had changed forever—when the woman he'd thought he loved had drugged his wine, stolen his hoard, and then imprisoned him behind iron bars, the one metal that could harm a dragon and which he had no power over, for half a century. The woman had taken everything that mattered to him, and centuries later, it still stung to realize the extent of his gullibility.

Eyes sharpening in the darkness, his dragon senses

assessed the night. A faint patter of rain against the bay windows drew his attention. The dragon inside him shifted, wanting to manifest itself and take flight. Over the years the beast in him had become almost feral, carrying with it a desire to fly in dangerous conditions.

Elizabeth's betrayal had dug deep into him, like claws raking old wounds open again and again. He had wanted her for his mate, she had been the one fate had chosen for him, yet she hadn't believed true mating was real, not until she was on her death bed, and by then it was far too late.

I was nothing but an unholy beast to her except in those final hours of her life. She saw me only as a means to take back those jewels to line her royal coffers.

Being rejected by her had nearly killed him. A dragon couldn't live without its mate. And while he hadn't completed the mating bond, his dragon had been driven half-mad with grief by losing her. Even now, five hundred years later, thinking of her made his dragon reckless, desperate to hurt itself because it didn't care to live, not without its mate. He could feel it stir inside him, wanting to plunge off the cliffs and test its wings against the light-ning and the rain.

Soon, he promised. *Soon.*

He swung his legs out of bed and stood. The stone floor was cool beneath his feet. He was surprised that it wasn't snowing outside. This time of year on the coast of Cornwall there should be a great, fierce storm raging against the shore, layering the rocky inland hills with wet, sticky snow.

It was not the kind of snow he was used to, however, even after living here for five centuries. He preferred his snow thick and fluffy, dry as vodka. Russian snow. The snow of his homeland. But that was lost to him. He could not go home until he recovered the jewels Queen Elizabeth had stolen from him. It was a matter of honor.

Mikhail left his bedchamber and walked down the narrow hall of his home. It was a stone country house, a mere mile from the cliffs. The secluded spot left him isolated, just as he liked it. It was dangerous to navigate the roads around the coast this time of year, and the self-imposed isolation left him melancholy, but he welcomed the dark tide of feelings.

He hadn't always been this way, the kind of man who preferred solitude to companionship. But he'd been burned too often by the friendship of mortals to fully trust them ever again, and he'd never felt at home among the English dragon families, except perhaps for the Belishaws. He was content to be an outsider...forever.

He paused at the foot of the stairs, listening to the old grandfather clock ticking away the hours. Two in the morning. Outside, the sea pounded against the cliffs, the sound reminding Mikhail of how alone and remote his country house was. The frothy white spray from the water struck the rocks and formed a thick, almost impenetrable mist that had lured many a ship to a watery grave. In many ways, Cornwall was like the edge of hell—a dark, harsh place, especially in winter, and yet somehow that made it beautiful as well. A place of endings, a place of darkness and loneliness that called to his wounded soul.

His eyes strayed to an oil painting by the stairs, one of the dark cliffs with the distant black figure of a dragon flying out to sea. The house was full of memories and the ghost of his friend James Barrow, the one human he had trusted. But James had died long ago, more than a hundred and fifty years now.

"Mikhail, stop brooding." James's laughter echoed through the hall, a flash of memory that made him smile. If there was anyone aside from his brothers who had understood him, it had been James. The human had been a friend to him when he'd needed it most, a brother when he had become brotherless. Their bond had run deep in a time when Mikhail had felt most alone because of his exile. When James had died, he'd left Mikhail the house, as well as all of the ghosts and memories that came with it.

Mikhail had no urge to return to bed, lest dark dreams come creeping back up on him. With that unpleasant thought, he headed for the living room. He collapsed onto the leather sofa and flicked on the television, flipping through the absurd number of channels before a news story made his body freeze.

He turned the sound up to listen to a breaking news report from London. A reporter spoke in front of the entrance to the Victoria and Albert Museum.

"We officially confirmed last night's immense discovery," the man said, excitement flustering his face. "Workmen installing a new wine cellar in the basement of a small bed-and-breakfast in Cheapside unearthed what turned out to be the remnants of a far older building. Tests confirm that the edifice was likely built around the middle of the sixteenth century."

He paused, catching his breath before continuing. "But the most amazing part of this discovery is the large pile of jewels that were uncovered in the remains of the old building beneath the inn. More than two hundred pounds of raw gems and finished settings, believed to have been from the Elizabethan era, have been transported to the Victoria and Albert Museum. Over the next two weeks, the items will be cataloged and transferred to the Thorne Auction House."

The female news anchor interrupted. "And I understand that this find is unusual for another reason?"

"That is correct. Because the finding is strictly made up of gemstones, they do not fall under the Treasure Act of 1996 and are therefore not required to be sold to a museum. As such, they remain the property of the bed-and-breakfast owners, a Mr. and Mrs. Elwes-Bush. The Victoria and Albert Museum representatives will be among the bidders at the auction, of course."

The TV cut away from the reporter to show photos of the jewels. Among the pearls and rubies, he caught a glimpse of a gemstone emerald watch made from a single large emerald, cut into a square box shape, with delicate gold roman numerals inside. A string of wild thoughts raced through him as he recognized what he saw.

My hoard...

Mikhail could barely breathe. The jewels, *his* jewels, were at the Victoria and Albert Museum. He knew those gems, had gazed at them for hours, burning their vivid colors into his mind so he would never forget. He'd spent five centuries trying to find them again, searching all of England for them, and they'd been hidden away somewhere in Cheapside.

She'd never put them back in the royal treasury, possibly because she knew he'd look for them. When he'd finally emerged from his prison, he'd sought word on their last location. What he'd discovered was that the hoard of jewels had been stolen while being transported from the Tower of London to one of Elizabeth's residences. The robbers were never caught, and the treasure was lost forever.

The listless melancholy that had colored the last five hundred years of his life faded. The jewels were in London. He was going to get them back, and he would finally be able to go home.

A slow smile curved his lips. This time, there would be no tempting virgin to stand in his way.

❧ 2 ☙

**The greatest treasures were most often guarded by the
slyest and cruelest dragons.
—Adam Nevill, *House of Small Shadows***

iamonds are my best friend... The words hummed through Piper Linwood's head as she stood in the showroom of the Victoria and Albert Museum, staring at the glass-encased display of jewels with longing and fascination. Never in her life had she seen such an impressive and awe-inspiring collection. As one of the premier gemologists in North America, she'd seen hoards that would make a queen emerald-green with envy.

But all of those paled in comparison to this.

No one back home in Massachusetts would have guessed she'd end up in glittering, aristocratic London, overseeing a trove of this magnitude. After ten years, multiple jobs, double course loads for classes, and a heavy caffeine addiction, she'd clawed her way up from small-town life to cataloging this remarkable find.

And I am going to help sell them. She still couldn't believe it when Thorne Auction House had contacted her for the position, along with her friend and colleague Jodie Harkness. As a consulting gemologist, her job was to identify and place a starting value on each piece in the collection. It was a huge honor. She was only thirty, but they'd chosen her over a handful of even better qualified gemologists.

She looked around the exhibit room, full of tourists snapping pictures and taking selfies next to the hoard of jewels, several of them pretending to make a grab for them. A group of blank-faced security personnel protected the collection. Only a small number of jewels were currently on display, and they would rotate the pieces between the vaults and the exhibit.

But this exhibit was temporary. The pieces would soon be sold at auction, so this was the only chance for the public to see them. A camera crew was recording the event, with a reporter standing next to a collection of salamanders encrusted with diamonds and sapphires.

The display room was crowded and warm and noisy. She was more accustomed to a tiny room with a gemological binocular microscope, a set of jeweler's loupes, a refractometer, and a dozen other tools of the trade she used to assess a gem's quality. The bustle of so many people made her slightly edgy, especially when they strayed too close to the display. She couldn't help but feel a little protective of the collection, even though they were secured beneath thick pressurized glass cases.

As she studied the room, her eyes lit on one person and stayed attuned to him as he stood next to one of the glass displays. She shifted her position and frowned, taking in the tall, dark figure, with black slacks and a dark gray sweater that fit him almost regally. Taking a few steps closer, she began to follow him slowly through the exhibit.

He meandered from case to case, like any tourist, but there was a precise, controlled quality to his movements. Whenever he stared at tourists blocking his view of the display case he was currently gazing at, the tourists moved away like startled rabbits. Piper couldn't help but look at him, fixated on his tall, lean form. He was handsome, very handsome, but in a too-intense sort of way that made her heart pound and her head feel fuzzy.

His hair was long enough to fall over his eyes, but he didn't brush it away or even seem to notice it. He stood transfixed at the final display in the exhibit case, which contained a bag of partially decayed pearls that had been uncovered where the trove was found. Next to the artfully scattered pearls on a blue velvet cloth was a clock made entirely of emerald. It looked like a pocket watch with an emerald lid that folded down to cover the delicate gold filigree face. The clock's hands had vanished sometime during the last five centuries, but one could still see the numbers around the dial. A few of the other gemologists who'd seen it believed the housing had been carved out of a single emerald the size of a man's fist. If that was true, then it increased the clock's value to nearly priceless.

With a flush of heat that she tried to ignore, Piper approached the man by the case. He wasn't dressed like a tourist, and he wasn't acting like one, either: no pictures, no casual flipping through the exhibit brochure. He stared at the case as though it contained all of his answers. His fixation was unsettling, but she had to admit, it was not unlike her own. Perhaps he was a gemologist? No one else would look at jewels that intensely.

"Beautiful, aren't they?" she said as she came beside him. Her words came out a little breathless, but he didn't seem to notice. He didn't turn to face her the way most men would when a woman spoke to them.

"The pearls..." he whispered, his tone dark with a smooth but bold Russian accent. "They used to be so beautiful. They gleamed like moonlight trapped in frozen drops of dew." He raised a hand as though he wanted to reach through the glass to clasp a handful of the age-pinkened pearls.

The features of his face, which Piper could only see in profile, were cut of marble and destined to break a woman's heart. This man was as beautiful as the pearls and the emerald clock, but far more dangerous. Jewels were a girl's friend. A handsome man was not. He looked like the sort who could seduce any woman he wanted and leave her brokenhearted.

Piper gave her head a shake and focused back on the jewels. Gems would never stand her up on a Saturday night.

"If left in the ground without proper protection, pearls will decay, just like any other organic material. They are far more delicate than the gemstones."

She felt silly rambling to this stranger. This was why she didn't have a boyfriend. They always said she talked too much about her work and never focused on them. They acted like it was her fault that she'd never really been that into them or their relationships.

The man slowly turned to face her, and she was struck by his green eyes, so bright, like emeralds.

Oh, wow...

Eyes didn't come in that color of green. They had to be contacts. His mouth—it was a thing of dreams, and its sensual fullness made her want to lean in and nibble his bottom lip and...what was she thinking?

"You understand treasure?" he asked.

"Treasure? You mean gems and..." She was flustered, too distracted by his eyes and lips. Was it crazy that she was picturing him leaning down and kissing her right now? Yeah, super crazy. Had she had too much caffeine today? Not possible—she'd only just had her fifth cup from the cafeteria. If anything, she was due for another.

He nodded, and his eyes now watched her with the same intensity he'd given the jewels. Her entire body flooded with awareness like some kind of sixth sense. Every hair on her arms seemed to rise, and her blood began to pound in her ears. A slow wave of heat started from her face and moved down to her toes. Her body rebelled against her, all because this dark stranger was staring at her in a way that reminded her she was a woman, making her think of all the things that a woman wanted from a man in the dark of night.

Whispers, sighs, limbs entwined and bodies writhing...

Piper came back to herself with a jolt and tried to remember what they were talking about.

"I'm a gemologist. My job is all about treasure." She couldn't help but use the word he had. Funny, she never thought of gems and precious stones as treasure, but they were. This amazing new discovery was by definition a treasure trove.

The man cocked his head and leaned toward her. His nostrils flared as he inhaled deeply. The predatory move into her personal space made her tense and try to move back, but she was too close to the jewel case. She'd bump into the glass and set off the alarms. The corner of his mouth twitched up as though he almost smiled at her realization of being trapped.

What the—?

"A *gemologist.*" He tested the word, making it sound decadent on his lips.

"Yeah," she answered, a little breathless, trying to regain her composure. "I've been hired to appraise the gems of this collection before they go to auction."

A sharp gleam in his eyes made her freeze in place.

"Have you now." It was a statement rather than a question, and for some reason that unsettled her. When she met his eyes again, the green seemed to melt into liquid gold. She jolted and he blinked, the yellow glint vanished. There was something predatory about him that made her both excited and uneasy at the same time. She'd always been into men who were dominating, but she'd never been around a man who actually put off those dominant vibes before. Her skin flushed at his dark, knowing look.

"I should leave you to—" she said, now trying to side-step him.

"My name is Mikhail Barinov," he announced, stopping her. There was a touch of pride in his tone, but it lacked the arrogance that she expected to go with it. It was almost as though he expected her to know of him, but she obviously didn't. Which begged the question, who the hell was he?

"I'm Piper, Piper Linwood."

Mikhail raised her hand to his lips and gave her a chivalrous kiss. His lips were warm and soft on the backs of her fingers. She shivered. It was impossible not to imagine his lips touching other parts of her. The wicked thought filled her with a wild rush of excitement and a hint of panic. She never thought about strange men like this. Was it because Mikhail was insanely gorgeous? Or was it because at the age of thirty she was still a virgin and her hormones were finally kicking into high gear?

"Will you be attending the reception at the Thorne Auction House tonight?" he asked her.

Surprise fluttered through her. "Why yes. How did you know about that?" She didn't think the reception was open to the public.

There was a flicker of hesitation before he replied. "I shall be there as well." His lips curved into a small crooked smile that sent her heart racing. "I shall look forward to seeing you again, Ms. Linwood. And the jewels."

Before she could reply, the mysterious and sexy Mikhail Barinov slipped into the crowd and disappeared. He hadn't even told her how he'd known about the private reception.

Her friend Jodie Harkness joined Piper at the display case. "Who was *that*?"

The emerald clock and the scattered pearls lay on the velvet cloth. They were beautiful and enchanting, but now when she looked at them all she could see were Mikhail's eyes. She remembered what he'd said: *The pearls...they used to be so beautiful. They gleamed like moonlight trapped in frozen drops of dew.*

It was as though he'd seen the original jewels before they'd been lost beneath an old inn for five hundred years. But that was impossible. She must have misunderstood him. He was clearly Russian, and English was not his first language. Yes, that was it—he'd gotten his tenses mixed up and hadn't meant to make it sound like he'd seen them before, but rather that he was sad to see them not looking brand-new.

"Hey, Earth to Piper," Jodie teased.

Piper finally drew her scattered thoughts together and looked at her friend. "What?"

"Who was Mr. Tall, Dark, and Devastatingly Handsome? Tell me you're finally exploring that kinky side you mentioned you had. He looked like he was into it."

Jodie tugged the ends of her gray suit jacket down and leaned against the wall next to the display case. Piper sighed with more than a little envy. Jodie was tall and slender, with dark hair and pretty brown eyes. She looked like she'd come out of a *Vogue* fashion ad.

Piper, on the other hand, was only five foot four and too curvy to look good in most off-the-rack outfits. Her hair was that boring color somewhere between brown and blonde, and her eyes were a light, almost washed-out blue. The only thing she really liked about herself was her face. It wasn't model caliber, but pretty enough if she put some makeup on. Not that she did that very often. When she was examining gems through her tools and viewing scopes, heavy makeup on her eyes posed a problem.

"I don't know him. At least, not before two minutes ago. He said his name is Mikhail Barinov. I believe he's Russian."

Jodie's eyes sparkled. "Russian? Oh, they are the *best* in

bed." Piper laughed, but her friend continued, her tone earnest. "I'm serious! They are dark and brooding and more than a little kinky. This could be good for you!"

Piper's heart jumped in her chest. "Kinky?" Although she was a virgin, she'd had plenty of fantasies, and she knew what turned her on. She'd begged her past boyfriends to experiment, but none of them had been into it, so she'd never been that interested in handing over her V-card. She wanted her first time to feel explosive, to blow her away, to fulfill her fantasies.

"Yeah." Jodie leaned in to whisper as a crowd of tourists strolled by. "Like tying you down, bit of spanking, bit of bondage. That sort of good stuff. I've dated a few Russians, and they're all like that. Dominating and sexy."

Piper's eyes widened as she imagined Mikhail in bed, pinning a woman down while he...

"Easy, girl." Jodie giggled. "If your face gets any redder, you'll set off the fire alarms."

That was the problem with having some seriously dark fantasies and a modest personality—they tended to collide in uncomfortable ways. She'd told Jodie only a few weeks ago that she'd like to have a man who would be a little rough, someone who would dominate her in bed, maybe spank or tie her down. Her friend hadn't laughed, but she'd never forgotten, either. The mere mention of it and her entire body heated up, and it always turned her face an embarrassing shade of fire-truck red.

Jodie changed the subject. "So what did you and Mikhail talk about?"

She could tell her friend was trying to suss out any details of a possible romantic encounter. Ever since she and Jodie had flown to London a week ago, Jodie had been hell-bent on finally getting Piper laid. But she didn't hold it against her.

I was the idiot who had too many cocktails at the airport bar, then told her I was a virgin and that I got turned on by a bit of domination. Smooth.

It was sweet, though, Jodie's desire to help her get rid of her pesky V-card.

"Talk about? Oh, well, we talked about the jewels at the reception tonight."

"Is he coming?" Jodie asked.

"It sounded like he is. I wonder how he got an invite. Only potential buyers and employees are attending." Piper bit her bottom lip, thinking it over. *Who does he know who could get him into the auction?* She'd met many of the potential buyers and seen lists with names on them from the auction house, but she hadn't seen any Barinovs on the list. Still, he might be a late addition, fresh off a private jet from Moscow or something.

"Maybe he's connected to the auction house, but we just didn't meet him before today?" Jodie suggested.

"There was something about him..." Piper murmured, once more thinking of Mikhail's green eyes and how, for a second, she'd sworn they'd started to turn gold. How he'd acted like he knew the jewels personally, which was, of course, ridiculous.

"He was crazy hot. You need to jump his bones ASAP before he flies back home," Jodie added and then brightened. "That's it. We're going shopping. We'll get you something totally amazing to wear tonight. I could see he was into you from across the room." Jodie seized her arm and hauled her out of the exhibit room. "We are *so* not missing this opportunity."

She wasn't really looking forward to shopping, but she did have a sudden urge to look her best for the sexy, mysterious Mikhail Barinov. She would've felt pathetic acting like this for any other man, but there was something about the man and the way he'd looked at her, the same way he'd looked at the jewels: with an intense hunger.

Was it foolish to hope he might be genuinely interested in her? Probably. But she wanted to take a risk. If there was a man worth risking herself for, it was definitely the man with bewitching green eyes and a Russian accent.

❧ 3 ❧

We men dream dreams, we work magic, we do good, we do evil. The dragons do not dream. They are dreams. They do not work magic: it is their substance, their being. They do not do; they are.
—Ursula K. Le Guin, *The Farthest Shore*

Mikhail walked up the steps to Berkley's Club, his skin tingling. It had been a long time since he'd scented a virgin woman in her prime. He'd stayed away from humans for so long that he'd almost forgotten how the sweet, floral scent of a naturally beautiful woman could tease his nostrils. The little virgin gemologist was as ripe as a red apple hanging low on the branch, begging to be plucked. His body hardened at the thought of getting her alone, stripping her naked, and inhaling that intoxicating, pure scent until he was drunk with the aroma.

He gave his head an almost violent shake. No—he refused to be a fool for a woman again, *especially* a virgin. Piper Linwood was no different than any other female, ready to betray a man the moment it was convenient. It didn't matter that she'd carried a loneliness in her eyes that called to his, or a hopeful blush in her cheeks when he'd leaned in close to her. It was a ruse and nothing more. His hands curled into fists as he rapped his knuckles on the club's front door and waited, his mind racing with thoughts of the past.

The memories of that night when Queen Elizabeth had seduced and betrayed him five hundred years ago had left him filled with a quiet rage. When he'd entered the jewel exhibit an hour ago, his heart had stopped at the sight of *his* jewels on display for the world to see like common trinkets. But they weren't.

The hoard was his family's payment for a treaty with the Belishaws, an English dragon family. The Belishaws had received those same jewels years before Elizabeth was born as a payment from King Henry VIII, when he was a young and weak monarch. In exchange, the Belishaws had provided the Crown with their support and protection. Now those jewels belonged to him and his two brothers, Grigori and Rurik. To see the hoard on display like this had upset his dragon. A dragon's hoard was supposed to be hidden deep below the earth in caverns where no one could steal it.

The door to the club opened. He took a deep breath as he stepped inside. A servant met him just inside the door.

"Good evening, sir."

Mikhail handed the servant his black membership card. "I'm here to see Randolph Belishaw."

The man's eyes widened as he examined the card. "Yes, of course, right this way." He waved for Mikhail to follow. They walked up a flight of gleaming, polished wooden stairs, softened by expensive carpets. Paintings of famous members from days long past lined the walls. He paused at the top of the stairs and noticed a portrait of a blond-haired man with laughing gray eyes. The man wore buckskin breeches and a blue waistcoat. The inscription beneath the painting read, "Charles Humphrey, Seventh Earl of Lonsdale."

He'd met the man once in an underground boxing ring more than two hundred years ago. Lonsdale had been one of the fiercest humans he'd ever faced. Mikhail hadn't stayed in London long after that match.

"You had one hell of a right hook," Mikhail said with a chuckle. What had happened to Lonsdale? Had he slipped into obscurity like most other men of his day? The thought was a sobering one. Good men always died, while dragons lived on.

The servant had paused a few feet ahead, apparently believing Mikhail had spoken to him. "Excuse me?"

Mikhail smiled. "Sorry, just lost in the past."

The servant looked older than him at forty or fifty years old, but Mikhail was over two thousand. It just so happened that as a dragon shifter he didn't physically age past his mid-thirties. Only far older dragons, those five or ten thousand years old, would start to show their age, and even then their hair might just have a few silver streaks in it. Dragons didn't grow old and wrinkled, but without purpose, many of the ancient ones simply remained in their dragon forms and buried themselves in caves deep in mountains and went to sleep, never to wake again.

It was why finding one's true mate was important—it gave a dragon a reason to stay alive, unless of course one's mate was human. He'd known many dragons who had given up on finding true mates and contented themselves to breed with dragonesses simply for the sake of continuing the bloodlines, but he'd never wanted that for himself. He'd been determined to find and claim his true mate—but that dream had been shattered centuries ago.

"The room is this way." The servant led him down the hall and paused by the door. "Mr. Belishaw is inside. I shall send someone to bring you drinks." The servant opened the door and allowed Mikhail to pass through.

The small private room was lushly decorated, furnished with leather chairs and a warm fire crackling in the hearth. A lone man with dark brown hair and aristocratic features sat in a chair, reading a newspaper.

"Belishaw," Mikhail greeted him.

Randolph Belishaw—or simply Belishaw to his friends—raised his head and grinned. "Been a long time since you came to see me. Still hiding in that little cottage in Cornwall?" Belishaw stood and clasped hands with Mikhail with genuine warmth.

"Cornwall is right for me. You know I love the cliffs—excellent for flying. You've always been more of a city dragon."

Belishaw laughed, his brown eyes twinkling. "True." He was the eldest son of the Belishaw family—a noble line of English dragons—and one of Mikhail's few friends.

Belishaw offered him a chair by the fire. For the first time in a century, Mikhail felt guilty for not coming to London more often. He liked to think he was all alone, but he did have friends here. *I am too used to playing the martyr, I fear.*

"You've seen the news?" Mikhail asked.

His friend grinned. "Of course. Bet you leaped at the chance to see the jewels for yourself."

"I already have." Mikhail's smile slipped at the memory of how the pearls had looked. Once a bag of opalescent joy he'd carried in a large red cloth bag, now a pinkish-gray and sunken looking. It was enough to break a dragon's heart. Jewels were meant to be guarded and cherished, not tarnished.

"Oh?" Belishaw looked surprised, and then it changed to a keen gaze of comprehension. "*That's* why you're here. You wish for me to bring you to the Thorne Auction House reception tonight, don't you?" There was a flicker of pain in Belishaw's eyes. It was clear that he thought he was being used.

Damn, I can be a bloody bastard sometimes.

Mikhail leaned forward in his chair and raked his hands through his hair. "Please, Randolph. I wouldn't ask, but—"

"Say no more. If the promise of gems draws you out of your little cave in Cornwall, then consider it done. I'll go with you, of course. I'm rather fond of the new American gemologist they brought here. I should like to see her again."

Mikhail's body went rigid. An American gemologist? His little virgin gemologist who smelled like heaven? The one he'd done a poor job of not thinking about for the last hour?

"Gemologist?" Mikhail forced himself to sound neutral.

"Oh yes. A succulent little creature with the biggest brown eyes and legs that go on for days, as the Americans say. I'd love to have them wrapped around my hips, if you understand my meaning." Randolph grinned wickedly.

Brown eyes? Not pale blue? So it hadn't been the woman named Piper Linwood. The small, curvy human with eyes like alexandrite, a bluish-gray that could change shade with whatever she stood close to. He'd taken one look at those eyes, and for a moment he was lost in fantasies of stripping the woman bare and draping jewels over her body. He wanted to see diamonds glinting across her stomach and strings of pearls rising and falling over the mounds of her breasts.

The fact that her profession was studying and understanding such treasures had made his dragon growl in pride and the man part of him hard as stone.

"So tonight we go to the reception." He looked at Belishaw, who was still grinning as though he, too, was lost in personal fantasies.

"Indeed, but you're going to need a suit." Belishaw eyed Mikhail critically. "You didn't bring one to London, did you?" Belishaw was known for his fine taste in clothing: the finest suits, the most expensive Italian leather shoes. Mikhail simply wore whatever was in his closet with little thought to it so long as it was dark in color.

Mikhail chuckled. "You know I did not. Rolling up a fine suit and strapping it to my leg during flight would have ruined it."

Belishaw burst out laughing. "I forgot you Russian imperials are always so rustic. British dragons don't fly anymore, not unless it's an emergency. I only fly now when I need to clear my head."

Mikhail shuddered at the thought of going so long without transforming. The dragon inside him could not go that length of time being caged inside his human body.

"I suppose I am more rustic." He thought of the cliffs by his home and how often he leapt from them, allowing his body to elongate and his skin to turn into scales. There was nothing more glorious than flight.

A pang of longing for home—his true home in Russia, the Fire Hills—slammed into him. He hadn't seen his brothers in two hundred years. He hadn't spoken to them for that long, either. He wasn't sure what to say to them after so long. The last time he'd gone home, his father and mother had been traveling the world. He'd defied his father's orders of exile and come home for that year.

He had brought the Englishman James Barrow with him. Barrow had been a friend and confidant. He had known what Mikhail really was, and rather than be afraid, he'd been curious. Fascinated. Barrow had been a naturalist, and exploring the world of dragons had been one of his greatest joys. Mikhail had worried that his brothers would not open up to Barrow, but they had been welcoming. Grigori, his eldest brother, was a man who lived for duty to his family, and the younger hotheaded Rurik was the Barinov battle dragon. Each brother had a duty assigned to him.

And I am the one who failed mine.

"I can see it, you know," Belishaw said, his eyes peering deeply into Mikhail's.

"See what?"

"Your pain. You came here to bring home a treasure to your family, but you were betrayed by a woman you intended to mate. I know your father blamed you, but you must stop blaming yourself." Belishaw set down the empty glass he had been holding. "It's been five hundred years. Your parents are gone, and from the way you speak of your brothers, they would take you back in an instant, yet you haven't talked to them for two centuries. Who are you trying to punish, them or yourself?"

Belishaw always had a way of reminding Mikhail he had a tendency to play the martyr.

"You are right. It is time I returned home to them," he admitted. His gaze drifted to the fire in the hearth, watching the logs pop and snap beneath the vermillion flames.

"So what's stopping you?" Belishaw's question was more of a challenge.

"Nothing. I will get those jewels back and return with my honor restored."

Belishaw grinned. "Ah. *Now* things are getting interesting. What do you plan to do, exactly?"

A slow smile curved Mikhail's lips. "My plan is to seduce a gemologist into giving them to me or aiding me in their retrieval."

Belishaw tensed. "Not my brown-eyed creature."

"No. It seems there are two here to help with the auction. You can distract yours all you like. I shall take the one with eyes like alexandrite."

"Then we'd better get you one bloody good suit. No

doubt it's been a while since you've seduced a mortal. You're bound to be rusty."

Mikhail winced at the truth. His skills at seduction might be rusty, but from the way Piper Linwood had looked at him when he'd kissed her hand, it shouldn't be too hard to convince the woman that he was interested in her. It would be his greatest pleasure to get Piper alone and show her just how good at kissing he really was.

❧ 4 ❧

*But there, beneath those rings, beneath the talisman
and gems and precious stones like blue eyes (lovers'
keepsakes) there still remains the silent crypt of sex,
filled to its vaulted roof with flower petals.*
—Rainer Maria Rilke

Piper Linwood was speechless.

The Thorne Auction House was nothing short of stunning. It was an old townhouse dating from the eighteen hundreds located on Curzon Street, and it had been converted into a boutique auction house and reception hall. The owner, Mr. Wesley Thorne, was an old English teddy bear who, as it so happened, looked a bit like Teddy Roosevelt, with ruddy cheeks, a bushy moustache, and rounded spectacles perched on his nose.

Piper and Jodie had come to the auction house earlier that evening and had been escorted to rooms upstairs where they could change into their evening gowns. He'd even offered to let them stay the night in case they had to work late. The reception was a black-tie affair, so she and Jodie had bought evening gowns at Harrods.

"Can you believe this place?" Jodie hopped onto the canopy bed, kicking her legs with a squeal of delight. "It's like something out of a Jane Austen novel."

Piper had to agree. She'd grown up in a small town outside of Boston and wasn't used to the elegance and splendor of many of the places she'd seen in London since she'd first arrived. Mr. Thorne had told them that this townhouse had been in his family a long time, and he had been living here until recently. Thorne's grandson was American and lived on the Gold Coast of Long Island, but he owned properties all over the world. Mr. Thorne was moving to America soon to spend more time with his grandson and his fiancée. It was so sweet.

She got to see a picture of the grandson and his fiancée, holding each other close on the porch of a beautiful ranch house in Colorado, snow glittering on the ground. They looked so in love and so happy. Piper felt a little ache in her chest. She'd never had a relationship like that, not even close. She'd dated a few guys, but there had never been a spark. And she wanted that spark. She'd gotten tired of looking and had given up... until today.

One look at Mikhail Barinov at the museum and she'd *felt* it, the spark, and when he'd lifted her hand to his lips, an actual electric spark had jumped between her hand and his lips. The thought that a spark like that could be more than metaphorical had so shocked her that she'd just stared at him as he'd left the exhibit.

And he's coming here tonight. Her stomach gave a fluttering flip for the hundredth time at the thought of running into Mikhail again.

It was a silly girlish thing to be obsessing over a man she'd known for less than five minutes, but *damn*... Any other woman would've been just as smitten with a hunk who had such bewitching eyes and a mouth that made her think of wicked things. And his gorgeous eyes had promised her that hint of edginess she desperately needed. She shivered.

"So..." Jodie's voice cut through Piper's thoughts. "We got you that knockout dress. Tell me you're going to make the most of it when that Russian hottie shows up." She sat on the bed, pointing one delicate foot like a ballerina. Piper wished she was more like Jodie, all elegance and effortless beauty. A man like Mikhail would want a woman who looked like Jodie, not her. She was just so *normal*.

"Piper, don't you dare think like that," Jodie suddenly snapped.

"Hmmm?"

"You're squishing your face again. I know what you're thinking, but it isn't true. There are plenty of men who think you're attractive."

Piper snorted. "Of course, like the creepy archivist at the museum—"

"No. I mean *yes*, but I mean that other men like you too. Ask me how I know that." Jodie climbed off the bed and approached one of her gown boxes.

"Okay. I'll bite. How do you know?"

"Because." Her friend paused as she lifted the lid of her box and stroked the silk of her new black dress. "I bumped into Mikhail when he came into the exhibit. On purpose. He barely glanced at me. I gave up and circled around to the back of the exhibit, and that's when I saw him talking to you."

Piper waved a hand. "He was only talking to me because I talked to him about the jewels."

Jodie removed her dress from the box and whirled it around so the skirt swayed. "Then you didn't see the way he was looking at you. There was just as much interest in you as those pearls. Trust me on this. If there's one thing I understand, it's men."

Jodie was right about that. She understood men, and they flocked to her like birds to a cartoon princess. If she hadn't been so nice when they met two years ago, Piper would not have wanted to get to know Jodie. Jealousy would have gotten in the way. Luckily, work had pushed them together, and they'd become fast friends.

Piper still couldn't quite believe it. It wouldn't be the first time she'd really liked a guy and misread the situation. "So if he's interested in me..."

"Then talk to him. *Flirt.* Do something that will encourage him." Jodie set her dress on the bed and started stripping out of her clothes. Piper fetched her own dress box and set it on the bed before undressing as well. Jodie had talked her into a dress she never would've picked normally, but since the company was paying her expenses, well, why not?

She was down to her black bra and panties by the time Jodie was dressed and ready.

"Hurry up." Jodie slipped on her black stilettos and checked the time on her slender wristwatch. "We've got half an hour before people start arriving, and I wanted to have a drink with Mr. Thorne. He's such a dear."

"I still need to put on some makeup. I'll meet you downstairs," Piper replied.

"Okay." Jodie smiled at her, then paused by the door. "He's going to come tonight, and you're going to look amazing. Trust me, Piper. I have a good feeling about this."

"I hope you're right."

Piper carefully removed her dress from the box. It was made of dark reddish-purple silk, the color of burgundy in firelight. The skirt was full from the waist down, and the hem was trimmed with black lace. It was nothing like what she'd normally wear to a party. A simple black cocktail dress usually worked, but she had taken one look at this in the store window at Harrods and swooned. It was sexy but not slinky, more like something Grace Kelly would have worn than Audrey Hepburn.

Piper stepped into the gown and shimmied it up her hips. Then she slipped her arms into the short sleeves and zipped it up to her lower back. Normally she felt awkward in fancy clothes, but tonight felt different. The dress was perfectly tailored, and she couldn't resist peeping at her reflection in the mirror. The dark cherrywood-framed mirror in the corner of the room reflected a cool, brown-haired seductress. She bit her lip and smiled before putting on her makeup. It felt so different from the way she usually looked. Her dress was alluring, miles away from a boring black business suit.

Maybe tonight would be special after all. Piper fetched her black pumps and leaned against the bed to put them on. Her stomach gave another nervous flip as she exited the room and headed toward the staircase. She paused at the top when she realized guests had started to arrive early.

The reception hall was filled with at least a dozen people in suits and cocktail dresses. Jodie was already engaged with some of the guests; she was a complete natural in social situations. Footmen bearing trays of champagne floated among the crowd. The glow of the chandeliers illuminated the bubbling gold liquid in the glasses.

Piper soaked up the moment. She'd come a long way since she'd been a kid in Boston, studying hard instead of going out. Nights like tonight had seemed impossible. Something to daydream about, not experience. She'd come from a middle-class home and had to scrimp and save to get to college. Now it felt like her entire life had led to this moment. She rarely stopped to pat herself on the back, but tonight was a good night to take pride in her achievements.

I earned this. With a smile, she took a step down the stairs, then froze. Two men had just come in the front door. Jodie gave a squeal of delight and approached one of the men, who immediately tucked her arm in his, and they walked deeper into the house, leaving the other man alone. He lifted his gaze as though Piper had called his name.

Mikhail Barinov.

Those green eyes of his almost glowed as he stared at her. For a second Piper panicked. Should she smile? Wave? What was the sexy, casual thing for a woman to do in this situation? God, she wished she were naturally flirty like Jodie. But no, she was awkward and nervous.

When neither of them moved for several long seconds, Piper tried to remember how to breathe. Everything around her seemed to blur at the edges, as though she were trapped in a dream. The sharp light from the chandeliers softened to a golden haze. Her blood pounded in her ears.

Mikhail had the raw, unadulterated look of a man who was picturing a woman without her clothes on. There was the barest hint of darkness there, too, which reminded her again of a predator and that she was his prey. Rather than be upset, Piper's skin burned at the thought of Mikhail looking her over and liking what he saw. The slow curve of his lips sent her heart skittering.

And then he broke the spell that had kept her rooted to the floor by turning away. Before she knew it, he had slipped into the crowd and vanished. *Again*. The man had a knack for disappearing.

"Ms. Linwood," Mr. Thorne called out to her from the bottom of the stairs. She recovered herself and rushed down to join him.

"Smashing. You look smashing, my dear. I'm glad your friend insisted on taking you shopping." The old Englishman chuckled and offered her an arm to escort her.

A blush heated her skin, but she was pleased to hear the compliment. "Thank you, Mr. Thorne."

"This way," he said as they cut through the throngs of people gathering in the large room.

The jewels that had been set up that afternoon at the museum were now on display in the main small ballroom on various daises beneath protective glass. Piper searched for Mikhail and saw him fixed on a display of ruby bracelets. The red and gold of the jewelry gleamed against the black cloth on which they lay. Once again there was a glint of recognition in Mikhail's eyes that didn't make sense as he stared at the jewels.

"Curious fellow," Thorne murmured next to her.

"Oh?" she asked just as softly.

"He seems most interested in the jewels, and he..." The old man shook his head, erasing whatever errant thought had strayed into his mind.

"Mr. Thorne, could I trouble you for some champagne?" She hated to impose upon his good nature, especially with an ulterior motive at play, but she was hoping to get a minute alone with Mikhail. It was silly, but she wanted to see if he would talk to her again.

"Of course." Thorne patted her hand and wandered off in search of a waiter. She composed herself, painted a cool smile on her face, and readied herself to greet him. When she turned back to Mikhail, she growled in frustration. He was gone. Again. She whipped her head around, searching for him, and caught a glimpse of him exiting through a door at the opposite side of the room.

Don't follow him. Piper ignored her inner voice and slipped after him through the crowds. Perhaps she should have heeded the voice in her head, but that voice had kept her living a lonely, bored life. Boring meant not getting her heart broken. Boring was safe. It was long past time she did something dangerous.

She found Mikhail in a small drawing room next to the reception hall. He stood before a fireplace in the dark as if he belonged there. His lean, strong figure and the dark navy-blue suit were lit by flames. The door clicked shut behind her, the sound far too loud in the soft silence of the darkened room. Piper sucked in a breath, watching the shadows play on his dark hair as he turned to her.

"Piper." The word was a silken caress that was straight out of her darkest fantasies. Even though there was a good distance between them, she could hear him clearly, his voice seeming to come at her from all sides thanks to the acoustics of the room.

"Mr. Barinov," she whispered so softly that there was no way he could hear it. But she swore she saw his lips twitch in the dim, shifting, gold-vermilion light.

"Straying off the map into unknown territory, are we?" He chuckled as though it was some private joke. "Here there be dragons."

Piper stared at him. "I followed because..." Why had she followed him? Because he was like the damn Pied Piper for women who had tall, dark, sexy stranger fantasies.

"You followed because you can't stop thinking about it." That voice poured over her like molasses, and she could feel a delicious burn grow in her belly.

"Thinking about what?" She didn't move, remaining by the door. But he did.

Mikhail walked toward her with a grace that seemed more panther than human. Her pulse spiked when he stopped mere inches from her. The firelight made the blue of his suit appear to be a dark, rich brown as he placed a hand on the closed door behind her and leaned in. The minty smell of his breath, warm and fresh, fanned her face, and his eyes, although out of view of the fire, seemed to burn with light—gold light.

"You are thinking about..." He moved closer, his lips a hair's breadth from her now. "*This*."

Her heart exploded as he slanted his mouth over hers. Waves of electric, pulsing pleasure at that exquisite kiss sent her head spinning. It was like curling up by the fire on a cold winter's night and putting a glass of warm brandy to her lips, with a slow burn followed by a powerful rush seconds later.

Piper moaned against him as he slipped his tongue between her lips to stroke hers. She was already curling her arms around his neck, dragging him closer. Mikhail pressed his body flush to hers against the door. He was so tall, a daunting wall of muscle, frightening and exciting all at once. He was a man who could take her without asking. The thought, as forbidden as it was, only made her hotter and wetter than she'd ever been before. She should have been ashamed of such thoughts, but in that moment she couldn't be. There was too much pleasure in this kiss, too much exhilaration in her surrender to it. She didn't want it to end, didn't want the distant sounds of the party to intrude upon this perfect unplanned adventure. It would likely never happen again.

He deepened the kiss, his mouth consuming hers with a fire that left her giddy. And then something happened—

strange flickers of images flashed across her closed eyelids. Not her imagination, which had been fixed on Mikhail's animalistic appetite. This was something else.

Men in doublets approaching a throne, a queen with a pale face and red hair, pearls glistening on the bodice of her gown. Then the images changed, a roaring sea beneath her, icy water crashing against a distant shore, a deep loneliness that seemed only to grow until...

She saw herself at the exhibit. Saw herself through *his* eyes, a beacon of color and life drawing him toward her like a moth to a flame. She could feel his heart jolt, his body hum to life as he zeroed in on her. It felt as though he would never look away from her ever again. It was seductive, powerful, frightening, and yet she embraced the rush of emotions that came from him.

What...how...?

He broke the kiss to nip at her throat, and she tilted her head back to let his exploration continue. "It's as though you were made just for me, *moya sud'ba*."

The way he said the words made her shiver. "What's *moya sud'ba?*" she asked.

"My destiny," he growled, his eyes bright. "I should have known the moment we first met." He inhaled again. "Even the way you smell, sweet and wild like Fire Hill flowers."

"Fire Hill flowers?" she said in a haze. His clothes were still warm from the fire, and even his skin was hot to the touch.

"The wildflowers from my home. The Fire Hills of Russia. They are soft and sweet, not too much, just..." He kissed behind her ear. "Right."

She blushed, unable to stop smiling. "I smell like wildflowers?"

He made a deep-throated purr against the column of her throat, and she dug her nails into his shoulders. "And your taste," he continued in a husky whisper as he kissed her again.

This was madness to be kissing a stranger in a darkened room lit only by firelight. What else could you call it? But she was tired of being boring old predictable Piper. Mikhail made her feel wild and reckless, alive in ways she'd never dreamed. She didn't want to stop, didn't want to go back to being responsible. She wanted to live in this moment forever.

"What about my taste?" she asked, her voice trembling with desire.

Mikhail stared down at her and slid his hand into her hair at the nape of her neck, his fingers coiling the strands tight. A slight pinch of near pain shot sparks into her womb. Piper gasped.

"It's like the sweetest of Georgian wines. It lingers upon my tongue until I ache to become drunk on it." He nuzzled her cheek, his breath echoing hers in quick pants.

All they were doing was kissing, yet it felt like a wildfire had burst to life inside her, and there was no stopping the coming inferno.

"You are to be my ruination." He nipped her bottom lip, and she whimpered.

Maybe this was all some fantastical dream. If it was, she didn't want to wake up anytime soon. She was kissing a man who made her see things, impossible things, and she felt...*wild*. She felt strong, as though the woman she'd always wanted to be was suddenly within her reach, as if he'd unlocked something deep within her. She wouldn't be able to go back to the cool, collected woman she once was. He'd breathed fire into her body, and she wanted the blaze to keep burning bright into the night.

The clang of a platter against the wood floor on the other side of the door made them jump apart. But the heat between them didn't evaporate. Far from it. Mikhail cleared his throat and brushed his hands down his suit. He smiled and ran his fingers once more through her hair, this time to detangle the mess his exploring hands had made.

"We should return to the party," he said. But neither of them moved. Then he glanced around. "Are you staying at the auction house tonight, or do you have a hotel?"

A hint of hunger gleamed in his eyes, warning her that if she answered correctly, this situation could be continued somewhere far more private. The old Piper would have shied away from something so reckless, but the new Piper was ready to take a leap of faith and see where a night with Mikhail would lead.

"I...well, I have a hotel, but I promised Mr. Thorne I would stay late to discuss a few of the pieces with him. He said I could sleep in one of the spare rooms if I needed to."

God, she was rambling, wasn't she? Cringing, she tried to flash what she hoped was a seductive smile. She never had much luck with that sort of thing, but she was trying her best. If she had the chance to spend one night in this man's bed, it was a risk she wanted to take.

Mikhail feathered his lips over hers in a final lingering ghost of a kiss before he whispered in her ear, "Wait for me here tonight." Then he gently shifted her away from the door and opened it, slipping back into the hall and down to the main room, where someone was giving a speech. Piper stayed put, counting the seconds and the steady but rapid beat of her heart.

When she finally entered the ballroom, she went unnoticed by the crowds. Prospective bidders were focused on the collection of amethysts and lapis lazuli that were gathered on a display table, arranged with purple mums to bring out the natural colors of the gems. Piper looked over the tops of the heads in the crowd, trying to see where Mikhail had gone, but there was no trace of him. Her heart sank with disappointment. She'd hoped he would stay.

"Ms. Linwood!" a reedy voice greeted her, and her shoulders tensed. She forced herself to turn and face Bartholomew Winston. He had been the curator of the jewel exhibit while the hoard had been at the Victoria and Albert Museum. He was a pudgy little man of thirty-four years with a thinning patch of hair and thick black glasses with harsh frames that slightly magnified his eyes.

"Hello, Mr. Winston." After spending just a few breathless moments with a man like Mikhail, she didn't want someone like Bartholomew to ruin her memories.

"Barty, please." He gave a conspiratorial wink that made her feel claustrophobic. In the last week, he'd made it more than clear he wanted to date her, even suggesting that he might be able to further her career with his extensive contacts, and she'd had to turn him down every time. But he still didn't take the hint.

"Right." She slid a step to the side, still searching for Mikhail.

Barty reached out and caught her hand, jerking her to a halt. "I was hoping to talk with you about your evaluation process."

"My evaluation process?" she asked, only half listening.

"Yes. You see, I'm most fascinated by it. I'm a student of history and have long researched the history of Cheapside in London. The process and the presence of goldsmiths in Cheapside—"

"You'll have to excuse me, Barty. I really need to speak with my colleague." She offered him a hasty smile and rushed toward Jodie and the man who'd arrived with Mikhail.

"Jodie!" She greeted her friend in relief.

"Hey! Piper, this is Randolph Belishaw. He's one of the biggest patrons of the Victoria and Albert Museum."

"Hi." She smiled at the handsome Englishman. There was something about him, a hint of danger that felt familiar.

"It's a pleasure, Ms. Linwood. Jodie has been telling me all about you." Belishaw's cultured English tones were almost as enticing as the rough and foreign edge of Mikhail's Russian accent.

"You came here with Mr. Barinov, didn't you?" she asked.

"I did." Belishaw glanced around, his extra height affording him a view she didn't have.

"Is he still here?" Piper asked.

"It does not appear so." He focused on her again. "Did you...?" His voice trailed off, and he shared a knowing glance with Jodie. The exchange made her blush.

"No, we didn't plan to meet up again." Not true, but she wasn't going to make herself sound desperate. It wouldn't be the first time a guy had sworn to call and didn't. Mikhail bailing on her and not coming back later was definitely within the realm of possibility.

"Ms. Linwood?" Mr. Thorne joined her, passing her the glass of champagne she'd asked for. The older man smiled at her expectantly. "I have a few prospective bidders who are most curious about the collection of toadstones in lot seventeen, and I was wondering if you could talk to them."

"Of course." She followed him, ready to explain that toadstones weren't actually stones but fossilized and polished fish teeth. The Elizabethans loved to wear the teeth as rings to ward off contagions. It was little facts like that which made her job as a gemologist fascinating.

As Piper trailed behind Mr. Thorne, she sighed. The party would go for another two hours at least. She had a long time to wait to see if Mikhail was going to come back tonight after the guests had gone. She prayed he would, or else she'd spend the rest of her life dreaming about where that amazing kiss might've led.

$$❧ \quad 5 \quad ❧$$

That was the deep uncanny mine of souls,
Like veins of silver ore, they silently
Moved through its massive darkness. Blood welled up
among the roots, on its way to the world of men, and
in the dark it looked as hard as stone.
Nothing else was red.
—Rainer Maria Rilke

Barty Winston seethed as Piper Linwood walked away from him.

Little American bitch thinks she's something special. Too good to talk to me—that much is obvious.

But not for long. He'd made a deal with the devil

tonight, and soon he'd be rich enough to take whatever he wanted, including her.

"Is that the woman?" a deep voice asked behind him. Barty jumped, startling a passing footman who barely avoided dropping his tray of empty champagne flutes before continuing on his way. Barty gave a short nod, afraid to look over his shoulder at the man lurking behind him.

Conrad Sinclair was a tall, imposing man of six foot three, with jet-black hair and eyes just as dark. But Barty never liked to look at him directly; there was something almost serpentine in the way Conrad never blinked, not even once. And there was something unnerving about a man in his thirties who behaved in such an old-fashioned way, yet he didn't seem to be posing or pretending to be something he wasn't. That was part of the reason why Barty was afraid of him. Nothing about him made sense.

It didn't help that he was also one of the most powerful men in the country by virtue of his office as a member of the British Parliament. And if the rumors were true, soon he'd be *the* most powerful when he became the prime minister during the next election.

Ever since the jewels had been uncovered, Conrad had been keeping discreet tabs on their location and condition. He had donated a hefty sum to the museum to obtain a donor's opportunity to see the exhibit privately and attend the auction and presale party.

"You did not tell me she was so beautiful." Conrad

stood beside him and placed a hand on Barty's shoulder, forcing Barty to turn sideways to look at him.

After a panicked gulp, Barty nodded. "Y-yes, Ms. Linwood is very pretty. If you enjoy that sort of dumpy look." Which he did, although he would've preferred her tall, leggy brunette friend instead. But she was clearly out of his league. Piper seemed more like an achievable conquest, which made her rejection sting all the more.

Conrad inhaled deeply, and his eyes seemed to redden in color, like blood mixed in oil.

"She's *pure*..." The word escaped his lips in a low growl that sent shivers stabbing down Barty's spine.

"Pure?" Barty's gaze darted to Piper, who stood next to Mr. Thorne, the owner of the auction house, and a couple who were admiring a display of toadstones.

Conrad inhaled again and closed his eyes. "Yes. Untouched."

"What? You mean you think she's a..."

"A virgin." Conrad's eyes opened, and his smile was cold and almost vicious as he flashed white teeth. "And I do not think. I *know*."

"Really?" Barty's mouth fell open. Untouched. The thought made his cock harden in his slacks.

"I will take her, in addition to the jewels," Conrad announced.

"What?" Barty sputtered. "But I—"

"She will be mine if you wish to receive the money I promised you." Conrad continued to watch Piper, who was smiling and then laughing at something the couple she was with had said. The sound was light and sweet. Barty scowled. He'd wanted her far longer than Conrad. But there was no way he could go against the man's wishes. His very tone conveyed a steadfast certainty of this being his right.

"The auction takes place in three days. I suggest we move up our date to tomorrow evening," Barty said. "Both Piper and her colleague will have access to the jewels while they are here in the auction house. They plan to do some last-minute examinations."

Conrad twisted a thick gold-banded signet ring on his pinky finger as he gazed hungrily at Piper.

"Tomorrow is acceptable. I will send men to collect the jewels and the girl. Once I have them, you will receive payment." Conrad grabbed a champagne glass from a young footman who'd paused beside them. The moment Conrad had his glass, the young man darted away.

"What do you plan to do with Ms. Linwood...after?" Barty held his breath.

Conrad's dark chuckle made Barty's skin crawl. "After? I suppose if there is anything left, I could give her to you."

Barty wasn't interested in taking a man's seconds, but Piper was attractive enough that he would take what he could get. Conrad shot him a quick imperious glance.

"Have everything ready by tomorrow night. Do not disappoint me."

Barty nodded. "Consider it done, Mr. Sinclair."

Without another glance, Conrad stalked from the room. People scrambled out of his way instinctively. Barty snatched a champagne glass of his own and hastily downed the fizzy liquid. He knew how they felt.

There was something scary as hell about Conrad Sinclair. Maybe he wouldn't worry about getting Piper afterward. Whatever Conrad wanted to do with her was his business. With a sigh, he smoothed his shirt and tie with shaky hands and headed toward the table of appetizers, putting as much distance between himself and Piper Linwood as possible.

CONRAD SINCLAIR STEPPED INTO HIS PRIVATE CAR waiting outside the Thorne Auction House, his nostrils still filled with the scent of Piper Linwood. A virgin, of childbearing age no less. It was so rare to find them in these modern days. Hundreds of years ago, there had been an abundance of sweet-smelling creatures he could pluck like ripe fruit, but now? It was almost impossible.

Conrad's skin burned at the thought of stripping the woman's clothes and shoving her onto her back so he could take her. He would enjoy her cries of pain and the feel of her nails clawing at him. He loved it when females fought him. He was a male dragon, after all, and enjoyed being dominant in bed and in life. Dragons did not breed with weak creatures. He would prefer a dragoness, of course, but they were increasingly rare and more resistant to the advances of dragon males than ever.

He watched the streets with their bright flashing lights and immense video advertisements and growled. The modern age was a dreadful thing. A hint of smoke escaped his nostrils as his body responded to his mood. His dragon was just beneath his skin, clawing to get out. It'd been two weeks since he'd allowed himself the luxury of changing form and taking to the air.

The dangers were too great here, so close to London. The Brotherhood of the Blood Moon had a large hub in London. The last thing Conrad wanted was to be on their radar. He'd worked too hard to erase the evidence of his family lineage, as the last of the Sinclair dragons. The Brotherhood shouldn't know he was a dragon, which meant that if his plans went accordingly, when he became prime minister they would never see the threat coming. But he couldn't resist going after the jewels. He would just have to risk being recognized by the Brotherhood as a dragon if they came sniffing around. It would be worth it, though, to have the Cheapside hoard in his possession.

He *needed* those jewels. Both for practical reasons and out of spite. They had once belonged to Mikhail Barinov, given in exchange for a treaty with the Belishaws. It was because of Mikhail that he had been robbed of the power that should have been his.

And it had gone so well for so long. Being immortal, dragons could be patient creatures. He thought nothing of spending a decade slowly becoming a trusted assistant and confidant to the man who would someday be the queen's court magician, John Dee. Teaching him a little of his people—not much, but enough to put him on the right paths of investigation.

He had planned to use the queen to rid himself of his greatest rivals at the time, the Belishaws. Dee learned much of the dragons' nature, including what plants and minerals could quiet their inner beast, to the point of making as them weak and vulnerable as any human. Finding a potion to bring out the words of truth in his kind had been an unexpected but not unwelcome bonus.

Conrad knew that once he used Dee to poison Elizabeth against the Belishaws, those potions would ensure their destruction and secure his place and power over all of England, queen or no queen.

Then Mikhail Barinov had arrived and ruined everything. As soon as he had begun making secret overtures to Elizabeth, Conrad knew his plans were in peril. If Mikhail were to bond with her, claim her as his true mate, she would never turn on the Belishaws. In the end, Conrad had not only been forced to speed up his plans, but to change his target as well.

It had worked well enough. Barinov had been locked up in a dungeon, kept weak and helpless, and his treasures taken. But then Conrad had to wait years before he could move on the Belishaws. Too soon and he risked exposure. Time. He had all the time in the world.

Or so he'd thought.

He buried the memories of the past deep, ignoring the flare of his dragon's rage.

"Soon we will have all that we are owed. Soon," he promised the beast pacing inside him.

I trusted her, that human witch, but she betrayed me. I will have the hoard at last and will stand laughing over her tomb.

He closed his eyes, imagining the gleam of the rubies in the firelight of his treasure room and the sweet scent of a virgin in his bed.

Some days it was good to be a dragon.

MIKHAIL WAITED IN THE SHADOWS OF THE MEWS outside Thorne Auction House, counting each heartbeat as he watched the lights in the windows being extinguished one by one. It reminded him of times long ago, with dark nights and firelight, eagerly waiting for any hint that Elizabeth wished to see him.

I was such a fool then to wait for a queen's command. For one who knew so little of lovemaking, the Virgin Queen had known exactly how to master and manipulate men. But that was long ago, centuries away from this moment and the woman he wanted to see now.

Piper Linwood. His true mate. The moment he'd kissed her, he'd caught flickering visions of a little girl chasing a fat white rabbit in a backyard before stopping to pick up some brightly colored eggs. The vision had changed to a young woman bent over a desk, staring at gems gleaming on a black velvet cloth, her focus intense as she studied them.

A dragon knew his true mate by the bonding that began with a first kiss. Invisible threads would slowly bind his heart and hers together over time, until they could share thoughts and emotions almost telepathically. But it all started with a shared memory during a kiss.

When he'd recognized Elizabeth as his true mate, he'd thought that losing her would mean he'd never get a second chance. But fate had sent him Piper. His dragon was hesitant, though, and didn't want to risk mating a woman if she would only betray him as Elizabeth had. It would kill him. He tried to send encouraging thoughts to his dragon.

She's a virgin. Something a dragon couldn't resist, it was like his own personal brand of drug. Her scent had haunted him from the moment he'd met her, and he couldn't resist luring her to the firelight earlier tonight. It was an old trick his father had once spoken of. A male dragon could use a fire's glow to draw a female dragoness to him. She wouldn't be able to resist the gleam, crackle, and spark. And once she was close, a kiss to claim and keep her. And it had worked with Piper, though not in the same way.

He smiled at the memory of glimpsing her at the top of the stairs, wearing that beautiful red gown. The dress had demanded to be touched, as did her body. The flush in her cheeks, the lips parted in surprise, and those eyes, an ever-changing blue-gray that fascinated him. Tonight he'd watch them change like a gem held up to candlelight, watching shadows darken and transform the facets of the jewel.

It had been impossible not to lure her closer, separate her from the crowd, and draw her into a dark world of hot, slow kisses and exploring hands. It had taken every ounce of restraint he possessed to go slow and simply taste her lips tonight. She had tasted like perfection, a sinfully ripe fruit that made him dizzy.

Now that he'd had a chance to kiss her and had seen the answering gleam in her eyes, he wasn't going to back down. She was his mate, and he would find a way to claim her...once he had stolen back his jewels.

She agreed to wait for me. He didn't plan to let her get cold feet, not when everything between them had burned hot enough to set the room ablaze.

The last light in the auction house went dark, and Mikhail slunk along the mews until he reached the back door that led to the kitchens. Belishaw had mesmerized the guards earlier that evening. As a longtime acquaintance of Thorne's, he had the run of the auction house and had used the last hour before the party ended to take care of the security detail. They all manned their posts, but they wouldn't see Mikhail or anything else unless he wished it.

A dragon's ability to mesmerize could be *very* useful.

He retrieved an old set of picks from his pocket and crouched by the keyhole. He made quick work of the lock and slipped inside. The alarm beeped his entry, and he turned to the small white keypad and entered the code a helpful female servant had provided him. It was always amusing to see a female lose her senses when a dragon turned on his charm. At least he was not as rusty in his ability to seduce as Belishaw had led him to believe.

Mikhail moved silently through the house. She had to be upstairs, and once he had her under his command, he'd take the jewels. His heart beat wildly as he eased open the first few doors on the upper landing and checked. No Piper.

The last door opened with a creak, and every muscle in him tensed. After a moment he pulled the door all the way open and froze. In the center of a large four-poster bed, he saw Piper. She was stretched out on her side, her curves on full display. The way her dress draped down her hips and her shapely legs peeked out from the skirts made Mikhail swallow down a sudden flare of desire.

No. Not yet...

Her scent was intoxicating. He growled as the dragon prowled and paced beneath his skin. Now came the hard part. He knew she would not help him willingly. She was a woman with honor, and she wasn't going to like what he planned to do next.

I am a bastard, but those jewels are rightfully mine, and I do not have the time to explain.

The wood floor creaked and groaned beneath his feet the moment he reached the bed. Piper stirred. Her long dark brown lashes fluttered up. Those pale blue eyes widened, and she tensed as she saw him, her mouth open in a silent fit of surprise. He leaned over and clapped a hand over her mouth. She fell flat on the bed, a muffled cry vibrating beneath his hand.

"Easy, love. I said I would be back, didn't I? I don't wish to hurt you. But you will listen, yes?"

Her eyes locked on his, and she gave a jerky nod. The scent of fear rolled off her, and he cursed silently to himself. He didn't want to do this, but he didn't have any options. It was the only way he could get to the jewels before they were sold.

"You're going to help me, aren't you?" he asked. The look of confusion in Piper's eyes told him she still didn't understand why he was here.

He continued to lean over her on the bed, his hand on her mouth. "You have access to the jewels?"

A tiny, shaky nod.

"Good. Now listen to me carefully." He studied her eyes and noticed the lessening of trembling in her body as his mesmerizing gaze took hold. Her pupils dilated, and she was almost glassy-eyed.

"I am going to remove my hand. You will not scream, and you will not be afraid. You are going to help me open the safe, and we're going to take the jewels to their rightful home." He carefully pulled his hand away. Piper released a soft gasping breath but didn't scream.

"Now." He reached for her, and she tensed. He growled in frustration and gripped her arm gently as he pulled her off the bed.

"You won't hurt me?" she whispered, still in a daze.

Mikhail cupped her chin and gazed down at her. "I will never hurt you. You have no reason to fear me and every reason to help me. Do you understand?" She had no reason to fear him, but the same couldn't be said of the consequences of their actions. While he didn't like making her an accomplice, he had to use her. She knew how to get into the safe. But his plan had accounted for all that— there would be no record of her helping him once this was all over.

She was barefoot, which was a good thing, and he nudged her ahead of him, keeping hold of her arm. If she got too far away from him, he risked losing control over her. Free will was important between mates, and a dragon's biology made it impossible for them to coerce their potential mates for long.

"Take me to the jewels." He had arranged for Belishaw to wait in the mews with a vehicle. Once Mikhail was ready, he would load the jewels inside the vehicle. Piper walked slowly ahead of him, and he nudged her lower back with his other hand.

"Quickly, love."

She jerked forward, and they returned downstairs to the ballroom. The jewels had been collected from the display cases, which now sat empty.

"This way. They were secured in the vault after the last guest left." Piper took him to a small door built into the wall. She released a hidden latch, and the door swung open, revealing a tiny reinforced room that contained a large vault built into the back wall. She glanced at him, biting her lip, and he nodded. Already his hold over her seemed to be fading, but he would wait to use it again if he could.

"Open it."

With shaking hands, she entered the combination on an electronic keypad. There was a series of beeps and clicks, and then the vault made a loud hiss. Piper cranked the metal wheel at the door's center, and the door swung open. A light turned on, revealing the collection of jewels tucked safely away in travel boxes. The sight filled Mikhail's heart with joy.

At last.

Pearls, opals, emeralds, rubies, amethysts, gold—it was all there. The tightness in his chest that had lasted for nearly five hundred years started to loosen. He was so close to bringing the jewels home and reuniting with his family.

"Help me carry the boxes," he urged Piper with a jerk of his head.

She stiffened, and her lips parted as though to protest.

Mikhail curled his fingers around the back of her neck, holding her still, not hurting her, but more in the way a male dragon would handle a rebellious drakeling as he reminded her who was in charge.

"Piper, now is not the time to test me," he warned.

"Why do I feel so strange?" she asked quietly. "It's like you're making me help you, but..."

Mikhail didn't answer her. Instead he met her gaze and worked his will into her again, reinforcing the belief that they were returning the jewels back to where they belonged. Which was true, for him at least.

He didn't miss the flash of anger in her eyes before they softened with obedience. That was also good. She was strong enough to fight his powers. That was a quality worth admiring in a female. His mother, gods bless her, had been both beautiful and fierce, and Mikhail had always longed for a female of his own with such qualities.

Piper lifted a box labeled "Emeralds" and waited while he grabbed a box of topaz gems. Then he nodded at the door.

"Go to the kitchens and exit through the door that leads to the mews. There will be a Range Rover waiting for us."

"Okay."

They were able to move the entire cache in less than ten minutes. When Piper moved to take the final box, Mikhail stopped her.

"Leave it. Those who found the treasure have done me

a great service. That is their reward." It was a decent-sized box, holding perhaps a tenth of the trove, but she had no reason to disobey. "Now, lock the vault and come with me."

Piper did as he commanded and followed him to back to the kitchens. The door was open, and he could see the car was ready. The back door behind the driver's side was already open. Belishaw slipped out the back door of the auction house.

"Cameras are still on loop, and the guards are still at their posts."

"Mr. Belishaw? What are you doing here...?" Piper stared at him, then at Mikhail as though pieces were falling into place. "You planned this together, didn't you? The guards, the cameras..." Her accusing tone stung him because it was true. They'd planned this quite carefully, and if she didn't get in the car soon, she would ruin his plans.

"We did. Now, get inside. You're helping take the jewels to their rightful home, remember? This is the right thing to do, Piper." He gestured to the car. Belishaw walked around to the driver's side door and climbed in.

Piper froze, her eyes full of fear. "But—"

"Get in or I will make you. You must come with me *now*." He wasn't going to leave her here. She was his true mate, and he wouldn't leave her behind. If he could convince her the jewels were rightfully his, she just might lose her fear of him and realize she *wanted* him.

That was a big *if*, however, because from the look in her eyes right now, the ones that burned with resistance, he knew that she didn't trust him. It was going to be a hard battle to win her over.

"*Please*, Mikhail, just let me go. I won't tell anyone." Her voice broke, and it crushed something soft and unprotected inside his heart. He didn't want her to cry or beg, didn't want to see her afraid of him. But he needed her to come with him. A true mate was sacred, a gift from the gods, and he wasn't going to let her go, not after living nearly two thousand years without her.

"Piper, I swore I wouldn't hurt you, but you need to listen to me. You cannot stay here. You helped steal the jewels. Come with me, and I will take you somewhere safe."

She shook her head and took a step back from him. It was the only warning he was going to get. She started to turn, ready to run. Mikhail lunged for her, grabbing her waist and hauling her back against his body, clamping a hand over her mouth again. He didn't want to entrance her again if he could help it.

Her teeth sank into his fingers, but he swallowed down a cry of pain as he carried her back to the vehicle. Mikhail shoved Piper into the back seat of the Range Rover and followed her. She jabbed an elbow into his face, catching his jaw. Pain radiated from the point of impact, but he shook it off and pushed her flat on her back. Then he snatched her wrists, pinning them against the leather upholstery.

Piper screeched and struggled but wasn't able to budge.

"Need help?" Belishaw chuckled as he glanced at them struggling in the back seat. "I can mesmerize her for you if you are tired of playing the villain."

Mikhail let out a soft hiss of warning. "Just drive!"

The car sped into the night. Mikhail focused on keeping his little human female captive. It wasn't going to be easy. Piper was a fighter.

❧ 6 ❧

My nightly craft is winged in white, a dragon of night-dark sea.
—Anne McCaffrey, Dragonsong

Oh God, this is bad. This is so bad. I've committed a crime, and now I'm on the run with a jewel thief.

The thought kept racing through Piper's mind in an endless loop. Somehow this man had convinced her to help him steal the Cheapside hoard. All of it. How the hell had he done that?

He just looked into my eyes, and I went all gooey.

She couldn't erase that feeling, the heavy compulsion to do exactly what he'd asked. Had he hypnotized her? Didn't someone need to swing a pocket watch or something to do that? She was in a hot mess, and now he was taking her to God knows where against her will.

But he'd also kept assuring her she was safe. Her natural instincts were torn between trusting him and wanting to knee him in the balls and escape.

Mikhail still had her trapped beneath him, his hands gripping her wrists. She'd stopped screaming once the car started moving. Some part of her was staying rational despite everything that had happened tonight. That voice was now warning her to save her energy. No one would hear her. She was being held hostage in a black Range Rover. Getting free was going to be difficult, and she wouldn't make it far, being barefoot in a party dress.

Mikhail watched her intently, his gaze hot and frightening. Dark hair fell into his eyes, and he licked his lips. How could she have fallen for a jewel thief? She'd been head over heels for him, kissing him and letting go of her control to just *feel* everything with him, only for it all to have been a lie. He'd been using her and had somehow gotten into her head. The memory of his mouth on hers now tasted bittersweet.

"Are you ready to behave?" he asked.

The word sparked a new fire inside her. Even though he'd hauled her into the car, she didn't think he would hurt her on purpose. It gave her the courage to stand up to him.

"*Behave?*" she echoed, her voice dangerously silky.

"You'd like that, wouldn't you? A little slave who would do whatever you tell her to?"

Mikhail chuckled. "You are no slave, not unless you wish to be." His own tone now turned dangerously soft. "Do you?"

It was then she became truly aware of her body in relation to his. He was lying on top of her, her thighs parted, his slender hips cradled by her body with her skirt bunched up to her waist in black and red ruffles. Memories of their kisses came back to her, and she hated how much she already missed them. Kissing a damned jewel thief. She was going to need some serious therapy after this, because his damned natural dominance was turning her on.

"You said you wouldn't hurt me," she warned. If he tried to do anything to her, she would castrate him, no matter how good a kisser he was.

"And I keep my promises, but sometimes a bit of pain intensifies pleasure." He let go of one wrist to twine his fingers in her hair and tug lightly, prompting a rush of heated memories from their kiss earlier when he'd done the same thing. It had felt so good, so hot, and it spiked new desires inside her.

She shook off the memories. This was not the time to let her fantasies play out. He'd made her help him steal a fortune in jewels somehow and then kidnapped her. Shame filled her at the thought that she was still turned on by him. She'd always thought Stockholm syndrome took longer to set in than this.

Piper turned her shame into anger. "Get off me!"

Under other circumstances, if she'd trusted him, the thought of him dominating her would have made her wet, hot, and panting. Right now she was just angry. He wasn't going to abduct her, turn her into a felon, and just expect her to swoon.

Mikhail's eyes softened. The strange gold gleam swirling at the edge of his pupils faded, and the summer-green jade returned.

"Easy, easy now." She felt that strange desire to do exactly as he said wash over her again. For a long while they simply stared at each other until she felt relaxed and collected. Not brainwashed, just...*calmed*.

He sat back, let go of her wrist, and loosened his fingers from her hair. She scrambled to the opposite side of the seat and curled her arms around herself. Strangely, being farther away from him made her feel vulnerable in a way that made no sense. As mad and scared as she was, when he touched her it felt...safe. Why the heck would it make her feel safe? Not having an answer to that question wasn't exactly comforting.

"Where are we going?" she asked.

"Cornwall."

"Cornwall?"

"Yes. To my home." His haunting green eyes entranced her even as they frightened her.

"Why...why are we going there? Are you planning to sell the jewels there? Have you already found a buyer? Or is that your hideout?" She didn't understand why he had brought her with him unless he was worried about witnesses. Didn't witnesses to crimes usually end up dead? The thought made her stomach roil and blood roar in her ears.

He chuckled. "All understandable guesses, but no. I've no intention of selling them, and I would never call my home a hideout."

"Why not?"

Mikhail smirked. "Perhaps it is, after a fashion."

She lowered her arm slightly, shivering. Mikhail removed his coat and held it out to her. She stared at it, then him, wanting to decline.

"Take it. It won't bite." Something about his tone made her think he was teasing her.

Piper took the coat hesitantly, but then after another shiver she slipped it on. The large coat made her feel so small, like a child wearing an adult's clothes.

"What are you planning on doing with the jewels then?" she asked.

"I'm taking them to Russia." He seemed to wait for her to react to that.

"Russia? But..." Her brow furrowed as she tried to puzzle out his intentions. "You really don't plan to sell them?" Why would a man steal jewels worth millions, leave some of them behind, go through all the trouble and risk to smuggle them to another country, and not get his money's worth?

"No." He settled back against the seat and put his arm around the back of it, his fingertips inches from her shoulder. Her body hummed with tension at his close proximity, and she noted privately that not all of that tension was from fear.

"So why steal them if you don't plan to sell them?" Piper asked, burrowing deeper into his coat. She lifted the edges of his coat up, inhaling his scent. Damn, it smelled good. She shouldn't like it, but she did.

"How about I ask you a question first?" His eyes glinted with mischief, which put her more at ease—not that she wanted to feel that way.

"Okay. Ask." She was curious to know what he wanted to ask, and she hoped that if she played along it might give her some small advantage. A hostage who did what she was told didn't give the hostage-taker much warning that she was planning to escape, right?

"Why did you become a gemologist?" His green eyes were a pretty shade in the dark, like emeralds covered by shadows.

"I...well..." She'd never really thought about it before. She'd started out in geology, then... "I've always been drawn to jewels and gemstones. I guess I'm just fascinated by the array of colors and knowing that they are found that way in nature. It's amazing."

"It is." He smiled wolfishly, but Piper didn't feel

threatened. She'd learned one thing about him tonight—that was a playful smile, not something to be afraid of. Maybe he wouldn't kill her after all. Her gut didn't think he would, even though her mind insisted there was no other reason to kidnap her after using her to steal the jewels.

"I like gems. There's something about their purity, the depth of their colors, and the endless facets that are possible. It's fascinating."

"I quite agree. I could spend days holding a ruby in the palm of my hand." He lifted one hand in the air, palm up, as though imagining a large red stone sitting there. "And watch the light play upon it." He tilted his head as though thinking about something. "When we reach Cornwall, I wish to show you something."

Piper bit the inside of her cheek as she tried for the hundredth time to figure out how she was going to get out of this mess.

"Why don't you sleep awhile? It will be a long drive before we reach my home," Mikhail said.

"Sleep?" She straightened her shoulders. "I couldn't sleep here..."

"Piper," Mikhail sighed, shifting his body closer to hers. "No one is going to hurt you."

"You're not planning to kill me?" The question popped out. She'd had no intention of alerting him to her fears, but it was too late now. She was exhausted, and it had just slipped out.

"Kill you?" Mikhail gaped at her. Belishaw chuckled from the driver's seat, and she glanced between them.

"Yes. Kill me. It's what the bad guys do with hostages, right? I'm a witness..."

Mikhail shook his head. "I swore to you that I wouldn't harm you. It should be obvious that includes killing you." He rubbed his temples with his thumb and forefinger. "Foolish little creature."

Piper studied his face for any hint that he was lying to her. He glanced back to Belishaw, then to her, and cupped her chin, forcing her to look into his eyes.

"I didn't want to do this again, little dove, but you give me no choice. You're exhausted, and you need rest. Now... *sleep*." His deep, rumbling voice and the gold flecks in his jade eyes, like dancing flames, lulled her into a strange, hazy, dreamlike state.

She felt her eyelids droop, and her brain went fuzzy. She could just close her eyes for a few minutes, catch a catnap...

◈

THE CAR HALTED, MAKING PIPER PITCH FORWARD A little. She woke up and blinked. She was warm and cozy, and the last thing she wanted was to move.

"As much as I enjoy you cuddling against me, little dove, I need to get you inside where you can sleep in a real bed." Mikhail's voice was a husky whisper close to her ear.

She glanced around and realized that she was practically on top of him. Her head was tucked beneath his chin, and he had one arm curled around her waist. Her legs were across his lap, and his other hand rested on her outer thigh.

"Oh!" She scrambled away from him, which only made him laugh. The rich, rumbling sound warmed her down to her toes, and she hated that. A kidnapper should not have that effect on her. But Mikhail did. This was definitely a bad case of Stockholm syndrome. There was no denying that.

"Why don't you come inside and warm up? I'll put a pot of tea on." Mikhail climbed out of the car. Piper watched him walk over to Belishaw by the SUV and speak to him. It was a whispered conversation, and whatever Mikhail said had Belishaw nodding and opening the trunk. Mikhail came over to her side of the Rover and opened the door for her. She stared at him, still debating her chances of escape, even though running off into the dark in Cornwall was a terrible idea.

His lips twitched. "I would advise you against trying to run. I would only go after you, and when I caught you, I'd likely punish you."

"But you said you wouldn't—"

"There are other ways to teach a lesson than to cause pain. Sometimes withholding something can be more effective."

Was he serious? "You'd deprive me of food and water?"

"No, of course not," he replied, his tone darker. "I would never do that."

"Then what do you mean?"

He leaned into the SUV. "I mean that I would strip you naked and put my mouth and hands upon your body until you begged for release—then I would deny you your desire for pleasure." His mouth sloped into a lazy grin. "Only after you begged would I grant you mercy and let you come."

Her temper flared to life. "I would never let you touch me, you—"

Mikhail caught her by the waist and dragged her against him, his mouth covering hers and silencing any protest. She clutched his shoulders, desperate not to fall as he stepped away from the vehicle. How had she forgotten how good he tasted? It was exquisite, like seventy-year-old scotch. She buried her rational thoughts, which warned her that this was a nonsensical thing to do—kissing the man who'd somehow forced her to steal priceless jewels—but damn, he kissed like the world was ending.

Flickers, like faded photos, began to flash through her mind again, confusing her. How was this not some wild dream? A woman in a Tudor-era gown danced with her, the woman's eyes alight with mischief as she placed her palm against Mikhail's hand and began to twirl in a courtly dance.

More visions, moving quicker, a kiss in the dark room outside the jewel reception, the feel of her lips against his and an overpowering sense of belonging. Piper's heart felt as though it was being tugged out of her chest toward his. On some deep level she sensed she was being bound to him, falling for him, but it was insane...wasn't it?

I can't love a stranger. I can't love a man who steals jewels and...

"Wrap your legs around my waist," he growled against her.

"Excuse me?"

"You have no shoes. I'm going to carry you inside." He gripped her backside, and she gasped, her legs locking around his waist like he'd flipped a switch. She dug her fingers into his shoulders.

"Please don't drop me!" she begged. None of her previous boyfriends had ever tried to carry her because she was too heavy.

Mikhail buried his face in her hair and kissed the shell of her ear as he walked. "How could I? You barely weigh anything."

A blush heated her cheeks, and she shoved aside the girlish excitement at the thought that he was carrying her. And she liked it.

He kidnapped you. This is not sexy or charming. This is a crime. That irksome voice of reason was shouting at her again, but she hushed it.

Mikhail paused at the door of the house. She'd been too distracted to get a proper look at it.

"Hold on." He turned the knob, and the door creaked

open. A rush of warm air escaped as they entered. Mikhail closed the door behind them and set her down.

"Welcome." He waved a hand at the entryway, and Piper took her time in appraising what a jewel thief's home was like. It was an old stone mansion with wooden walls and cloth wallpaper that had been painted to look like wooded glens. The walls were warm and rich, with art hanging from the walls along the staircase that led to other rooms. Her bare feet sank into a red-and-blue Persian rug. It was the most surreal moment she'd ever had in her life.

"Come. Let me get you some tea before you settle in for the night." Mikhail grasped her hand and led her to a quaint kitchen. He offered her a chair at a small table in a cozy nook with a window that overlooked the sea. She pulled his coat tighter about her to keep out the slight chill from the single-glazed windows where a stiff breeze from the ocean drifted through.

"Mikhail..." she began, wondering how many times she'd have to beg him to let her go.

"We will talk about your situation in the morning. Tonight you will sleep." He set a kettle on the stove and clicked the burner on. Blue flames erupted around the pot.

Piper stared at him through bleary eyes, completely exhausted. She didn't feel afraid now. She couldn't explain it, but something felt...*different*. The rough, dark man Mikhail had been when he'd kidnapped her in London was not here. The man in the kitchen was a relaxed country gentleman. Was it because he'd successfully stolen the jewels and felt he no longer had to worry? That had to be it.

She remained silent as he poured a cup of tea and sat down at the table beside her. The honey and chamomile felt good and soothing as it went down. She'd always enjoyed tea before bed, even as a child.

"This is your house, but you're from Russia, right?" She tried to puzzle the pieces together even through her fatigue. There was so much that didn't fit together. The more she knew about him and this situation, the easier it would be to explain to the authorities once she made it back to London.

"Yes. I have lived here for many years, but my true home is in Russia. I haven't been home in a long time." The look in Mikhail's eyes seemed so far away, as though he were seeing ghosts from his past.

"Why do you live here then? Is there a reason you can't go back?" She couldn't resist studying him more closely as she sipped her tea. She realized that he was dressed differently now than when they'd kissed at the public reception. He now wore dark blue jeans and a black button-up shirt. He must have gone to Belishaw's house to change into his thief clothes. She'd imagined thieves ran around in all black with ski masks. But this wasn't a movie. This was real life, and he'd clearly gotten away with the robbery just fine.

"I made a mistake a long time ago, and my father exiled me. Eventually, I stayed here with a good friend for a time. When he died, he left me this house."

A pale shaft of moonlight came through the window, illuminating Mikhail's green eyes. The unexpected pain she saw in them made Piper tilt her head with curiosity.

"I'm sorry about your friend." She'd never lost anyone close to her and couldn't imagine what it must be like.

"It was a long time ago, but I have many memories of him to fill my heart." His sad smile only made him more beautiful somehow. His affection for the man was still there, but a bittersweetness hung about his lips. Piper had the strange desire to lean over and kiss him, to try to banish the sorrow inside him.

Piper hastily drank the rest of her tea and tried not to think about kissing Mikhail anymore. She'd done it enough already today, in situations that seriously called her sanity into question.

Mikhail stood and held out a hand. "Do you want more tea?"

Piper shook her head and handed him the empty mug. He set it on the counter and extended his hand again. After a long hesitation, she placed her palm in his and tried to ignore the spark she felt when he curled his fingers tightly around hers. They left the kitchen, and she followed him down the hall lined with tiny landscape paintings. Someone in this house had loved art. There were piles of folios on a corner table by the stairs, and sketches peeped out at uneven angles from old worn leather bindings.

"Are you an artist?" she asked.

Mikhail chuckled. "Me? No. Those belonged to James. My friend. He was quite talented." Mikhail paused at a painting at the base of the stairs. It was a cliff-side view of the sea. The waves crashed against the rocks as though announcing the arrival of a storm. There was a distant, almost black-colored bird painted in the distance. Strange to paint a single bird, she thought, a bird that didn't seem to resemble a bird, actually. The wings were far too spiked, more like a bat than a bird. *How odd.*

Piper nodded at the scene, which still managed to look stormy despite the hall lamps that painted everything with gold light. "Did he paint this?"

"He did. James was a naturalist, what you'd call a scientist now, but there was a part of him that was untouched by logic and thrived on emotion and the arts. He was one of the few humans I trusted with—" Mikhail suddenly stopped, and with a rueful smile he continued up the stairs. He was a man of more secrets than she realized.

They walked down a short corridor and paused in front of a heavy oak door with intricately carved designs. The latch was an old brass contraption that had not been updated like other parts of the house. It was stiff when Mikhail gave it a jerking twist with his hands. She guessed that most people would have taken a home like this and done their best to update everything so it was new and modern, but Mikhail hadn't. His home was ancient. The stones by the window were covered in moss, and the walls were thick enough that the roar of the sea outside couldn't slip between the cracks and stones, though the windows were still a problem. It was a place that filled one's mind with dreams of days long past and the lives people might have once lived. The house was a haunting place full of surreal beauty.

The wooden door opened, and Mikhail led her inside. A four-poster bed sat on a small dais, with blue-gold brocade curtains draped over the bed, shadowing it from the light of the chandelier.

"You can sleep here," Mikhail said. "The windows are locked, and I wouldn't advise breaking them. The glass is thick and old, which makes it more dangerous for you." He leaned on the bedpost and watched her intently.

Piper walked away from him and examined the delicately designed vanity table, inlaid with mother-of-pearl. The surface was cold and silky to the touch, covered with a fine layer of dust. She tilted her head back to see cobwebs strung like fine spun lace along dozens of perfectly cut glass pieces of the chandelier hanging above their heads.

It'd been a long time since anyone had stayed in this room.

A breeze slipped between the panes of the windows, making Piper shiver despite Mikhail's heavy coat.

"I'll fetch you something to wear tonight and start a

fire to keep you warm." Mikhail nodded at the fireplace against the wall that backed up to the outside, directly opposite her bed.

Piper sat down on the edge of the bed to wait. He didn't lock her in the room, but she suspected he would if he felt the need to. Escape could come later. Right now she just wanted to curl up in a soft, warm bed and sleep. Nothing about tonight had gone the way she'd planned. She was supposed to have met up with Mikhail, sure, maybe have a glass of wine, and, well, do what she'd been wanting to do for more than a decade.

Instead, she was his prisoner on his estate. In *Cornwall*, of all places. Yeah, she definitely hadn't planned this. To think she'd been worried he wouldn't show up at the reception tonight or that he'd stand her up afterward. Those fears seemed rather silly now, all things considered. She closed her eyes and tried to take in a slow, calming breath.

Mikhail returned with a stack of clothes which had a large shirt and boxers.

"I'm sure these will be too big for you other than to sleep in." He closed the door with his foot and set the clothes beside her on the bed. Then he knelt beside the fireplace and placed several hardy-looking logs on the rack, then set some kindling beneath them. She was only half paying attention when flames suddenly erupted over the logs and a healthy fire began consuming them. How in the world had he started a fire that fast? Piper shook her head. *Must've been a Boy Scout.*

"I'll come wake you in the morning," Mikhail said as he rose and walked to the door. "But please, do not run. Between the cliffs and the fog that shrouds the shore this time of year, it isn't safe." His earnestness was so startling that she simply nodded. He lingered in the doorway, his face a mixture of doubt and worry. "Good night, little dove." Then he closed the door.

Rather than feeling safe from him, however, she felt more alone than ever.

Little dove. She hated that she liked being called that. She strained an ear to listen for a lock turning, but she heard only soft footfalls as he walked away. Piper rose from the bed and went to warm herself by the fire. Distant eerie whines trickled down the fireplace as the wind passed over the chimney outside. It reminded her of her grandmother's tales of banshees in Ireland, crying out to foretell someone's approaching death. The sound was an unearthly wail, but it was muted by the sounds of the sea.

She padded over to the window and stared out into the darkness. A car was driving away, its taillights already distant spots in the night. Belishaw had finished whatever he'd been doing, probably hiding the jewels for Mikhail before he left. They were truly alone.

Piper faced the stack of clothes and shivered again.

"Suck it up, Piper. If he wanted you dead, you'd already

be in the ground," she muttered. She stripped out of her dress and donned the black T-shirt and plaid blue boxers she'd been provided. The boxers were actually just the right size for her full figure.

There was a tall wardrobe in one corner, and she couldn't resist investigating. The doors creaked, and the front panel shimmered slightly as gilded paint caught the light from the chandelier and fire. A musty smell, mixed with a lingering hint of perfume, teased her nose, making her sneeze.

Inside the armoire was a collection of clothes. They were very old but in good shape, rather than moth-eaten and faded. Piper tugged on the sleeve of a dressing gown made of red silk, causing it to fall off the hanger. She lifted it out of the armoire and glanced at the closed bedroom door before she examined the outfit.

He won't know if I just take a little look, right?

The red silk was dark, like burgundy wine, with gold embroidered dragons. She didn't know how to describe these dragons, except to say that they felt more European than Asian in design.

Her fingers traced the dragons that battled on the back of the dressing gown. Even though it was made of silk, the item was well made and warm. She shrugged it on, feeling a tad guilty, but it was freezing in the room unless she stood directly next to the fireplace. She missed her fuzzy slippers back in her hotel in London. Mikhail didn't strike her as a man to have fuzzy bunny slippers lying around to borrow.

An exhausted, hysterical giggle escaped her. She covered her mouth with her hand to stifle the sound. There was a long moment of silence in her room, broken only by logs snapping and crackling in the fireplace.

I'm losing my mind. That's it. I'm going all-out bananas. There was nothing funny about being stuck in a mansion on the Cornwall coast after being made an unwitting accomplice in a jewel heist.

Even though she was exhausted, she couldn't sleep. Piper tiptoed to the door, the dressing gown trailing behind her, the silken train whispering on the carpet, then the stones. She tested the knob, wincing as it creaked. She froze, then waited for Mikhail to come charging down the hall, but nothing happened. She opened the door and peered around it into the corridor.

The door to a room two doors down was slightly ajar. It had to be Mikhail's bedroom. Gold light could be seen, inviting her to come inside, but she ignored the lure. Strains of music drifted down the hall toward her. It sounded like Tchaikovsky. Mikhail was a classical music fan? She was as well. So few people seemed to have an appreciation for classical music anymore.

In the small blue-collar working town where she'd grown up, there hadn't been much of a chance to listen to music like that. When she'd gotten her scholarship and had taken art history and music classes for her electives, she'd discovered a beautiful, artistic world she'd never known existed. One Mikhail seemed to share.

Mikhail was so different from the men she'd known growing up. He was mysterious, worldly, completely intoxicating. That whole tall, dark stranger thing women joked about being attracted to? It was totally a real thing.

Piper walked down the hall, away from Mikhail's room, intending to explore the first floor of the house. She'd just put her foot down on the top step when an arm shot around her waist, lifting her into the air. She was jerked back against a hard male body.

"Going somewhere, little dove?" Mikhail whispered in her ear.

❧ 7 ☙

I would rather be adorned by beauty of character than jewels. Jewels are the gift of fortune, while character comes from within.
—Plautus

"No! I wasn't going anywhere!" She gasped and dug her fingers into his arms, trying to make him release her.

"Why do I get the sense that you're lying?" He chuckled, but the sound was dangerous. "Does this mean I must keep watch over you, even while you sleep? Or shall I tie you to the bed?" He carried her back down the hall to his room and tossed her none too gently onto his massive bed.

"Stay," he ordered and went to lock the door, blocking her only way out.

"How *dare* you!" Piper snapped, even though her heart was racing again. She hadn't forgotten what he'd threatened to do to her in the SUV...about how he would punish a woman. She also hadn't forgotten that his dominance turned her on.

I'm going to need major therapy after this.

Mikhail opened a drawer from his dresser and turned to face her, a pair of silk neckties in his hand. He wound a blue one around his fist and pulled, as though testing its strength. When he looked up at her, his lips split into a wicked grin.

"Be a good girl and stay still." He came toward her, but Piper scrambled onto the other side of the bed and grabbed the first thing she could find. A candlestick. There was just one problem. It had a candle in it—a *lit* candle. Hot wax spilled and dribbled down her hand. She yelped at the sharp sting of pain.

"Ow!" She dropped the candlestick, and Mikhail dove for it, dropping the ties. He used his thumb and index finger to extinguish the candle. Then he set the candlestick back on the table.

Piper clutched her hand to her chest as it throbbed. She was too stunned to react when Mikhail scooped her up and carried her to a large connected bathroom. He set her down by the sink and, with surprising tenderness, took her hand and held it under the faucet. The icy water hit her skin, making her whimper. But she was not going to let him see her cry again over a minor burn, not after everything she'd been through tonight. Soon the pain that had burned so fiercely faded, and the wax cracked and peeled off, sliding into the sink.

"There now," he said. Then he spoke softly in Russian. The meaning of his words was a complete mystery, but they were sweet-sounding. He rubbed the back of her hand, his fingers stroking and massaging not just her skin but the muscles beneath. The action was hypnotic, and she couldn't resist leaning back against him as he caressed her.

"I will take care of you," Mikhail said and feathered a kiss against her ear.

A wave of desire battled with the confusion building inside her. This would've been perfect if she hadn't been kidnapped. Why was she letting this man get to her? Was she so sex-starved that even the tiniest bit of intimacy would affect her this strongly? She really hoped that was not the case. Womankind everywhere would be ashamed of her.

After a minute he dried her hand with a soft cloth and examined the slightly reddened skin.

"You will sleep with me tonight since you cannot seem to stay in your cage, little dove."

"I am not sleeping with you. You had your chance back in London before you decided to kidnap me! And why do you call me *little dove*?"

"Your eyes. They are blue-gray, like the belly of a dove." Mikhail didn't bother pulling her back into his room; she came willingly because the bathroom was icy. But she wanted to make it crystal clear she was not going to sleep with him, even if the crazy side of her brain seemed fine with that. He pulled off his shirt and tossed it onto the back of the chair by his fire. She gasped.

A massive dark blue tattoo between his shoulder blades caught her eye. A dragon. Its wings were spread wide, the clawed tips arching over his shoulder blades, and it seemed to move when he moved his muscles. It was not unlike the dragons stitched on the dressing gown she wore. He must have an obsession with dragons. It was a bit odd, but who was she to talk when it came to obsessions? She loved old stones, and not because they were old or because they were sparkly or valuable, but because they were something pure and amazing that the earth had created.

"Yes, you will sleep with me. *Only* sleep. You're too tired for anything else, as am I."

She almost hissed at him. "Tired? It's not because I'm tired. You've kidnapped me. You stole the Cheapside hoard, and you somehow got *me* to help you!" She jabbed his bare back with a finger. He turned and captured her wrists, pinning them against the bedpost. Startled, she didn't fight when he retrieved a tie from the floor and tied her wrists to the post above her head. That sense of being entranced, of not being fully in control, had returned.

Mikhail cupped her chin, and she parted her lips when he pressed his fingers gently against her cheek. Then he slipped another tie between her lips, gagging her. He tied it behind her head, and she growled at him when he stood back to admire his work. The spell broken, she let loose a string of curse words that would've shamed even him if they hadn't been muffled into a series of unintelligible sounds.

He trailed a fingertip down her throat, to the V-neck of the oversized black T-shirt she wore. "I find you bound and gagged a most arousing sight, little dove."

Piper tried to breathe past the panic, but the danger of her situation was hitting her hard again. She was tied up and gagged, completely vulnerable with a thief and kidnapper. Aside from how she'd ended up here, this was part of the fantasies she'd always imagined and been ashamed of. Surely he wouldn't touch her. If he did, he'd know how aroused and embarrassed she was.

Mikhail frowned. "You're afraid." He raised one brow and crossed his arms over his chest. "You need never fear me."

Piper stared at him, silently pleading with him for mercy, but not because she was afraid of him. She was afraid of her own dark desires because he could make them a reality.

"I will tell you a secret that I haven't told anyone besides Randolph Belishaw. The jewels we stole tonight are *mine*. They belong to my family. Elizabeth I stole them from my family. We received them from the Belishaw family as part of an ancient agreement. They don't belong to the Crown or to England. I have letters dated from 1559 that prove the treaty, and they list the jewels included as payment. I am no thief. I was simply taking back what rightfully belongs to my family."

That was not what Piper had expected him to say. She was freaking out over what he might do to her, and now he was telling her he wasn't a thief and he had proof with Elizabethan-era letters? She worked at the gag, finding it loose enough to spit out.

"If you have the letters, then why didn't you just show them to the authorities? Make your claim public?"

A shadow flitted across his face. "It is not that simple. I can show you the letters, but not the world. Shedding light on my family's past is...undesirable."

"Undesirable?" she pressed. She didn't understand.

"One day I will tell you, but not tonight."

She scowled at him. Having proof but not being able to go public with it? That had scam written all over it. "You're really not giving me much reason to trust you. You're just creating more questions than answers. And you're scaring the hell out of me!" She jerked on her bound hands again.

"You were never in danger tonight. Nor were you ever truly in control, and for that I apologize. I have ways of making people compliant. It's a talent I was born with. I didn't want to use it on you, but I needed to make sure you stayed quiet and helped me retrieve what was rightfully mine. I won't use that little trick on you again unless I have to. We have chemistry, you and I, and I want to explore it, if you're willing."

"And if I'm not willing?" she challenged with a fiery glare.

Mikhail crooked a brow and smirked. "Tell me you aren't. Speak the truth and I will let you go."

Again that weird sensation that she had no control came over her, but this time, she knew that her words as they left her lips were true, not lies that he put there to satisfy his male pride or his lust. She spoke a truth she couldn't even fully admit to herself.

"I...I do want you, and..." She growled in frustration, hating that he'd somehow made her admit that much. "Dammit, stop that! Stop whatever you're doing to me!"

"We both needed to hear you tell the truth. You want me. So you will stay, then, won't you?"

She glared at him, less afraid now, not that she could explain why. "I'll stay. For a day, but after that, if I want to leave, I'm leaving."

"If after a day you still wish to leave, then you will be free to do so." He then came back to her and touched her lips. "Now, you wish to ask me questions, and I will answer them." He stroked his fingertips down her throat, then pulled them away and gave her space again.

Piper sagged in relief. She drew several calming breaths before she finally spoke. "Why did you kidnap me? I was totally ready to go out with you tonight, you know. I was waiting for you to come back, and I thought we could go grab a drink or something. But then you went all hypnotic jewel thief on me." And ruined the night she'd been hoping to have, one where she and Mikhail ended up in bed together.

Mikhail grinned. "I am from the old country, little dove. You showed me your desire, and I wanted you as well. It's a custom in my family for a male to take a female away to his lair and seduce her there. I would never force you to my bed, but I sensed that you might like a bit of fire and power in your partner." He reached up to her wrists and stroked a hand down her arms as he leaned in. "And I can give it to you, but you must be ready to admit you *want* it. You cannot deny it, not after you told me the truth just now. You want me."

She started to say she didn't, even if it was a lie, but he covered her lips with his finger.

"You don't have to argue with me to prove your strength, Piper. I know you are strong. Strong females, not weak ones, need a strong male, and I am here for you when you decide you are ready. So tonight we sleep, and you will sleep beside me."

"Why do you want me to sleep with you?" she asked. What did he get out of her just sleeping next to him if it wasn't for sex?

He was still leaning close, his body heat warming hers. "Because it is a cold, old house, and you will want the heat my body can provide." He brushed a thumb over her bottom lip, then feathered a hot, slow, seemingly innocent kiss on her lips.

"And if I don't want to?"

He reached a hand above her head and freed her wrists. The silk tie slid against her skin and dropped away. She lowered her wrists, touching them, but she wasn't bruised or tender at all. Just as he'd promised.

"The door is that way. You know where your room is." He turned his back on her, and she had another glorious view of the dragon tattoo on his skin. For a second, in the dim light of the fire and the half-lit lamps, she swore the dragon *moved*.

Mikhail walked back into his bathroom, disappearing from view. Piper heard the water begin to run. He'd said he was going to make her sleep with him, but then he hadn't even done that. She really *did* have a say in what would happen between them. That gave her more reassurance tonight than she could have hoped for. She took the chance to flee his room and go back to her own.

Her bed was ice-cold, even with the fire roaring in the fireplace. She burrowed deep into the covers, shivering. She closed her eyes, trying to pretend the sheets weren't like layers of ice against her skin. As she lay in the dark, Piper made a vow to install heaters if she ever had to live in a house like this.

Everything would be better in the morning. She'd find a way back to London, and then she'd call the police and explain everything to them. It would be fine. It had to be.

She drifted toward the dark realm of sleep. As her mind eased its control, her thoughts wandered more freely. She wished she hadn't been afraid of her desire for Mikhail tonight, because being under his control like that, at least in a sexual way, had been unbelievably stimulating.

But she couldn't forget how she'd gotten here. Even though he hadn't harmed her, he had still stolen a fortune in jewels, had her help him do it, and then kidnapped her. That wasn't okay. She wasn't going to be some silly fool who let Stockholm syndrome get the better of her. No matter how sexy he looked without a shirt, how green his eyes were, or how much she wanted to trace the outline of the dragon tattoo on his back...

MIKHAIL STOOD OUTSIDE THE DOOR TO PIPER'S bedroom for a long while, listening to her shift and toss under her sheets. When he heard the faint chattering of her teeth, he'd had enough. He eased the door open and peered cautiously inside. She was asleep but still cold, despite the mountain of blankets on her bed.

With a growl of frustration, he approached the bed and carefully slipped her out from under the blankets and into his arms. Her chattering teeth stilled, and she murmured something fretful in her sleep before she nuzzled his chest and sighed.

Unable to stop a cocky grin from spreading across his face, he carried her back to his room and settled her beneath his blankets before he turned out the lights and joined her under them. Her feet were like ice, and her hands were just as cold. He tucked her body close to his and placed her feet on his shins. Soon she'd warm up. A dragon gave off more body heat than a human, one of the perks of being a shifter, such as being able to extinguish or start a fire with a wave of his hands. Both had come in handy tonight. Mikhail curled an arm around Piper's waist and buried his face in her sweet-smelling hair.

"You have nothing to fear from me, little dove." He whispered the words, hoping she would hear them in her dreams and know what he said was true. "I vow on my life and my brothers' that you are safe."

He wanted her desperately, but he would wait as long as it took to earn her trust. *Because she is my mate.* It was a thought he'd been afraid to embrace before now, but it was harder and harder to deny how he and his dragon felt about this fiery beauty.

The only problem was that she was human...like Elizabeth. When dragons mated, they tied their lifespan to that of their mate. If he mated a dragoness—an admittedly unlikely prospect—he would live another five thousand years, but if he mated a human? He would draw his last breath mere hours or days after she did. Unless he found a way to change her.

Being a dragon shifter meant his life and his body were controlled by ancient magic. Ever since he was a child, he'd heard legends of humans who had, after great sacrifices, earned the right to join their ranks. They lived immortal lives alongside their dragon mates. He remembered his mother telling him stories about the first dragons, how they had been creatures of magic and how the early humans had bonded with them, combining the dragon's soul with the human's body. Those had been the first dragons. The later generations had been born rather than made. Those first dragons had come from another realm by virtue of special gemstones, ones which held great magic. But no one had done this in a long time, longer than he had been alive. The knowledge of how to do it had been lost, even in the oldest of his people's memories.

Mikhail didn't like the idea of Piper having to make any great sacrifice, so he would not ask her to change for him. He closed his eyes, holding his precious human close. If he only had another sixty years with her, it would be enough. Every moment would be a treasure. He didn't want to make another mistake, not like he had with Elizabeth.

That was why he had taken Piper tonight. He had to be in control at first, until she could decide if she wanted him. If she did not, he would let her go, but not before he was certain he could trust her with the truth of who he was and, more importantly, what he could become.

Five hundred years ago, being a dragon had been dangerous enough. He could've been captured and killed. But now? In the digital age where cameras were everywhere and scientists were eager to dissect creatures like him? Not to mention the damned Brotherhood of the Blood Moon, who had a stronghold in every major city these days, always watching and waiting for one of his kind to make a false step. It was crucial for himself and his race to stay hidden in the shadows.

His hold tightened on Piper, and he settled deeper into his bed. He had been alone for five centuries. It felt so good to have a woman in his arms again, even if he had to face letting her go when the morning came. Until then, he would dream as he hadn't done in years, of his gray-blue-eyed dove and the hoard of jewels hidden in the cellar of his house.

A smile curved his lips as he slipped into the realm of a dragon's dreams.

8

Those who build walls are their own prisoners.
—Ursula K. Le Guin

Piper woke slowly, in that hazy way one does on a winter weekend when one has snuggled deep into the blankets. Bright, clear sunlight bathed the room and bed in stark pale colors, washing everything out and making it feel surreal.

She blinked and studied the bed hangings and the dying fire in the fireplace. Where was she? Bit by bit, memories of last night came back to her. She winced as she realized it hadn't been a wild and fantastical dream. She was *really* in Mikhail Barinov's house in Cornwall and had been forced into helping him steal the Cheapside treasure trove.

It took her a few seconds longer to realize she was in a warm bed, but not the bed she'd gone to sleep in. She whipped her head up as soon as she recognized where she was: Mikhail's bedroom.

How had she gotten here? Surely he hadn't... She lifted the sheets and breathed a sigh of relief. She was still clothed. Nothing had happened last night, as far she could tell. But why had he brought her back here after she'd been given the freedom to choose where she slept?

Frowning, she slipped out of bed. A pair of jeans and a sweater lay beside her on a chair, along with boots and thick woolen socks. There was a small note propped up beside them.

PIPER,

Belishaw brought your clothes down from London this morning. Your suitcase is in the other bedroom. Feel free to freshen up and shower. Come down to the kitchen when you are hungry.
—M.

BELISHAW? HOW HAD HE GOTTEN INTO HER HOTEL room? Scratch that—given what they'd pulled off last night, breaking into a hotel room couldn't have been difficult.

She set the note down and glanced at the bathroom. She really could use a shower. She had to start her day feeling clean or else she got cranky, and that was the last thing she needed if she was going to escape.

The bathroom was stunning, with smooth marble surfaces and expensive faucets. She'd been too busy focusing on the scalding wax last night to appreciate it. The shower was a massive glass box against one wall. There was a heated floor tile switch, which she experimented with when she got in and turned on the water. So much of the house she'd seen so far hadn't been modern, yet this bathroom certainly was. It seemed Mikhail had kept the renovations to just the rooms he lived in most.

The rest of the house might have been cold, but not this room. The water warmed her chilled skin, and the heated tiles made her feel as cozy as a kid by a roaring fire in a pile of blankets. She got out, dried her hair, and got dressed. Then she returned to her bedroom to check her luggage. But there was only so long she could put off the inevitable and face Mikhail.

She followed the heady scents of eggs and bacon down the stairs into the kitchen. Mikhail stood in front of the stove, wearing jeans and a button-up white shirt, holding a cast-iron skillet over a blue flame.

"Good morning." He offered her one of those sexy smiles that hit her right behind her knees.

How could he always make her want to forget that she was supposed to be resisting him, trying to get away? It was so hard to ignore the "Fuck me, baby" vibes that rolled off him in waves. It gave her way too many wild ideas, like curling her arms around his body from behind and breathing in that woodsy pine scent of his.

Get a grip. Piper gave herself a little shake and placed the stovetop island between herself and the sexy Russian jewel thief.

"How do you like your eggs?" he asked as he scooped a helping of scrambled eggs onto a plate.

She couldn't help but lick her lips. "Er, scrambled is fine."

He added shredded cheese to the eggs, just like her mom did. "And bacon, I assume?" He raised a gloved hand with a second skillet where several fat, thick strips sizzled.

"Yes, please." She held back a moan as he plucked the strips from the pan with a fork and set them on the plate next to the eggs.

Mikhail turned to the fridge. "Coffee, tea, or juice?"

"Orange juice, if you have it," she replied. She picked up a spare fork on the counter and sat down at the nook table with the plate.

A tall glass of orange juice was soon sitting in front of her. When she finished eating, she looked up to see Mikhail leaning against the counter, watching her with open amusement. She chose to ignore him. She didn't want to know what was making him smile. It was likely at her expense. Having breakfast with a jewel thief was something she'd never thought she'd experience in her life, yet he acted so casually and put her at such ease that she could *almost* forget how she'd ended up here.

"So..." she said. "Is Randolph Belishaw somehow involved with your connection to the jewels or just your getaway driver?"

Mikhail shrugged. "A bit of both."

Piper raised a brow. That answer left the door wide open for a dozen more questions.

"Last night you said the jewels were yours, that the Belishaw family gave them to your family as part of a treaty long ago. Was that true?" Maybe she could catch him in a lie now.

"All true." He walked over to a small side table near the fridge and retrieved a packet of letters bound with twine. He carefully slid a letter out of the middle of the stack and set it down in front of her. He kept the other letters carefully out of reach.

"I pulled these from my private safe earlier this morning. I thought you'd want to read them."

The yellowed parchment was crinkled when she unfolded it to read. The ink had changed from black to brown with age, but she could see the date, 1559, inscribed at the top of the letter. She squinted at the letter but was eventually able to stumble through the words. It was from the Belishaw family to the Barinov family, detailing a treaty between the two noble houses with a payment of an immense hoard of jewels to the Barinovs. In exchange, the two families would be tied by an oath to come to the defense of the other in times of war.

There was an itemized list of jewels which included: boxes of rubies, an emerald watch, diamonds, emeralds, amethysts, a cloth sack of pearls, and many other special items, including a fist-sized ruby in the shape of a person's heart. That one she remembered clearly, the Dragon Heart Stone. The piece was so valuable that they had not even put it on display at the V&A museum or at the reception last night. It had stayed safely locked in a vault at the Thorne Auction House. Piper read the rest of the letter. It was clear the jewels had belonged to Mikhail's ancestors, assuming the letter was real.

She set the letter down. "How did the jewels end up in Cheapside if they belonged to your family?" She was ready to unravel his story if she found a single thread to pull on. A lot could happen to a family in five hundred years, and it was entirely possible that the jewels could've been lost, sold, or stolen. They could rightfully belong to someone else now. The options were endless.

Mikhail collected the letter and carefully tucked it back into the stack before he finally answered her.

"My family was betrayed. Elizabeth I took advantage of—my ancestor—and drugged his wine and tricked him into revealing where he'd stored the jewels. My ancestor was forced into prison but he never forgot what she did with the jewels."

"But why?" Piper asked. "It wasn't out of some kind of greed, was it?"

Mikhail considered his words. "No. She believed herself to be in the right. She believed the jewels were a part of her father's royal treasury, and they had been, once. But her father had given them to the Belishaw family in the early years of his reign for their services. And the Belishaws, in turn, had given them to us. Henry, however, grew to resent the deal in his later life and no doubt told all who would listen that he believed them to be rightfully his. He was a bitter man, petty and vengeful. And there were other voices that poisoned the queen against my ancestor..." Mikhail's face darkened, a host of storms surging in his green eyes, and once again he spoke as if he had been there.

"So Elizabeth imprisoned him? Your ancestor, I mean?" Piper asked.

He nodded, his eyes solemn. "Yes. For forty-four years. And the real tragedy was that he loved her. And she might have loved him, had things been different. Instead, she repaid his love with shame and imprisonment. To make matters worse, his own father exiled him from the family afterward. He was not allowed to go home until he recovered the jewels."

A tic worked in Mikhail's jaw as he spoke, his words soft and heavy with sorrow. Piper was lost in the lingering pain behind his eyes that seemed centuries old, as though he knew how his ancestor must have felt.

"That's awful." She had no other words to express her thoughts of such suffering.

"Five centuries is a long time for injustice. But now my family will have peace." The last of his words was barely more than a whisper.

"How long have you been trying to find the jewels?" she asked.

"A long time," he said with a rueful laugh. "Feels like centuries sometimes." He rapped his knuckles on the wooden table in an affectionate gesture, then smiled brightly. "Well then, little dove, am I still a fierce villain?" He reached over and brushed a lock of her hair away from her face. His fingertips left a delicious tingle that traveled down her body.

"Maybe you aren't so bad," she finally replied, a blush flaming her face.

His responding laugh was dark and sinful. "Oh, I am bad. *Very bad.* But you haven't had a taste of that yet." He stroked a fingertip down her nose in a playful gesture and then collected her plate and put it in the dishwasher.

She got up to follow him. "But you just said you were trying to prove you aren't bad."

He turned to face her, a smug smile on his face. "I'm not someone you should fear," he said. "But I am a very bad man, in a very *specific* way." He slid closer, his hands settling on the counter on either side of her hips, trapping her. Piper's heart jumped in her chest, and she tried to catch her breath.

"What—way?" She knew where this conversation was going to lead, and her body was begging for it.

"In the last half hour, I've imagined no less than a dozen ways to strip you of your clothes. I want to take you in a dozen different positions until you can no longer move." He growled as he leaned in, nuzzling her cheek.

His breath was hot against her, stirring the tiny hairs on the back of her neck. A sharp shiver ran through her, and her womb clenched in anticipation. God, he knew just what to do to make her crazy with desire. This time there was less fear. He wasn't as scary as she'd thought last night, and knowing that made her body's response to him feel less like she had betrayed herself.

One of his hands cupped the back of her head, and the other gripped her hip possessively as he sank his teeth into her neck in a playful bite. Her clit throbbed in response, the nipping sensation turning her legs to jelly. She fell against him, grabbing his arms as she tried to stay upright. His rumbling laugh moved through her.

"*Beg me*. Beg me for it," he murmured against her ear. "Ask me to take you upstairs and possess you...every part of you. I could pleasure you for hours if you wish. All you have to do...is beg." He licked up the side of her throat and bit her earlobe. A rush of heat exploded between her thighs, and she clamped them together, but it didn't stop the almost violent need that slithered just beneath her skin.

"*Beg*," he rasped again. His hand on her hip slid to her

lower back and then beneath the waistband of her jeans and under her panties. He cupped her bottom, squeezing it hard. That was all it took to drive her out of her mind. She opened her lips, ready to beg, but the jarring sound of a cell phone vibrating nearby was a splash of cold water over them both.

After a breathless moment that left her inwardly cursing, Mikhail let her go and picked up his phone from the counter.

"Belishaw, what—" Mikhail went silent and turned away from her, raking his hand through his hair.

Piper blew out a slow breath as her body descended from the heights she'd been climbing as he'd teased her in every way possible.

"But she isn't a part of this. I thought we—" He cursed softly in Russian and faced her, keeping the phone to his ear. "Fine, keep me informed." He hung up, his green eyes as dark as a primordial forest where the foliage was too thick for the light too penetrate.

Her heart lodged in her throat. Something had happened. "What is it?"

"It seems there was one hidden camera we missed last night. Before I left the reception at the auction house, I accessed the camera feeds of the rooms I planned to enter. They were all looped to show empty rooms. But I missed one." He paused, and Piper waited for the other shoe to drop.

"I'm afraid you were seen helping me load the jewels

into the car. Scotland Yard is searching for you. Your friend Ms. Harkness spent all night being interrogated as to your involvement and whereabouts."

Piper gasped. "Jodie was with the police? Oh my God, is she okay?"

"She is fine. Belishaw has connections and influence. She isn't a suspect, so they couldn't hold her for long."

Piper exhaled in relief and leaned back against the counter.

"But you *are* a suspect," Mikhail said. His lips firmed into a thin, grim line.

"Me? But I...you *made* me!" Panic seized her entire body. The terror and stress of the previous night flooded back.

Mikhail caught her by the shoulders, staring down at her. His green eyes smoldered, and the irises seemed to shift and swirl with honey-gold fire. "Calm down, little dove. I won't let anything happen to you. You will not take the blame for my actions. Understood?"

She gave a shaky nod, but she didn't know how he could make a promise like that. Scotland Yard was searching for her, and they had proof that she'd helped Mikhail. There was no evidence that she'd been coerced, no way to back up her version of the story. To all outward appearances, she'd helped Mikhail of her own free will and run off with him like a modern-day Bonnie and Clyde.

"Breathe, just breathe," Mikhail urged her, one hand on her hip again, but she shoved him away.

"Breathe? That's your advice? This is all your fault! If you hadn't used me to get to the jewels, they wouldn't think I was part of your plan!"

She brushed past him and dashed up the stairs to her room. The harsh, explosive sound of her slamming the door and the echoing rattle of the doorknob offered her only a tiny bit of satisfaction.

"Piper," Mikhail said through the door. "Let me in."

"I just want to be alone. *Please*," she begged. "Haven't you done enough?"

There was a long, deafening silence, and then he spoke again. "Very well. But I promise, I will clear your name."

His soft footfalls retreated, and the creak of the stairs assured her that she was indeed alone. She should've been glad about that, but Mikhail's absence left her feeling strangely hollow inside. She walked over to the windows and looked at the cliffs by the sea.

She lost herself in her thoughts for a long time, until she noticed a figure walking away from the house toward the cliffs. It was Mikhail. Despite the biting wind and the misting spray of the sea butting against the rocks, he was outside without a coat, walking straight toward the cliffs.

$\maltese$ *9* $\maltese$

There were cliffs there,
And forests made of mists. There were bridges
spanning the void, and that great gray blind lake
which hung above its distant bottom
Like the sky on a rainy day above a landscape.
—Rainer Maria Rilke

The mist rolled through the coast of Cornwall like a silent wave, blanketing everything with dampness and chill. For the first time in a long while, Mikhail felt cold. A dragon's blood runs hot, even in the deepest of Russian winters. But today he felt a bone-numbing ache and cold. It seemed to cut deep, freezing the edges of his very soul.

Belishaw's call had been a grim reminder of reality. He'd lived so long outside of the world that he'd lost track of the rules, forgotten about things like consequences. He'd involved Piper, and now her life was crumbling around her. He could see how much it might cost her, and it wounded him as much as it had terrified her. The last thing he ever wanted was to hurt his future mate.

I never think things through. Not five hundred years ago and not now. His father had made a grave mistake choosing him to oversee the transport of the jewels from England. The treaty with the Belishaw dragons had been crucial; if his family ever needed to fight the Drakors back in Moscow, they would need as much support as they could get. While the treaty itself still held fast, the shame of losing the jewels had weakened the Barinov reputation. It was why, even now, he could not go home to Russia, not until he'd seen his mission through and brought the treasure back with him.

Mikhail let the icy wind cut through him, but the punishment would never be enough for his sins. Sometimes when the wind, fog, and rain built around the coast like this, he felt his dragon stir with madness, a sense of unfathomable grief that couldn't be contained.

It wasn't the first time the past had come back at him, dragging old memories into the light. His dragon became too strong then and took over their shared body. He closed his eyes, remembering nights long past, even though he wished he could erase those memories forever.

The dungeon had been cold and damp, the smell of smoke from the torches of the guards thick and cloying. He lay there in the corner of his cell, his food always drugged and leaving him weakened. It had been midday, but there was no light here, not in the dungeons.

"Bring me a light." Elizabeth's voice had cut through the heavy darkness, and he'd stirred.

"My queen?" he croaked, hopefully. He'd spent the last two years hoping for this, or was it longer? But his cries had gone unanswered. Had she finally come to free him from this place?

Fire blazed suddenly past the iron bars, and he could see Elizabeth. She was wearing a gold-and-cream gown, pearls studded her sleeves and bodice, and a white ruffle was laced around her creamy neck. Her red hair was bound up in a fashion suitable for court, and her hand gleamed with jeweled rings.

"My dear, sweet Mikhail," she said with a tragic tone. "I am so sorry. I've learned the truth, but I fear it is too late. I can't fix what is broken, my love, but I can ensure there is some measure of justice."

"What do you mean?" asked Mikhail. "Are you here to free me?"

Elizabeth looked away. "I wish things were that simple, but they are not." She studied one of the rings on her fingers. His ring. The one that had a serpent biting its own tail. An emerald stone was set in the snake's eye. That ring had never belonged to her family. His father had given him that ring on his two hundredth birthday.

"My...ring, that is mine. A gift from my father," he whispered

and stumbled to his feet. He collapsed against the bars, relying on their strength to hold him up. Whatever his jailers had put in his food had been doubled in its dosage, no doubt because they'd been warned that this meeting would take place.

"It is. And I am afraid I must keep it, as I must keep you. Though not like this. Not for much longer."

"I don't understand," said Mikhail.

"I have been used, manipulated most cruelly by one who saw you as a threat to his own plans. He taught my most trusted advisor just enough about your people to distrust them, and he learned just enough on his own to know how to weaken them. It is because of him that you now rot here."

Mikhail found some strength in his bones and shook the bars. "Then free me. Free me, and I will destroy him."

Elizabeth's eyes hardened. "No. I will destroy him. Slowly. In the way I had at first devised for you. You do not realize the depths of this man's treason. It goes far beyond driving a wedge between us. He wanted to use me, to rule this kingdom, and drive away all opposition, starting with your friends, the Belishaws."

Mikhail's eyes widened upon hearing the name.

"In a way, I must thank you," Elizabeth continued. "It was because you sought to woo me that this man was forced to change his plans and turn his eye toward you. Because of that, I became suspicious of him later when he sent whispers my way about the Belishaws and how he felt they should be dealt with.

"That was when I learned the truth, all of it, both about your people and the evil schemes laid against me. Despite his words of

praise and flattery, I believe he always felt I was a weak and feeble woman. He knows now that this is not the case."

Mikhail tried to smile, tried to hold on to some hope. "Then you know my feelings for you were true. That you are my true mate."

Elizabeth looked away but nodded. "I do. And I feel the same for you. But not even love can be greater than the needs of a country and its people. If your family were to learn of what I did to you..." She played with his father's ring on her finger. "If I killed you, they would have no reason not to declare open war upon me. But as a hostage, their hand is stayed."

"My queen, please," he begged as he never had before. "It does not have to be this way. Set me free. I—"

"And have you burn London to the ground?" She shook her head. "Or return to your family to plan revenge? I know what you are, Mikhail, what you can do. And as much as I wish I could believe you, trust you, my own betrayals have doomed me to this path. It is far too dangerous to let you out. You will remain here, but your comfort will be looked to. You have my word. I only wish I could do more for you. Goodbye, my love." She turned away and left him in the dark.

"Elizabeth!" He roared her name, and the walls of the prison rumbled, but he couldn't get past the iron bars. Iron, the one metal his people held no power over. Combined with the elixir they always mixed with his food, he was as close to mortal as he might ever be.

She was true to her word. He remained imprisoned but was moved to better quarters, with a comfortable bed, a library, and whatever he asked for, within reason. The elixir dosage was reduced, for the walls, floor, and ceiling were all reinforced with iron.

Of the man behind his woes, he never learned his name and never clearly saw his face. They met only once, as he was being moved to his improved accommodations in a different part of the castle. It seemed the villain was to take his place chained and shackled in the darkness, bound by iron, forever.

Elizabeth never came to see him again, nor wrote to him, but whatever he asked for, short of his freedom, the staff did their best to provide. In time he came to understand the impossible position she had been put in, and he felt only pity for her. When it came to personal matters, it seemed the most powerful person in England had absolutely no power at all.

Forty-four years later, he'd heard the church bells tolling. The virgin queen had died. His dragon had keened inside his head, mourning the woman who could have been its mate. The pain had been strong enough that he'd felt his life hanging by a thread. Would the mate-grief kill him as it would a fully mated dragon? Or would he lie there suffering in the darkness on the edge of death?

An hour after the bells had stopped ringing, a man had come into the dungeons and set him free, handing him a handkerchief with the queen's emblem embroidered in red and gold. Mikhail had taken the small bit of cloth and unfolded it. There tucked safely at the handkerchief's center was his serpent ring.

"It was her last wish to give you this and your freedom. She also had a message she wished to pass on to you."

Mikhail put the ring on his finger and folded the cloth back up. "What did she say?"

"She said she knows she will see you soon and hopes you can forgive her when you do." The man left. Mikhail wandered from the prison, which had almost felt like a home at times, feeling even weaker than before.

So Elizabeth had known about the mate-grief. That was why she had released him. She believed he would soon die, but she'd wished for him to die with his freedom. It was her last gift. The only gift left she had the power to give.

He had watched from the shore as Elizabeth's coffin was carried downriver to Whitehall. The barge was lit by torches, the fiery glow the only source of light on such a black night.

Even then, broken and defeated as he was, his heart grieved the loss of his once-intended mate. For a dragon's heart is the strongest thing about him. His love and his loyalty could last centuries, even beyond death. Only the fact that they had not fully bonded saved him now, though in the centuries to come he would question whether or not that was a blessing.

He watched the barge vanish out of sight and twisted the ouroboros ring on his finger, then turned his back on his once-beloved Gloriana.

I can forgive you, my love, but I will not join you.

Mikhail buried the memories, now bitter in his heart. The past was the past, and he should not dwell on those dark days and forget to live. He looked out to the sea. Beneath the mist-covered cliffs, the white froth of the ocean churned against the rocky beaches, forming tiny inlets that had once hosted a place for the men and women of Cornwall to catch fish or raid the shoreline for the flotsam and jetsam of shipwrecks, provided by unfortunate captains who'd underestimated the dangers of the coast.

His dragon paced in the prison of his mind, demanding to be set free, even for a few hours. The weight of his sorrow at Elizabeth and now Piper left Mikhail weak. With a sigh, he allowed the dragon to come soaring to the surface.

Mikhail stripped out of his clothes and leapt off the cliff. He flung his arms wide, and for a moment he dove like an Olympic athlete. Then the transformation roared through him like a riptide. His muscles stretched, his skin hardened into dark moss-green scales, and his fingers became clawed tips on his webbed wings. Fire burned through his blood and he exhaled, causing flames to hiss from his jaws, turning the mist to steam, warming him as he flew higher and higher. He climbed the clouds, scaling the air with a series of strong flaps.

At last he broke through the stormy cloud bank and rose toward the sun. The bright rays hit his scales, brightened them to an emerald-like sheen. The beast was in control now. The human side of him faded to the background. The pain of spending half a century trapped in a dungeon had vanished, and he was free to fly and forget. But the dragon couldn't shake the image of Piper from its mind. The way her eyes had filled with tears, or how she'd locked him out and wouldn't let him comfort her.

A roar escaped the dragon, and more fire escaped from his jaws. He allowed his frustration and depression to rule him. He dove back down through the clouds, letting the storm surge around him as he plummeted into the raging seas. The cold water would have tested even the strongest of dragons, but he was used to the punishing feel of the icy waves. He used his powerful back legs to swim to shore, the movement difficult, then almost impossible as his muscles seized and he struggled to breathe.

He embraced this torture, part of him wishing he could sink beneath the surface and never come up. A dragon's grief could be overpowering. What little part of Mikhail that still had power inside the beast urged him onward until he was clawing onto the rock-strewn shore. Jagged stones and tide-softened pebbles stirred beneath him as he writhed on the beach. Minutes later, his body shook violently as he shrank and transformed back into a man.

Teeth chattering, he struggled toward the small cave by the shore where he kept extra clothing in a waterproof gym bag, and he jerkily dressed. The jeans and shirt clung to his damp skin, and the sand still felt gritty against his palms, but he didn't care. His bones almost cracked against one another as shivers began to rack him.

The dragon had gone too far this time. Tonight it had truly tried to hurt itself. The flight and the swim had left him spent, and he had no doubt his dragon had hoped it would kill him. He'd always had a knack for punishing himself, no matter what form it took. But it had been too much this time. Too much.

Shuddering, he left the cave, his body slowly shutting down as he tried to reach the cliff-side path that would take him home. He never made it. Collapsing to his knees, he squinted at the shrinking tunnel of his vision and the woman who cried out as though from a vast distance, a lifetime ago.

❧

PIPER COULDN'T BELIEVE WHAT SHE HAD JUST SEEN.

It wasn't possible. One minute she'd been running toward Mikhail when he stood at the edge of the cliffs, and then he'd stripped naked and jumped. She'd been too far away for him to hear her scream his name. The sea and approaching storm had drowned out any warning she could give him.

Now it was too late. He was gone. No one could survive that jump, and if the fall didn't kill him, the icy water and rocks below would. Piper fell to her knees by the cliff's edge, shivering and staring at the tumultuous water surrounded in mist below her.

And then she heard it. A deep, echoing sound that vibrated the air and shook her to her bones, like a noisy fighter plane taking flight overhead. But she didn't see any plane. She looked up, squinted, and then her heart stopped. Something dark rose up through the clouds.

It was a beast with massive wings and a long whipping tail. There was another sound, much like the one before. Flames burst from the creature's mouth. Piper stared at it, and only one word came to mind.

Dragon.

It was impossible. It was...*impossible*. She was dreaming. This could not be real.

The bank of clouds above swallowed the creature. It had to be a trick of the eyes, or perhaps she had snapped under the stress of everything that was happening to her.

There are no such things as dragons.

She continued to tell herself this until the creature suddenly dropped from the sky and plunged into the sea. She screamed again. When it resurfaced and swam toward the shore, she saw it being struck again and again by the waves, battering it as it clawed its way through the water, its long green serpentine body huffing and fighting for breath. She stared at it, frozen in place until it reached the shore, and she saw it begin to shrink and change, becoming more and more human. She ran toward a small path cut into the cliff side. She had to see it...no, *him*.

The dragon had become Mikhail. She lost sight of him as he entered a cave, but she kept running until she caught sight of him again. He was dressed now, but he looked hurt. There was lethargy to his movements, and without warning he fell to his knees.

"Mikhail!" she screamed and ran toward him, just as he fell face-first on the icy wet sand. He didn't move, didn't stir. When she reached him, she touched his skin with her hands. It was ice-cold.

"What happened?" a voice bellowed from somewhere behind her, bouncing off the rocks. She turned to see Randolph Belishaw racing across the beach toward them.

"He's—He's a—"

"A dragon, yes. But what *happened* to him?" Belishaw knelt by Mikhail and rolled him onto his side. Mikhail coughed, and some water escaped his lips.

"He...he leapt off the cliff and then into the water. I saw him climb out of the water and go into a cave, but when he came out he collapsed."

"We need to get him close to a fire," Belishaw growled. He started to lift Mikhail up from the ground. "Come."

Mikhail blinked, his green eyes cloudy. "Beli...shaw..."

"Mikhail, what the bloody hell did you think you were doing?"

Piper put one of Mikhail's arms around her shoulders. Belishaw did the same. They walked him along the steep, rocky path back up the cliffs. No one spoke as the three of them struggled. Piper slipped twice; her knees banged against the rocks which cut open her jeans. She knew she was bleeding, but they couldn't afford to stop.

She didn't know how long it took for them to make it back to Mikhail's house, but once they did, Belishaw dragged Mikhail to a couch in the living room that was near the fire. Piper collected as many blankets as she could and covered him up. Mikhail closed his eyes and let his head fall back on the couch, letting out a deep, shaky breath.

"Do we need to do anything else to help him?" she asked.

"No, he just needs to warm up by the fire." Belishaw sighed. "Ms. Linwood, I need to speak with you." He waved her to come closer the fire place. He held out his hand, and a small burst of flames shot out at the fresh set of logs. They caught fire in an instant.

"Holy shit!" Piper lunged backward. "You're a dragon too?" This couldn't be happening. She was definitely dreaming.

"Yes," Belishaw said. "A dragon *shifter*, to be more precise."

"And what is that exactly?" Her body swayed as a wave of dizziness swept through her. Belishaw took hold of her wrist until she steadied herself.

"We are a race of beings who have existed for thousands of years. Our ancestors in the distant past were humans who learned to use magic to bring dragon spirits from another realm to this one. They bound the dragons to them, and the two beings coexisted in one body. We are essentially half-human, half-dragon, or depending on how you look at it, fully human and fully dragon. Either form can take over at our choosing. The ability to bond like that, the ritual of it is lost, but when we mate with others of our kind, we can reproduce more dragon shifters. We live most of our lives as humans, but sometimes the dragon takes over when the human side is weakened." He paused, his honey-brown eyes searching her face—for what, she didn't know.

"Okay…" Dragons came from another realm and bonded with humans to form one shared being? She was going to have to process all of this later. Much later.

"For some reason, Mikhail's dragon attempted to harm itself. Do you know why?"

"The dragon? He can't control it?"

Belishaw's face darkened. "Most of the time the man and the beast have the same desires, the same needs, but sometimes a trauma can occur, and the dragon's will becomes too strong." He struggled forward. "Like when a dragon shifter loses his mate, the dragon's grief is too strong to survive. The dragon dies, and the human dies with it. It's why dragon shifters rarely mate mortals. When a dragon's human mate dies within eighty or so years, the dragon perishes within days of their mate's death."

"Is Mikhail…mated?" Piper asked. The thought of him belonging to another woman while he'd been kissing her…

"Almost, but no. She turned her back on him and broke his heart. After she died, he was overcome with grief. I believe part of him still mourns her as though he'd mated her. There have been other times I've seen an unmated dragon mourn the loss of a potential mate. The dragon, unable to die from its grief, attempts to harm itself."

"You mean like suicide?"

The grim expression in Belishaw's eyes made Piper uneasy. She glanced at Mikhail, who was still on the couch, eyes closed.

"But what would make him like that?" she asked.

"That's what I was hoping you could tell me." Belishaw frowned as he looked at Mikhail. "It's been many centuries since I've seen him like this. The last time was when..." He sighed. "When he was released from Elizabeth's dungeons and watched her funeral procession down the Thames."

Piper's lips parted in shock. "Centuries?" He couldn't mean *that* Elizabeth. *That...no...*

"We have lived a very long time, he and I. He hasn't told you, of course, but..." The man paused again, suddenly looking sheepish. "I should say no more. It's not my story to tell. We need to keep him warm. A dragon can withstand much, but cold water gets under the scales, chilling even the human half. And it seems he was battered badly against the rocks." Belishaw gestured to the bruises on Mikhail's ribs.

"Are they broken? Should we call for a doctor? Would they be able to tell that he's not human?" she asked. The bruised patterns on his beautiful chest made her heart ache. Had he really tried to kill himself? Or rather, had the dragon tried to kill him?

"We cannot be taken to hospitals or seen by human

doctors. At least, those who don't know what we are. Our blood possesses certain qualities that would be noticed immediately by mortal physicians and raise too many questions. He will heal. He has suffered much worse before this. But I fear the dragon is regaining control. I was going to return to London after I checked on you both, but now I think it's best if I stay for a while longer." He headed for the door. "Keep him warm. I need to make a few calls."

Piper hesitated for a minute before she settled on the couch beside Mikhail. He used to radiate with heat, but now she could practically feel the icy chill within him. She came closer and laid a hand on his cheek. Her fingers were bloody around the knuckles where she'd cut herself, but she ignored the sting. Mikhail shivered and leaned his cheek into her palm.

"So warm," he whispered and gave another full-body shiver. Piper bit her lip and crawled beneath the blankets on top of him, pressing her body against his. His shirt was still wet from his fall on the shore. He needed to get out of those clothes. They weren't helping him keep warm. She should have thought of that when they first brought him in. She reached for the buttons on his shirt and slipped them open. Then she peeled his shirt from his shoulders.

"Sit up for me," she said and leaned forward so she could remove his shirt completely.

He chuckled, but the sound was slightly ragged.

"Trying to undress me? You need only ask." When she looked up at his face, she saw that his green eyes weren't as glassy now, but his gaze was still distant and unfocused, and that bothered her.

"Come on, Mikhail. Stay with me, okay?"

Every moment of this was completely surreal. But when she touched him, those wounded, haunted eyes grounded her in the reality of the moment. Maybe that's why she'd not been able to resist him. Something about him had drawn her in like a moth to a flame. Dragons, Queen Elizabeth—all of it she could decipher later. Right now, this beautiful, mysterious man was on the verge of being lost, and everything inside her begged to rescue him.

"Jeans next..." She reached for the front of his pants, but he shook his head.

"I just need to lie down." He shifted beneath her, and she gasped as he stretched out on the couch and she fell on top of him. "Feels nice." He curled his arms around her and his head fell back, his breath softening in sleep. Piper moved to get more comfortable and adjusted the blankets to make sure they could keep the heat inside.

She rested her chin on his chest and counted his long dark lashes that spread out on his cheeks, envious of them. Only a woman should have lashes like that. Rather than take away from Mikhail's masculinity, they added to his devastating appeal.

Piper soon found she couldn't keep her eyes open, and

she let herself catch a few minutes of sleep. When she awoke, Belishaw had returned. He sat in a chair by the fire. His elbows rested on his knees, and he stared unseeing at the flames. He, like Mikhail, had haunted eyes. She hadn't noticed them before when she'd first met him. She'd been so focused on Mikhail at the reception. But now she could see it, the weight of centuries as a dragon, living a thousand lives while others died around you, while the world changed. No wonder she could see such sorrow there.

"Belishaw?" She was relieved he was here, but she was unsure of what she needed to say.

He replied without looking at her. "I've managed to find his brothers. They were hard to track down."

"His brothers?" It was another mystery to add to the growing list of things she didn't know about this Russian dragon shifter.

"Yes. Grigori and Rurik. He has not seen either of them in two hundred years."

Pieces of the things Mikhail had said about his family and himself started to fit together. "It was never his ancestor who lost the jewels. It was *him*." She stared at Mikhail's face in stunned silence.

Belishaw's brows rose in surprise. "So he told you some of the story?"

"He said the jewels belonged to his family but that Elizabeth believed they were rightfully the Crown's. He said his ancestor was robbed of them, and he showed me a letter between his family and yours stating that the jewels were part of a treaty between you."

Belishaw steepled his fingers. "Yes, that was all true. He and I were the two mediators between our families, and it was I who gave him the jewels. And they did indeed once belong to the royal family. You see, when Henry VIII was a young king, he came to my clan and offered many rare jewels to us in exchange for our aid. We agreed, happy to support him in exchange for such a hoard. But what you saw in the auction house was only a portion of what we were given. Some of the rarer pieces we gave to the Barinovs in our treaty. And some we regret having given up."

"Which ones?" she asked. She knew the entire Cheapside collection by heart.

"The most important one was a fist-sized ruby called the Dragon Heart. It's a very rare and dangerous stone."

"Dangerous? I examined it thoroughly. It's only a ruby."

Belishaw smiled a little. "It is far more than that. The stone has been passed down in my family for generations." He paused, staring into the fire again. "Sometimes, when I was in the presence of the stone, I could hear it whisper. Objects that house magic have a voice. It doesn't speak in words but more in flashes of images. It's hard to explain. Only those who can sense magic would feel it. Thankfully most humans have long since lost their sixth sense when it comes to magic."

Piper glanced at Mikhail, who still slept, and she

couldn't believe she was sitting in a Cornwall mansion, talking about dragons and magical rubies.

"Why do you think it's dangerous?" she asked. She hadn't noticed anything other than the purity of the gemstone and its stunning size.

"It's just a hunch, more than anything. My family was happy to trade it to the Barinovs because we didn't know the extent of its powers. England isn't like Russia. When our dragon clans fight, it's often deadly. You won't see us burning down the city, but entire family lines can be wiped out in a matter of weeks when clans go to war. The Barinovs have only one family whom they see as a threat—the Drakors. We believed sending the Dragon Heart Stone with Mikhail back to the Fire Hills would be safer than keeping it here in England. But the treasure never arrived. That's why I agreed to help Mikhail. He's lived in exile for five hundred years. Far too long. Now that he has the Cheapside hoard, he can finally go home." There was a hint of melancholy in Belishaw's eyes as he said this. It was clear the bonds of friendship between dragons ran deep.

She scowled. "His brothers wouldn't let him come home?" If they were that level of cruel, she didn't want them anywhere near Mikhail.

Belishaw shook his head. "It was their father's order to exile Mikhail, and he died more than twenty years ago, but Mikhail felt honor bound to continue his search. His brothers are eager for him to come home regardless."

"Oh, that's good. I didn't want them to come here if

they were the sort who would banish their own brother." A wave of protectiveness for Mikhail had grown inside her the moment she'd found him unconscious on the beach. She knew her face was red enough that Belishaw could see because he laughed. He leaned back in his chair, seemingly more relaxed.

"You're protective of him. That's a good sign."

"Why?" she asked.

"Because he feels the same toward you. It's good for two people to be protective of each other."

There was something in the way he said it that made her sense he wasn't telling her everything, but she doubted he would admit it.

She focused back on Mikhail. The worried, restless look on his face seemed to have faded a bit. "When will his brothers arrive?"

"Rurik, Mikhail's youngest brother, is in Russia. He is staying put to protect their landholdings there. The Drakors give them trouble from time to time, and he cannot leave their boundaries unguarded. The eldest, Grigori, and his mate are in America. They should arrive in a few days."

"So dragons mate with other dragons?" She felt silly for asking, but now she couldn't help but be curious. She had been kissing a dragon, after all. She wanted to know if humans and dragon shifters were...compatible. Belishaw had mentioned something about mating humans, but she'd been so worried about Mikhail that she hadn't been focusing on much of what the other man had said.

God, I'm an awful person. He almost died today, and I'm wondering whether we can have sex when he's better.

Belishaw's dark eyes sparkled like fractured topaz. "We do mate with dragonesses. But they do not like to mate with us. It is why we are slowly dying out as a race."

"Why don't dragonesses like to mate male dragons? That doesn't exactly mesh with how evolution works."

His lips twitched. "Because we are creatures of magic, not evolution. We are too dominant for the females of our kind. Our bed play is a little rough, and we like to..." He hesitated. "Be in control. Dragonesses do as well, and it makes sex less satisfying for the female dragons as well as the males."

Wow. That put some serious mental images in Piper's head. She couldn't forget how Mikhail had so easily tied her wrists and held her against the bedpost. The memory made her thighs clench. She became even more aware of lying on her half-naked dragon shifter on the couch.

"But you do...sleep with humans?"

A slow smile spread on Belishaw's lips. "We do indeed. And we quite enjoy it." He rose from his chair by the fire and pulled out his cell phone. He started to walk toward the kitchen. "Which reminds me, I owe your friend Jodie Harkness a call."

Piper cleared her throat. "Does she know about...what you are?"

Belishaw paused in the doorway, his face half in shadow. "No. If things become more serious, I will tell her. But it's safer not to for now." He disappeared into the kitchen, leaving Piper alone with Mikhail.

Once more she focused on his face, on the beautiful shape of his lips and the marble-cut features that would make angels weep. A dragon. Who would have imagined? There was a part of her that still couldn't believe it. Maybe her wild attraction to him came from the fact that he was a dragon? Maybe they were irresistible to humans? She wanted to think that his hold over her was something as simple as that, but deep down she knew it wasn't a simple fascination or some magical sway he held. No, it was something deeper, something purer that she could not name but only feel.

Tonight he'd gone over the cliffs, and the beast inside him had tried to—

She shuddered. She found within her a new drive, not to reclaim her life in London, but to save his here. To prove to him that life was still worth living. She reached up to stroke his cheek and traced his brow with a gentle caress. She'd seen the beast he was, but she was not afraid.

"I'm here. You're not alone." She hoped Mikhail's dragon could hear it too. "Stay with me."

$$\text{❧ I O ❧}$$

*And though I came to forget or regret all I have ever
done, yet I would remember that once I saw the
dragons aloft on the wind at sunset above the western
isles; and I would be content.*
—Ursula K. Le Guin, *The Farthest Shore*

Fitful dreams and haunted, shadowy nightmares chased Mikhail through the halls of his mind as he slept. The dragon stirred, trying to reclaim control as images of Elizabeth, his sweet Gloriana, betraying him played over and over. For five centuries his dragon had held the pain of the past at bay. But the moment Piper Linwood came into his life, the fortress around his dragon's heart had begun to crumble.

He had dared to desire a mate once before, and it had cost him everything but his life. The dragon inside him didn't want to take a risk like that again. It had nearly killed him. And Piper... She could be his mate. The chemistry was there, and the hunger in her blue-gray eyes when she looked at him made it all but impossible to keep his distance.

He had to have her. Even if it meant his death.

As the dreams faded into the recesses of his mind, he could feel the delicious heat of a woman's body on top of his. The smoky scent of burning logs and the slight chill of his clothes all came together in a slowly building awareness. His body was still cooler than normal, but the icy dread that had been drowning him when he'd crawled from the water had receded.

A delicate scent, floral with a hint of honey, teased his nose, and he took it in deeply, like he was scenting a freshly poured glass of wine. Piper's hair was spread out across his chest in wild tendrils. He moved one hand to twine a lock around one of his fingers. His dragon rumbled in confusion. It desired closeness, intimacy, but it was afraid after everything that had happened before.

He understood. More than forty years confined to an English prison, unable to transform, unable to escape, had almost turned his dragon feral. If he hadn't been so devastated by Elizabeth's death, he would've let his dragon go unchecked. London would have indeed burned to the ground from his rage.

Instead, when he'd seen her funeral procession, all of the fight in him had died. He'd had long years to think over what she'd said to him, and in the end she had been proven right. Though she had learned the truth, she had been powerless to do other than what she had. As a queen, she could not act upon her desires and what she wanted, only what she must do for her people.

He wondered for a moment about the man who had taken his place, chained and tormented in a tiny cell. Though there could be no happiness for Elizabeth and Mikhail, she had hoped there would be some measure of justice. Perhaps there had been, but it had not made his life any easier to bear.

Mikhail returned to the present, studying the way the firelight caught amber and bronze in Piper's light brown hair. It was a beautiful mix of colors. He remembered that she'd tried to remove his jeans earlier and smiled. The time for that would come soon enough.

Familiar footfalls caught his attention. Belishaw came out of the kitchen and paused when he saw Mikhail.

"You're awake," Belishaw said, his eyes hard and serious. "We need to talk."

Mikhail frowned. He did not want to talk. Not about the beach or how his dragon had tried to end him.

"Tomorrow," Mikhail replied. "I assume you will stay here? Or are you going back to London?" He hoped his friend would stay, though Mikhail admitted he wanted Piper all to himself.

"I had intended to go back, but I think you need me here. Piper won't be able to stop your dragon if it tries anything."

It filled Mikhail with a quiet joy to know he and Belishaw had formed such a deep friendship over the centuries, but he didn't want to be a burden.

"She is the key. The closer I get to her, the farther the past is pushed away. The dragon can't fight her forever."

His friend's eyes filled with understanding. "You mean to mate with her?"

Mikhail glanced down at Piper's sleeping face, her slightly upturned nose, kissable lips, and the gold-brown lashes on her cheeks. He nodded.

"I think I do." His answer still came as a surprise. "My dragon and I both sense she is a true mate."

"And the fact that she is mortal?" Belishaw asked.

"Elizabeth was as well, and I didn't care," Mikhail reminded him. "I never expected to live as long as my father. My brothers are still alive. They don't need me to carry on the Barinov name. I would rather be happy for seventy years than alone for the next five thousand." It was a decision all dragons eventually faced.

"Speaking of your brothers..." Belishaw cleared his throat. "I was able to track them down. Rurik has to stay in Russia, but Grigori and his mate are coming straight here. They were visiting her family in America."

"Grigori has a mate?" The news shocked him. Strong,

sensible, disciplined Grigori had never seemed like a dragon who would give in to his instinct to mate.

"He does."

"Is she a dragoness?" he asked. Somehow he couldn't picture a female dragon responding to Grigori's overly protective nature too well. He must have found one very tolerant female.

Belishaw shrugged. "I'm not sure. He didn't say. But if he mated a dragoness, I would have heard about it. Mating a Barinov would have been important news."

Mikhail hoped his brother hadn't mated a human. That would mean carrying on the Barinov line would be up to Rurik. Their youngest brother was a rough, wild man who would never settle down, and surely no dragoness would take him. Since only two dragon shifters could produce a drakeling, the Barinov bloodline would be doomed.

Mikhail wondered what had happened to his older brother since he last saw him. Clearly, he had changed in the last two hundred years if he had mated, especially if he had chosen a human. Grigori had always been the responsible one, dependable and in charge, the one who never took risks. Mating a human was completely out of character for him.

"You should go back to London," Mikhail said. "You don't want to miss out on time with your brown-eyed gemologist."

His friend grinned. "I do miss her. She's quite anxious

for me to return." He sobered. "She's worried about Piper too and I must reassure her that all is well. I will go, but you must call me if you feel it taking over. I don't...I *can't* lose another friend. I don't want to attend another blasted funeral." The gruffness in the Englishman's usually refined voice was a bit startling.

Mikhail nodded. "Very well."

With one last farewell, Belishaw collected his coat and keys and left. He had a long drive back to London.

Several minutes passed before Mikhail took a chance and moved beneath Piper. When she didn't stir, he pulled himself to a sitting position and rolled her sideways until she was cradled in his lap. Then he rose with her in his arms and carried her to his bedroom upstairs. He needed to get out of his damp clothes and to make sure she was no longer wet. The last thing he needed now was for her to get pneumonia.

He set her down on his bed and unwrapped the thick blanket. He touched her pants and sweater. They were still damp. She only stirred once as he slid them off her. He tucked her back beneath the blankets and loaded the fireplace with fresh logs, then held up his palm, and soon the logs began to pop and crackle with flame.

He returned to Piper and placed a kiss upon her brow before he stripped out of his jeans and climbed inside the bathroom shower. The hot water warmed his skin, and he sighed. Centuries of stress bled out of him and onto the warm, heated tile. He didn't think about the jewels hidden away, or the icy chill of the ocean, or even Elizabeth. He closed his eyes and pictured Piper and how she'd felt in his arms the moment he kissed her in the antechamber to the ballroom at Thorne Auction House. How she'd tasted, like brandy and fire, burning from the inside out.

He couldn't forget the flashes of her memories that had been passed on to him, either. When he'd kissed Elizabeth, he'd never seen the unguarded parts of her heart, only her memories that showed her moments of fear and mistrust of those around her. He'd assumed it was simply because she was a young queen in a dangerous court full of betrayals. Now he knew it was because her heart had never been open to him at all.

It wasn't so with Piper. She had opened her heart to him from the moment he'd first met her. And he had responded, opening himself to her. How could he not? The passionate, determined, but shy woman who had pushed herself harder than anyone he knew to become the woman she was. He felt proud that fate had seen fit to give him a second chance with a woman like her.

His body hardened, and he couldn't resist grasping his erection, stroking its length. By the gods, he needed a release. It had been too long since he'd—

A soft sound drew his attention to the shower door. Through the steamed glass he saw Piper standing there, wearing only bra and panties beneath the blanket wrapped around her like a cloak. She stared open-mouthed as he fisted his cock.

Did she want to watch? Her cheeks pinkened, but she didn't look away as he continued to pump his hand. His balls ached with the need to release, and watching her watch him was hotter than hell.

"Like what you see?" He swung the shower door open with his free hand. Steam rolled out and wrapped around Piper's frozen figure. She didn't reply, but her grip on the blanket began to slip as he unleashed his seed. She gasped and the blanket fell to the floor. She wore only the bra and panties now, and he got hard all over again at the sight. He didn't wait for her to think. He pulled her into the shower with him and shut the door. She jumped as the hot water splashed on their bodies.

"Wait, my bra—" she said as he dragged her deeper into the spray.

"Let me help you." He slipped his fingertips under her bra straps and unclasped it from behind, then lowered them off her shoulders. Her bra fell to the floor with a wet smack. She covered her breasts and backed up until she had the shower wall behind her.

Mikhail's instincts took over. He cornered her against the wall, placing his hands on either side of her shoulders and leaning in to kiss her. Her startled lips parted, and she opened up for his exploring tongue. Gods, he could kiss this woman over and over and never want to stop.

"Touch me," he urged her. Her hands crept hesitantly up his arms.

"Not there..." He rolled his hips and hers, letting his shaft bob against her belly. "*Here*."

When one of her hands curled around his cock, he groaned in pleasure.

"Like this?" she asked on a whisper. He managed a nod and began to rock his hips, using her hand to build toward a new release. She seemed to understand what he wanted and gripped him tighter. He cupped the back of her neck, holding her still so he could kiss her fiercely. The water rained down around them, but everything seemed to be on fire.

He hissed out as the climax hit him like a freight train. His seed splashed on her belly, and he panted as it began to wash away. An animalistic rush of joy unexpectedly came at marking her like that.

Mine, the dragon growled inside his head, the word unmistakable.

Yes. Ours, he agreed.

He opened his eyes and stared at Piper as she uncurled her fingers from his cock and lifted her head to meet his gaze.

"Tell me you want me," he said in a low growl. "Because I *need* to be inside you."

Piper bit her bottom lip, her eyes luminous like a full moon, a bright, thrilling silver-blue that made him think of polished moonstones.

"Okay...but I'm..." She faltered. "I'm a..."

He brushed a lock of wet hair behind her ear. "I know. I'll be gentle."

She nodded, and he wanted to crow with victory. It was an ancient urge the dragon couldn't resist, the need to connect to such purity, like they did with the gemstones. He turned off the shower and then took her by the hand, leading her out of the shower. He grabbed a fluffy white towel from the rack. After drying their bodies, he led her to the bed, and she sat shyly on the edge of it, her thighs clasped together and her arms crushed over her chest.

He smiled and leaned over her. She tilted her head back to welcome his approaching kiss. The sound of the fire and the distant roar of the sea felt like home for the first time, because he wasn't alone.

"I can't believe I'm really doing this," she whispered.

He chuckled. "Having sex with a dragon?"

"Having sex, period. I've imagined it for so long, and now I'm finally going to do it."

Mikhail nibbled her bottom lip. "I'm glad your first time is with me."

He meant that. He loved knowing that her first time would be with him, this beautiful, compassionate, intelligent woman whom destiny had seen fit to give to him. She was his second chance at life, and he would never take her for granted. They were sharing something intimate and special. No man would replace him in this moment. And if he had his way, no man would replace him ever.

"Lie back." She did as he commanded. Seeing her bare

except for those tiny wet black panties made every fantasy he'd had for decades come roaring back to life.

"What is it?" she asked, a hint of worry in her voice. "We could turn off some of the lights if—"

"No," he said. "I wish to look at you. *All* of you." He leaned over and hooked his fingers into her panties so he could tug them down her legs. She lifted her hips, her face bright red. Her shyness was endearing, but he never wanted her to feel unsure of herself, not with him. When he dropped the panties on the floor, he grasped her knees and pushed them apart. Her breath hitched, but she didn't ask him to stop.

"Please, go slow," she breathed as he crawled up her body on the bed. He nodded and nuzzled her stomach, pressing slow kisses there before moving up to her breasts. The full mounds were an irresistible temptation. He settled his hips between her legs but didn't put his weight down on her. Piper's hands settled on his shoulders as he kissed one nipple, then sucked on it until she moaned and dug her hands in his hair, urging him on.

She murmured something when he slid one hand down her body to touch her folds. Then she said it again more clearly. "Distract me." She was wet and hot to the touch, but she tensed when he stroked a fingertip between the sensitive folds.

"Distract you?" He moved back down her body before she could react. He placed his shoulders between her thighs, stopping her from closing up on him. He kissed the top of her mound before moving lower. He licked her, like a cat with a bowl of cream, growling in delight as she tried to wriggle away but couldn't. The tiny bundle of nerves peeped out of its hood, and he closed his lips around it.

She gasped in shock as he slid a finger inside her, probing her. He felt the barrier of her innocence as he pushed deeper. She let out a whimper, and Mikhail smiled before he sucked harder. Her body responded with a flood of heat, which he happily licked. She thrashed her head, and he sensed she wouldn't make it much longer. He moved quickly, sliding back up to kiss her. Then he guided his swollen shaft to her entrance and pushed in. Her body resisted, but he couldn't go slow, not if he wanted to cause as little pain as possible.

"Forgive me, little dove," he whispered. He slanted his mouth down over hers in a ruthless, distracting kiss as he drove deep into her. Her hips bucked, and she bit his lip, her nails digging into his back, but he welcomed the bite of pain. They moved slowly, gently, in a way he'd never imagined. It wasn't in a dragon's nature to mate like this, but right now the man in him was in control.

The cadence of whispered words and sighs as they moved toward a shared climax was breathtaking. The universe seemed to shrink to an infinite space between their breaths. Her blue eyes lit with a fire that matched the rolling heat surging through his chest. There were no words, only the awe-inspiring sensation that this moment would change him forever. His body and soul belonged to this woman now. As they reached the zenith of their pleasure at the same moment, Mikhail gave Piper everything that he was...including his heart.

The glow inside him did not fade as he collapsed next to her, sweat dewing on his body. Tears stung his eyes, and his throat closed as raw emotion choked him. He cupped Piper's cheeks and pressed his forehead to hers, whispering to her in Russian.

"You are mine; I am yours. Take my body. My heart. I am yours to command."

Piper's sweet sigh and bashful smile seized his heart. Loving Elizabeth, his beautiful Gloriana, had never been like this. He could measure his heartbeat against Piper's, and his breath and his body were for her and her alone.

She wriggled closer, and he reached for the blanket, pulling it up over them. "What did you say just then?"

"Nothing," he lied, but she pinched him, so he relented. "Only that I belong to you." He held his breath, nervous to see her reaction. Piper stroked a hand on his throat and then down along his shoulders, and a blush tinged her cheeks.

She nibbled her lip. "You belong to me?" He nodded. "No one's ever belonged to me before." Awe filled her voice, and finally he could breathe again. She understood what this meant, that what had just happened between them was more than sex. He had mated her. She didn't know the full importance of what had just happened, but she would soon, once he'd summoned the courage to tell her. Elizabeth's betrayal still left him on edge.

"I still can't believe you're a dragon," she said, her eyes fixed on his. "A real, honest-to-God dragon."

His lips twitched. "I suspect you will have many questions once you get used to the idea."

Piper chuckled. "I have questions now. How old are you? Where did the first dragons come from? Belishaw said the dragon and the man are sort of separate. How does that work? How does *any* of it work?"

"So many questions." Mikhail slid one arm around her waist, tugging her closer. "We dragons have been around for millennia. The old ones, ones so distant even history has forgotten them, were the ones who first joined with humans. I do not know much of that past; it seems more myth now than truth. My race is scattered across the earth now, and most who would know the truth have perished in battles. While we are immortal, we can be killed." He thought of his parents. How his father's desire to hunt Thunderbirds, another ancient creature, had gotten him killed, which in turn had killed his mother through the mating grief.

"But you're separate?"

"Yes. The man and the dragon are two full beings who share one vessel. The body is fully human and fully dragon, but only one part can be expressed at a time. When the dragon takes over, the human part of me is locked away. I can see, hear, and feel what happens to the dragon, but I'm no longer in control."

A shadow passed over Piper's eyes, but it was so fleeting he couldn't help but wonder if he'd imagined it. "What did you do to me to make me help you steal the jewels? I would never have done that willingly."

Mikhail nodded. "Dragons have the ability to mesmerize others. I hesitated to use it on you, but it was necessary. I needed you to come with me. I knew from the moment I saw you that you and I were meant to be together."

He didn't tell her about the consequences of their mating. She wasn't ready to know yet, and he wasn't ready to tell her. She'd been through so much with him in the last two days that he didn't want to scare her with talk of true mates.

She bit her lip, studying him. "Would you ever use that on me to do things I didn't want to? Aside from jewel stealing, I mean?"

He shook his head fiercely. "No. I would never force you to do anything, unless it was to save you. If you're ever in danger and you refuse an order I give to protect you, that's when I would use it on you, but only then."

"That's not good enough. You could twist any situation into saying it's for my own safety. Free will is important. It might be the most important thing there is." She scowled at him, and he saw a hint of warning in her eyes.

"I agree. I wish I had never done it in the first place, but I could think of no other way."

"Then promise to me now that you will never do it again, no matter what. Even if you believe it's for my own safety." Her gaze softened, and his heart swelled in his chest. God, he loved it when she looked at him like that, like she cared about him.

Mikhail did not want to make that promise. She did not know what his world could be like at times. But he also saw how important this was to her, and he understood. "You have my word," he said, stealing a quick kiss.

She sighed against his lips in a dreamy way that made his dragon purr in contentment.

"Any other questions?" he asked.

"Tons, but maybe in a little while," she said and tucked her head beneath his chin. What he had said earlier had caused her to worry. He didn't like that. She was his mate now, and he wanted her healthy and happy. He wouldn't make the same mistake he'd made with Elizabeth.

But this would be different. Piper wouldn't betray him, and he would see to it that she had the world at her fingertips. He held her close, breathing in her scent and letting it banish his dark memories. Letting it bury the past.

❧ 11 ❧

*People who deny the existence of dragons are often
eaten by dragons from within.*
—Ursula K. Le Guin

"What do you mean the jewels are *gone*?"

Conrad Sinclair stared at Barty Winston from across the expansive mahogany desk in his office. The wood had been so finely polished that he could see his own ghostly reflection if he leaned close enough to the surface.

"There was a burglary." Barty shifted uncomfortably in the chair opposite Conrad's desk. "Someone came in through the kitchen door that connects to the museum from the mews."

Conrad frowned, his temper roiling like magma beneath his skin.

"But the auction house has security cameras and alarm systems. The jewels were in a safe." He'd been working with Barty to acquire the information needed to make his own heist possible, but it seemed someone had beaten him to it.

"It was an inside job. The security cameras were put on a loop. The kitchen alarm was disabled with the correct code. Oddly enough, they left a small amount of the gems behind. But..." Barty nudged his thick glasses up his nose with his index finger. "There was, however, one camera that they missed. I believe the thieves forgot about it."

"Thieves? More than one?" Conrad didn't like the idea of chasing down two people. The odds they would separate and break up the hoard of jewels were high. That made his job of recovering them much harder.

"Yes." Barty scowled. "Piper Linwood, the gemologist you wished to acquire, seems to be involved. The lone camera that wasn't hacked shows her and a man carrying the jewels out to a vehicle parked in the mews and driving away. Her role in the burglary seemed to be voluntary."

Barty dug through his pockets and his coat until he found what he was looking for, a small thumb drive. He held it out to Conrad over the desk.

Conrad made no move to take it. "What is that?"

"The recording of the security video. I have a friend at

Scotland Yard who owed me a favor. I thought you might want to see it."

Only then did Conrad accept the drive. He inserted it into his computer and pulled up the video file.

It was dark by the mews, but he could see Piper clearly as she exited the kitchen door carrying a box of jewels. A man followed her, his arms also laden with boxes. The man was dark-haired and tall, and he moved with a grace that was unnatural for humans. The man moved like a dragon. Conrad paused the video and zoomed in on the man's face.

"You have no idea who this man is?" he asked Barty.

"No. Scotland Yard is currently running him through facial recognition, but they won't have any results for another couple of days."

Conrad studied the blurry face of the mystery man, and then it hit him—a flash of memory, centuries old. A man he had seen only once, as they'd passed by each other in a darkened cell. The memory was brief, faded around the edges, but Conrad was sure it was the same man. Mikhail Barinov...the Russian dragon he'd convinced Queen Elizabeth I had been there to betray and use her. She'd thrown Barinov into prison only to later change her mind and throw Conrad in as well as punishment against all dragons.

"Thank you, Mr. Winston." Conrad removed the drive from his computer and handed it back to Barty. "I will handle everything from here on. I no longer require your services."

Barty gulped. "And my fee?" Each word shook as he spoke, and Conrad couldn't resist scaring the sniveling little mortal. He stood up and placed his hands on the desk as he leaned over to stare at the man.

"And what, exactly, do you think I owe you? You were unable to fulfill your end of the bargain."

"But—"

"But nothing. You are fortunate I am letting you leave here with your life."

"My *life?*"

Conrad let his dragon start to claw its way to the surface. His dark eyes turned to bright gold, and he lifted one hand from his desk, his fingers suddenly wreathed in flames.

Barty let out a terrified screech and fell flat on his back as his chair tipped over. Conrad watched the pathetic human scramble away on his hands and knees out the door. Well, there was one less vote for him come the general election.

When Conrad was alone, he sat back down at his desk, thinking. Mikhail Barinov had only one set of allies that he knew of in England, the Belishaws, which meant he could use that connection to find him.

The one problem was that the Belishaw family was still considered the current ruling family of the dragons in

England. He would be putting himself at great risk if he forced his hand early.

Conrad snorted at the irony. Once again, Mikhail Barinov had inadvertently forced his hand, made him have to move ahead of schedule. But he needed those gems for an alliance of his own, for the final pieces of his plan to fall into place. Then the coming election would be all but guaranteed.

And then the fun would begin.

Conrad smiled and leaned back in his chair. There was a knock at his door, and his smile faded.

"Mr. Sinclair?" His assistant, Brenda, a small mousy woman, appeared in the doorway, smiling hesitantly.

"Yes?" he asked, watching her intently. He did so love to make her squirm.

"The prime minister is in the conference room. I believe she is a tad early for your meeting." Brenda glanced at her smartphone, no doubt checking their shared calendar.

"Tell the prime minister that I will see her in fifteen minutes," Conrad announced. He wondered if she was having doubts about stepping down. Well, it wouldn't take much to remind her it was the right thing to do. For the good of the country.

After Brenda closed the door, he laughed for a good long while. Even in five hundred years, he had not lost his ability to control humans. After the prime minister stepped down and called for a new election, things would move very fast indeed. A fiery campaign, preying on the fears and prejudices of the population, convincing them he would be their salvation. It had worked before, and those politicians didn't even have a dragon's charisma.

And then, when the country put their trust in him, he would watch it all burn.

Oh, Elizabeth, I swore to you that I would destroy your precious nation for what you did to me. I just never said when.

PIPER WOKE SLOWLY, HER BODY STIRRING WITH A languid, relaxed feeling of bliss. She'd never known her body could be so limp. Heat radiated from behind her, and warm breath fanned against the back of her neck. A large masculine hand cupped her right breast, offering a slight squeeze as she stirred.

Mikhail.

She was in bed with a man who could shift into a dragon. And he'd made love to her. Her thighs quivered with the memory, as did the soreness deep inside her.

She'd *done* it. She'd finally had sex, and it had been scary, a bit painful, and then *amazing.* He'd been slow and gentle, and she'd felt herself come apart beneath him. The memories warmed her all over. She was going to be embarrassed when he woke up, but at least right now, while he was asleep, she could enjoy this. Jodie had been right. This was *so* worth it.

But as much as she wanted to stay right where she was, nature was calling. She gently pried Mikhail's hand off her breast and slipped out of bed. He made a soft growl but didn't open his eyes and rolled onto his back, still asleep.

The dressing gown with the dragons stitched into it lay beside the bed on the floor. She slipped it on and went into the bathroom.

Afterward, she stared hard at herself in the mirror and almost didn't recognize the woman she saw. This woman had swollen lips, and her hair was in a wild tumble of waves, looking more golden than plain light brown. The red satin gown hugged her full figure in a sensual way that made her look like a lingerie model rather than a timid, curvaceous virgin scientist who knew almost nothing about sex. She couldn't help but smile. If Jodie could see her now, she'd totally freak out.

Hello, sex kitten; goodbye, prude!

Piper pulled the robe tight around her as a chill slithered though the bathroom window. Struck with a sudden inspiration, she tiptoed back through Mikhail's bedroom, pausing by the bed long enough to stroke her fingertips along his chest before she left. She had no idea what time it was, but it was still daylight out, and she was going to make them both something to eat.

She was almost to the kitchen when she noticed a door open at the end of the hall. It hadn't been open before. Curious, she padded down the hall and peeked inside. It was a study, but from the look of it, no one had used it in a very long time. A layer of dust coated the gilt writing desk and the bookshelves against one wall. The fireplace here had amassed an army of dust bunnies, and the sunlight had faded the rich fabrics of the couch and chairs.

Piper approached the bookshelf and noticed that there were more than just books on it. A few small animal skulls, a framed set of pinned butterflies, large exotic seashells, and a collection of nautical compasses were tucked between heavy tomes with titles such as *Exploration of India*, *The Classification of Mammals*, and *Scientific Discoveries with Plants in Medicine*.

This must have been the study that belonged to Mikhail's friend, the one who was a naturalist.

Ignoring a small flare of guilt, Piper approached the writing desk and sat down in the chair. She played at the desk's edges until she found a small, oddly placed bit of wood. When she pressed on it, a hidden drawer popped out. Piper had seen desks like these before on *Antiques Roadshow*.

She opened the door farther and found it contained only one thing: a leather-bound sketchpad. She set it on the desk's surface, ignoring the wave of dust it kicked up. Motes of dust caught and spun in the light streaming through the windows in a haunting dance. For a moment Piper thought she could see the ghostly form of a man pacing by the windows, but she blinked and the vision was gone, the dust drifting in gold waves as it settled.

The initials *JM* were pressed deep into the leather

cover. She opened it carefully to the first page. A gasp escaped her. It was a sketch of Mikhail. He sat in a chair by the fire, brooding. His dark hair was long and slightly wavy as it was now, but in the sketch he wore breeches and a waistcoat with a white shirt. Written beneath were the words, *"Heavy weighs the soul of a dragon who has lost his honor."* Then another line of words below. *"December 25, 1820, Mikhail Barinov as I remember him."*

The drawings were full of emotion, as though the artist had been fascinated with his subject. She carefully turned the page. Next was a drawing of a beast, one she remembered only too well. It stalked a herd of sheep over a hill, its wings tucked back against its body as it tried to creep up on them. The artist had written another description. *"Mikhail can't resist Mr. Bailey's sheep. One of these days the old farmer will realize who is eating them."* Piper could almost hear the laughter in the artist's voice, as though he were in the room with her. It was an eerie but not unwelcome feeling.

She turned another page. This picture was not of people, but a place. And it was painted with watercolors rather than drawn. It was a valley with trees in a hundred fiery shades. Nestled in the valley were three small structures with onion domes painted with bright colors. The sight was breathtaking.

The artist had only written one word beneath this. *"Home."* But it wasn't the artist's home. Perhaps it was Mikhail's?

Piper turned one more page, and her heart clenched. Three men stood facing each other, smiles lighting their eyes. The familial resemblance was unmistakable. A name was written beneath each. *"Grigori, Mikhail, Rurik. Brothers reunited after three centuries."*

A voice from the doorway behind her made her jump. "He was a very good artist." She turned to see Mikhail watching her.

"I'm sorry! The door was open, and I..." Great, she got caught. She could only hope he wasn't upset.

He only smiled. He wore only jeans as he leaned against the doorjamb. "Where did you find that? After James died, I searched for it everywhere." He approached her, and she handed him the portfolio.

"It was in a hidden drawer." She showed him the compartment. "I opened it by pressing this button. I recognized this style of desk and thought it might have a hidden compartment." She showed him how she'd triggered the release.

"Clever man, James." Mikhail moved to a couch and had her sit beside him. She shifted so she leaned back against him.

"Who was he?" she asked.

He curled an arm around her waist to set the portfolio between them. "An old friend. I was an outcast for a long time here in England, but he reminded me how good people could be. He took me into his home and offered me his friendship when I needed it most. He was my family in many ways, a brother of my heart but not by blood. Staying here with him was something I never regretted. And when he died, my dragon and I mourned him for decades."

She turned back to the picture of the three men to show him. "He met your brothers?"

"Yes. There was a point in the midst of my exile when Grigori sent word to me that our parents were touring the world and would be gone for a year. Grigori begged me to return home. I knew I shouldn't disobey my father's orders, but I missed my home. And my family." His voice was rough, and his hold on her tightened. Piper leaned into him, wanting to offer as much comfort as she could.

"So they let you come home? Your brothers, I mean?"

"They did. They never agreed with my exile, but I couldn't disobey my father. Yet I did. I brought James with me as well. By then he knew what I was and was fascinated by us. My brothers and I swore him to secrecy, which he readily agreed to. He never breathed a word of what we were. Back then we would've been killed. Now..." He didn't finish. But Piper had a sick feeling in her stomach.

"Now they'd probably turn you into a lab rat and do experiments on you."

He nodded. "And it would reveal the other supernatural creatures that are living among them as well."

Piper stared at him. "Wait—what other creatures?"

Mikhail's lips hovered in a near smile. "Surely you

didn't think we were the only unusual creatures out there?"

"Well, I mean, I thought you were..." Piper really hadn't thought about the possibility of other creatures. She was still stuck on the fact that dragons were real. But she supposed if one mythical species was real, then why not others?

"So..." She snuggled closer to him, loving that she could and he didn't push her away. "What creatures are we talking about here?" She tried to play it off casually, like she wasn't freaking out on the inside.

"Oh, let's see. Vampires and werewolves, phoenixes and other kinds of shifters, and then there are ghosts..." He ticked them off one by one on his hand.

Piper stared at him. "Vampires and werewolves?" *Holy shit.*

"Yes, but I assure you the stories you've heard of both have been greatly exaggerated, except perhaps the fact that they don't get along too well. I'm actually friends with a few members of the London Blood Society. They can be a bit too brooding and melancholy for my tastes, but I like vampires well enough."

She ran over the rest of the species in her head. "What's the difference between werewolves and shifters? I mean, are there wolf shifters or just werewolves?" She couldn't believe she was having this discussion with him, but for the moment she was just trying to learn as much as she could.

Mikhail twined his fingers in her hair and bent his head to nuzzle her cheek.

"So many questions," he purred against her ear. "I don't think I've distracted you enough."

She lay lengthwise on the couch with him, her body on top of his, her back to his chest. He took full advantage of the position and set the portfolio on the ground. Then he parted the satin dressing gown and cupped one of her breasts. Her nipple pebbled in the cold, and he played with it until wet heat pooled between her thighs.

"You're the most wicked man I've ever met," she moaned. He growled, and his erection hardened beneath her as she wriggled her hips.

"Teasing wenches get bitten and then bedded *roughly*," he warned in a dangerous voice, but it only heightened the building erotic charge in the air around them.

"*Wench?*" She took his hand from her breast and slid it down between her thighs. She moaned as one of his fingers played with her, dipping into the wet heat. Mikhail knew just how to torture her to the brink of exploding.

"Yes, wench." He chuckled and bit her earlobe. A zing of pleasure shot straight to her clit. "You forget how old I am. I was born in an age where a man took a woman when he wanted her."

That shouldn't have turned her on, dammit, but it did. His words, so delicious and forbidden, took her fantasies of dominant men to a whole new level. She wanted to pretend she was a medieval wench. Unable to resist, she leaped up from the couch, laughing as she spun to see a shocked expression on his face.

"This *wench* needs to be caught, m'lord." She blew a kiss at him and ran from the room. Even though she was playing a game, her body responded wildly to the chase. Her heart pounded against her ears, and she could already imagine how it would feel to be captured by him, to be drawn back into that dark, erotic world he created when it was just the two of them, bodies pressed against each other. He knew what she needed, that edge of domination, that hint of fear without actually being afraid. It heightened everything, made it all too intense, too over-powering, and utterly, devastatingly perfect.

Her dressing gown flowed behind her as she rushed for the stairs. The sound of footsteps behind her warned that Mikhail was coming fast on her heels. She reached his room a few seconds ahead of him, but she couldn't get the door shut because he shoved an arm through, catching the frame. She abandoned that plan and darted around the massive bed, keeping it between them. He stood on the other side, watching her with golden eyes. All trace of the bewitching green was gone. The honey-fired depths seemed to hypnotize her.

"Nowhere to run, little dove."

✻   1 2   ✻

Dragonman,
Dragonman,
Between thee and thine,
Share me that glimpse of love
Greater than mine.
—Anne McCaffrey

A crooked smile curved Mikhail's lips, and it made him that much sexier. He stood there in nothing but unbuttoned jeans, showing the dark trail of hair from his navel leading down to his waist. The indentions of his hips made her mouth run dry. She was thirsty for a taste of him.

"Surrender and I won't be too rough," he said in a smug

tone. A hint of the medieval badass he had been six hundred years ago crept through, which might have scared any other woman. But she *wanted* that rough edge in him. She didn't care that she was still sore; her body wanted— *needed*—to be owned and possessed by him.

She started to crawl over the bed, her eyes wide and soft as though she planned to give him what he wanted. He placed his hands on his hips and came closer. When he reached the bed, she leaped off and sprinted for the bathroom. But he moved too fast for her. She was grabbed from behind and lifted into the air, then tossed onto the bed. He grabbed one of her ankles and with a gentle tug flipped her over onto her stomach. Then he pulled her back toward the edge of the bed. Her legs fell off the side of the mattress, and cold air hit her backside as he pushed the dressing gown out of the way. She was completely exposed from behind and bent over the bed. Piper dug her nails in the bedding, her breath coming fast.

"Naughty little wench." Mikhail's deep growl was more animal than human, and that dangerous undertone made her body flush with heat. Damn, this man could role-play like a god.

"Guess you have to be rough then," she said, hoping he would take the hint.

He leaned over her. His jeans and hips pressed into her bare ass until she felt the bulge of his shaft. His fingers twisted into her hair, tugging just hard enough that a wisp of pain skated down her spine.

"Like that?" he asked. He gave another tug, and she whimpered as her womb clenched and her thighs quivered. It was a good thing she was bent over the bed because her legs wouldn't be able to hold her up much longer.

Mikhail stroked a fingertip down her neck, then traced down the line of her spine and finally slipped that finger between the cleft of her ass, down to her slit. She buried her face in the bedding as he thrust his finger in. He soon found a spot inside her that made her whimper. Her hips gave an involuntarily jerk. He found it, instinctively, that spot some men swore didn't even exist. And he was killing her with it.

"Beg," he commanded. Darkness edged his voice, but it was a darkness she craved and did not fear. If she needed him to, he would stop in a heartbeat. That's what made this all so much better. He could give her what she *needed*.

"Please..." The word barely escaped as he continued to rub that spot with the pad of his finger.

"Please, what?" His tone was indulgent now, like a cat who'd allowed a captured mouse to get free, only to hold on to it by the tip of its tail. She bit her lip as he withdrew the finger and gave her ass a light slap.

There weren't words for how good that felt. The stinging subsided to a slow burn. He rubbed the spot with his palm, a possessive, affectionate gesture that sent fresh heat flooding through her. He traced her folds with his fingers. The way he owned her was intoxicating. There wasn't anything outside this room, this breathless struggle between them to reach the heights of pleasure.

"Such a hot, wet little wench. I wonder how you taste." He dipped his finger into her again and withdrew it. She glanced over her shoulder and watched him slide his index finger into his mouth. Those gold eyes burned as they met hers, and he popped his finger out.

"Like ambrosia." He hissed low, as though he was picturing how it would be to eat her out. She swallowed hard. If he went down on her now, she'd die.

"Please, Mikhail..." She wriggled her ass, trying to entice him.

He was no longer smiling; there was only a serpentine hardness to his features as he unzipped his jeans and let them drop to the ground. His massive cock jutted out, and he ran one hand along its length and leaned over her, grasping her by the back of the neck. She buried her face in the bedding again, but her mind's eye still pictured everything that was happening to her.

The tip of his shaft rubbed along her slit, teasing her as he coated his cock with her arousal.

"You belong to me." That was the only warning she had. He thrust into her, hard, and she saw stars. He was too big, too full for her sore channel, and for a moment she couldn't breathe.

"Oh God." The words were muffled by the pillow as he shoved in deep, withdrew, and thrust in again.

They were so deeply joined that she couldn't remember what it felt like not to be a part of him and he a part of her. The flash of exhilaration made her vision hazy. She closed her eyes, panting as he fucked her the way she imagined a dragon would a mate. That was the only comparison that came to mind. This wasn't just sex—it was a thousand times more intense than that. Her skin started to burn just beneath the surface.

Suddenly she could feel the wind across her cheeks and the heavy condensation of clouds freezing along the tips of her wings as she climbed higher…higher. Then the sun was blazing above her, the air getting thinner…

She came crashing back to the earth. The climax roared through her like a tornado, tearing down every wall she'd built, and something wonderful happened as it always seemed to when she lost control with him.

Flashes of memory swam across her mind. Memories that weren't hers. Darkened halls, flickering torchlight, the whispers of a long-dead queen, the stumbling heaviness of a body drugged with wine…and the darkness of a dungeon around her, suffocating her. No, not her…

"Piper!" Mikhail's voice was a shout, but it sounded so far away, as though through a distant tunnel. It bounced off the walls inside her head.

"Stay with me!" he shouted. His voice verged on panic.

Panic? She jolted, her eyes flying open. She was lying on her back on the bed. Mikhail held her in his arms, his hands cradling her face. His green eyes were wide in terror, his fear creating shifting silver glints in their depths.

"Piper...you're safe. You're safe." He crooned her name with tenderness as he stroked a fingertip over her lips. "Stay with me, little dove." He lowered his head and brushed his mouth over hers. The waves of soft, sweet emotions that filled her head made her want to curl up in his arms and forget the outside world.

"What happened?" Her voice was hoarse. The memories this time had been too dark, too real. They had choked her with despair. Was that how he'd felt when Elizabeth had imprisoned him? Her heart ached for him, knowing now why his dragon had been driven half-mad all those centuries ago.

"You fainted, I think," he said. He moved his hand from her cheek and curled his arm around her waist, holding her close. "Your heart rate spiked and then plummeted, and it scared the hell out of me."

"I saw something from your memories." Her eyes narrowed as she tried to remember what she'd seen. "A dark hall with torches. A redheaded woman in a cream-and-orange gown, and suffocating darkness." Her body shivered at the terrifying final memory.

Mikhail blew out a shaky breath. "That was the night Queen Elizabeth betrayed me. She drugged me. I told her where my jewels were, and the next thing I knew, I was imprisoned. For forty-four years I couldn't shift, and it drove my dragon mad. That must have been what you were experiencing." He gave his head a little shake.

"That was incredible...and honestly a little scary." She closed her eyes, but the images were already beginning to fade, as though they'd never been in her mind.

"I was afraid I was too rough—you shouldn't have taunted me. I can't be like that with you. You're fragile, and I should be gentler with you." His words were painted with sorrow and frustration. "This was a mistake."

Piper prickled with anger as she faced him. "Oh no you don't. You can't pull away from me. I want the *real* Mikhail. I need you to be yourself. The rough, fire-breathing animal that you are. I don't regret a second of what we did. It was incredible. *You* were incredible."

She ignored the rising blush in her cheeks and the realization that she was completely naked. The old Piper would have been scrambling for a blanket to hide her curves under. But she was changed now. There was no going back to who she was, who she had been. She wanted to be this new version of herself, and she wasn't about to let him pull back after what had happened.

Mikhail pressed his forehead to hers, and they stayed close and quiet for a long while. Time seemed to be suspended. Even the sunlit motes of dust seemed to hang motionless in the air.

Mikhail coiled a tendril of her hair around his fingers. Piper studied his face, the way a shadow of a beard had already formed across his strong jaw. She trailed her fingertips along this line, letting the faint stubble tickle her. There was nothing more perfect than this moment. She felt giddy, unable to resist asking the question that had sparked the explosive sex they'd just shared.

"So what *is* the difference between werewolves and wolf shifters?" she asked.

He laughed and kissed her. "Werewolves are bitten; shifters are born. It's a little more complicated than that, though. Shifters are more like us, their ancient ancestors born from binding to the spirits of animals, while werewolves are creatures of dark magic binding, a corruption that manifested itself to where the ability to shift can be transferred by bites."

"So werewolves are bad? When you say dark magic..." She shivered at the thought.

"Not at all. Their ancestors might not have had good intentions when they bound their bodies to wolves, but the descendants are quite normal, some good some bad, just like dragons and humans."

She tilted her head. "Why didn't you want to tell me that?"

He grinned. "I wanted you to think about me, not some big hairy dogs." He rubbed his nose against hers in an Eskimo kiss, and her heart turned over. The man was romantic as well as sexy. He couldn't be more perfect if she'd wished upon a shooting star.

"I am definitely only thinking of you." She kissed him, letting the passion burn like a winter fire in the middle of a snowstorm. Kissing a dragon was the most intoxicating thing she'd ever experienced. But then, all too soon, she had to bring herself back to reality, if only for a little while.

"Mikhail, what are we going to do about the jewels? Or the police, for that matter?" The last two days had been a wild sort of dream, but she had to face facts. She was a suspect in a jewel heist, and if she wasn't already fired, she would be the moment she came back. Her life, the one that she'd worked so hard to build, was over.

He stroked a lock of hair behind her ear. "I have friends in high places. Or, more accurately, friends who have friends in high places. I will make sure you won't suffer for what I've made you do."

She shook her head. "It's not that easy. This isn't a trivial robbery. I don't think anyone can call them off."

He was silent for several long seconds. "I'll figure something out."

She closed her eyes and tucked her head under his chin. He didn't seem to understand the depth of their situation. She couldn't just leave with him and the jewels and live happily ever after. They'd stay on every major agency's wanted list for the rest of their lives. Mikhail could easily mesmerize his way out of trouble if he had to, but what about her?

That voice inside her head, the one that whispered negative thoughts, came to the surface.

He doesn't love me. He's just infatuated. He'll get tired of me like all my other boyfriends, and what then? I've destroyed my career and put a target on my back. For what? Great sex?

Piper wasn't going to be stupid, not when it came to men. No matter how perfect Mikhail felt, she couldn't just pretend that they could walk off into the sunset and live happily ever after. He was a dragon, so he would stay young and beautiful forever, and she was just a human. One who would grow old and die. She hadn't forgotten what Belishaw said about dragons mating humans, about how it would kill him. But if they weren't fully mated yet, perhaps there was still time.

But she couldn't tell Mikhail that she was planning to leave. He wouldn't understand. He would feel betrayed, and he'd had enough of that in his past already. But she had no other choice. He could run off to the wilds of Russia and never have to worry about his life or livelihood. But she couldn't.

We aren't mated, and we aren't in love. We're just…

She didn't want to label the wild and passionate experiences she'd had with Mikhail. It was everything she'd always wanted with a man, but at the end of the day it was still lust. She couldn't destroy her life simply because she wanted a few more nights in his bed and in his arms. Even as she tried to convince herself of that, she knew deep in her bones that there was something more, something deeper between them.

It can't be love, but whatever it is, it's scaring the hell out of me.

If she let her heart stay in control rather than her head, she'd stay with him, and damn the consequences. But someday, when he grew tired of her, her heart would break and her life would be over. She would have risked everything for him, and it would only destroy her. There was no way she could stay, facing that outcome. Piper could only pray that someday he'd forgive her for what she had to do.

❧ 13 ❧

Dragon kind was no less cruel than mankind. The Dragon, at least, acted from bestial need rather than bestial greed.
—Anne McCaffrey

Randolph Belishaw could still taste the sweet flavor of Jodie Harkness on his lips when he left the London residence she was renting. He was growing more and more attached to the woman, and that was dangerous. From the first kiss they'd shared, he'd glimpsed her as a little girl, running about a large backyard, her pigtails bouncing as she'd chased a puppy. He'd known then that Jodie was his true mate, and the longer he stayed around her, the more his dragon would bond with her, demand to claim her.

But Randolph could not afford to mate a human, not when they lived so short a life. He was the eldest son of his family. He had duties and traditions to uphold. Better to find a dragoness someday and continue the line.

His dragon keened with a sharp, protesting cry inside his head. It wanted Jodie—it wanted her and no one else. With practiced patience, he pushed the dragon back down inside his head, taking control.

Still, the thought of never seeing Jodie again made his chest tighten. He shook himself as he descended the townhouse steps and began the journey home. He usually took a car, but tonight he wanted to enjoy the bite of wintry air. He stayed on the pavement, watching the streetlamps glow, creating a hazy halo around the opalescent domes that protected the lights.

"Mr. Belishaw." Someone called his name. He turned around. A man stood only ten feet away. A man he recognized.

"Mr. Sinclair!" He nodded and gave a bow of respect. Though the man was not part of the prime minister's inner cabinet, he was one of the most powerful men in Parliament. Word was he would be running for the top position in the next election. "This is unexpected!"

"You can be a hard man to find. One has to take an opportunity when it presents itself." Conrad Sinclair stepped closer. "I was wondering if you might have dinner with me. You see, I have something of a sensitive nature that perhaps you could shed some light on."

Belishaw's brows rose in surprise. "Me?" He hadn't the faintest clue what Sinclair would want to talk to him about, either as a member of Parliament or as a dragon. He only knew the man by the briefest acquaintance in the dragon world and not at all in the human world, other than in the capacity every human with a TV knew him.

"Yes. Very important. Do you have time this evening?"

Belishaw checked his wristwatch. "I suppose I could."

"Excellent. My car is just here." Sinclair waved at the black sedan parked along the street.

The lights turned on, momentarily blinding Belishaw. He raised a hand to shield his eyes as Sinclair stepped out of the way to allow him to climb inside. He was halfway in when he was suddenly shoved from behind. He collapsed onto the seat, and something sharp jabbed into the side of his neck. The beast inside him, the one that always surged to the surface when his life was threatened, now sank deep into a dark abyss beyond his reach. The cool leather seat pressed against his cheek, and it was the only relief he felt as a flood of heat surged within his body.

"What is happen—ing?" His breath came in short, thin pants as his vision began to tunnel. The last thing he remembered was Sinclair climbing into the driver's seat in front of him. Sinclair looked back at him, a cold, all-too-dangerous look in his eyes. Then everything went black.

When Belishaw struggled back to consciousness, he

couldn't move or think all that quickly. Everything felt muddled. He fought to push away the hazy quiet of darkness still drifting like a night fog inside him.

"Welcome back, Randolph," a voice said from the darkness. A single light above illuminated him, and he stared down at his body. He was seated in some sort of chair, but his hands and wrists were clapped in iron manacles. The one metal that a dragon's strength could not break. Dragons were weakened by iron just as silver affected vampires, werewolves, and other magical kin.

"What the bloody hell is going on? Release me at once!" Belishaw tugged on the restraints, foolishly hoping that the metal cuffs had a weak spot that would break under pressure. They didn't. He sank back in the chair, his breath ragged. It felt as though he'd been running for an hour and his body was starting to tire.

"Randolph, please do not insult me by assuming that I did not come prepared."

The owner of the voice stepped into the light, and a flash of memory returned. He had started to get into Conrad Sinclair's car to go to dinner with him. Then...

"You drugged me."

"It was necessary." The man lifted up a syringe, the metal needle glinting dangerously in the bright light. "As is this." He stepped toward Belishaw.

Belishaw roared, but the sound was human. His dragon was gone.

"You'll just feel a little stick." Sinclair chuckled as he plunged the needle into Belishaw's arm, injecting a yellow liquid into him.

"What the bloody hell did you give me?" Despite the strength behind Belishaw's voice, he was panicking. The dragon inside him had never left him before. It had been suppressed and buried, yes, but never gone.

"The first cocktail was a little something special I helped design long, long ago. For a day or so it makes you as human as the next man." He chuckled. "Well, maybe not the next man, since that's me, but suffice to say your dragon won't be able to surface. I had originally planned on it being used against your family five hundred years ago, believe it or not. But things got unnecessarily complicated. It was eventually used against me, so I can vouch for its effectiveness." Conrad smiled darkly. "There's nothing so frightening as being effectively turned into a *human*, is there?"

Human? I'm human? Belishaw swallowed hard.

Sinclair lifted the second syringe. "And this...is a truth serum. Useless against normal humans, but I found it works surprisingly well on dragons once they are sufficiently weakened. Funny, isn't it? The dragon protects us so much more than we know. Not just on the outside, but the inside. Poisons, serums, medicines—none of those work while we have a dragon inside us, alive and kicking, as the Americans would say."

"Why did you give me truth serum?" Belishaw asked. He felt something crawl through his veins like slow-moving currents in the sea, well below the surface.

"Because I need a few questions answered, and I know you, Randolph. Your family has always been plagued by a sense of honor and loyalty, even when you back the wrong side. You wouldn't willingly betray someone, which means I have to get creative."

Sinclair set the syringe down on the small metal stand where a table was laden with sharp scalpels and other implements.

Bloody Christ. I should've stayed in Jodie's bed.

"Now, the serum should be reaching your head in a few seconds, and then I can begin my questions."

Sinclair pulled the chair in front of Belishaw and sat down, patiently watching him.

Slowly, bit by bit, a fuzzy warmth blanketed his chest and his head. The panic and anxiety of the moment faded into a relaxed calm.

"How are you feeling?" Sinclair asked. The words seemed to come from deep below a lake, distorted.

"Fuzzy..." Randolph said, then chuckled at how odd his voice sounded.

"Good, good." Sinclair leaned forward. "Randolph, do you know who took the Cheapside hoard from Thorne Auction House?"

He pictured his good friend Mikhail. He loved that

Russian bastard. Shadows flitted across his thoughts, and he blinked. The little voice in the back of his head murmured, *Don't tell him.*

"Uh..." He dragged out the word and then laughed at the funny sound.

"Randolph, you feel good, don't you?" Sinclair asked.

"Yes," he answered without thinking. He was simply floating now.

"I can make it feel even better if you just say yes or no."

"Yes or no." Belishaw snickered like a schoolboy now, and the voice inside his head did too.

Sinclair's black eyes turned reddish-gold with anger. He grabbed a scalpel from the table and slashed Belishaw's cheek. Pain tore through him, far sharper than he expected.

"Humans feel physical pain much stronger than we do." Sinclair's voice was smooth again as he set the scalpel down.

Belishaw gave the other man his full attention, despite the throbbing pain and the hot blood trickling down his cheek.

"Now, let's try this again. You know who stole the hoard of jewels?"

Belishaw didn't speak, but his body betrayed him with a tiny nod.

"Good. Now give me a name."

His lips parted, but his tongue was frozen against the roof of his mouth.

"The fact is, I already know who stole the jewels, Randolph. I just need you to confirm it for me. Since I already know the answer, you aren't betraying anyone by confirming it."

Another nod and a wave of nausea passed through him.

"Give me the name, Randolph."

Belishaw struggled to stay silent, but it was like trying to catch grains of sand. Sinclair sighed and lifted the scalpel. This time he didn't move out of anger. He flicked his wrist and sliced Belishaw's other cheek. A cry escaped his lips, but he did not let the name out.

Sinclair set his weapon down. "I wonder if I need to bring additional motivation for you? Perhaps the human woman you've been seeing. Jodie Harkness? Would she loosen your tongue if I had her to play with?"

An icy wave of dread drowned him. "No," he begged, tears flooding his eyes. He couldn't control his emotions. Not with this drug in his system. But now he was mortal, and they were simply a sign of weakness.

"If you don't want her involved, then you need to tell me a name."

Forgive me, Mikhail. He sent his silent plea to the gods that his friend would understand.

"Mikhail. Mikhail Barinov."

"There, was that so hard?" Sinclair mused. "So it was

him after all. Again our paths cross. How interesting to have him prowling around my city like this, after so many years.”

“London doesn’t belong to you.”

“*England* belongs to me, or it will soon.” He leaned back in his chair, more relaxed, no doubt because he had the name he wanted. “So where has Barinov run off to with my jewels?”

Belishaw growled, though the sound wasn’t as deadly as it once was.

“The jewels are his. My family gave them to the Barinovs five hundred years ago as part of a treaty.”

“And they are mine now, because I wish it. Who currently holds them is immaterial. I need those gems for my own little treaty. Now tell me what rock Barinov is hiding under, or I’ll go see if Jodie wishes to join us in this little chat.”

The thought made Belishaw sick. There was no stopping Sinclair if he chose to bring Jodie here. He couldn’t protect both her and Mikhail. He would have to choose. Unfortunately, there was no real choice to be made. Mikhail at least had a chance to defend himself.

“He lives on the coast in Cornwall, at the old Barrow house.” He gave Sinclair the address.

“Thank you for cooperating, Randolph.” Sinclair stood and disappeared behind the wall of darkness that the circle of light did not penetrate before he returned with a new syringe in his hand.

"But I told you—" Belishaw cursed as the needle plunged into his neck.

Sinclair patted his cheek. "Can't have you running off to warn your friend, now can I?"

Belishaw blinked once, twice, and all went dark.

We need in love, to practice only this: letting each other go. For holding on comes easily; we do not need to learn it.
—Rainer Maria Rilke

Piper crept downstairs to the kitchen, her boots dangling off her fingertips so she could tread as softly as a cat. Mikhail was asleep in his bed. They'd spent all night making love, each time more desperate and hungry than the last. A tide of guilt rolled through her, battering her like waves in a cold, numbing way. But she couldn't ignore it any longer. She had to do the right thing and go back to London. Dragons and humans didn't belong together. He was immortal, and she had another sixty years at best.

We have no future. It's the right thing to do. We have to break this up before we get too tangled up in each other and it hurts even more.

Her hands shook as she reached the kitchen and set her shoes down. The empty room still felt welcoming and warm, which only made what she was about to do even harder. But first she had to find the letters he'd shown her. If she didn't have those, she might never have a chance of explaining what had really happened and why. She doubted he would have moved them somewhere else; he had no reason to suspect she'd want to take them.

The letters were right where he'd left them, tucked safely in the drawer by the fridge. The clock in the kitchen reminded her with each steady tick that time was running out. But she had to make sure she was right. Settling into a chair, she unbound the twine containing the letters and began to read them one by one. Some were addressed to a woman he called "Dearest Glory." Elizabeth...

He had loved her dearly, passionately. She was surprised by the pangs of jealousy she felt, even though this had all happened more than half a millennium ago, but she pushed onward. She had to find the letters with evidence of the jewel trade between Belishaw and Mikhail because it could prove his ownership of the jewels. And if she could prove his family's ownership, Scotland Yard would have to admit he couldn't steal what rightfully belonged to him, wouldn't they? There would be a mountain of paperwork involved, but at least he'd be free to leave England with the hoard, and she'd hopefully not be sent to jail for aiding and abetting him in the burglary.

Mikhail, why didn't you think sensibly and tell Mr. Thorne who you are, the descendant of the rightful owner of the jewels? All this could have been avoided if you'd only thought it through.

Pride, stubbornness, fear of exposure—who knew what his reasons had been for the subterfuge and theft. But it didn't matter now; what was done was done. Piper opened the next letter, its first words catching her eye immediately.

"My perfect pearl...lit by firelight...my beloved Gloriana."

Her heart skipped a painful beat. It was no wonder he was slow to trust anyone. To feel that way for someone, only to have her turn on him... Piper just hoped he didn't see her as doing the same thing.

She finished the last letter and folded it back up, putting them back in order. They were her only evidence of the truth, and she prayed they would be enough. She knew enough of law enforcement to know that the police wouldn't just take her word that he'd forced her to help steal the jewels. There was video footage of her carrying the boxes to the car, and that in itself was damning. She had to convince them she was innocent, but also that Mikhail had every right to the hoard. It was the only way she could see to clear her name and set him free.

She rebound the letters with twine and searched the kitchen for a pad of paper. She had to tell him what was in her heart, to explain everything. She didn't want him chasing after her, not to rescue her or stop her from contacting the police.

When she finished she dried her eyes with her hands, then picked up Mikhail's cell phone and a spare set of car keys for the Range Rover parked out back in the garage. She'd seen another SUV there, which meant he could come after her, but she didn't think he would, not after she left him like this.

Piper got into the driver's seat and set the letters down beside her. The jewels were still hidden away in Mikhail's wine cellar. She had no intention of bringing them back with her. They belonged to the Barinovs, and nothing was going to change that.

She drove out of the garage and down the winding path that would take her away from the one thing in life she didn't want to give up. But to be with him she would have a life on the run, and that wasn't fair to either of them, especially when his time with her would be so short.

She bit her lip as the rocky coastline echoed the ragged tears of her heart. That was the real reason she was leaving, the one she had trouble admitting, even to herself. She couldn't be the cause of Mikhail's untimely death.

Mating a human was effectively a death sentence for a dragon. This way, maybe someday he would find a drag-oness to mate with, one who would live many more millennia beside him. Not just the short amount of time she had to offer, if he was lucky.

Tears stung her eyes. Piper knew she was doing the right thing, she had to be. But the farther away she got, the more it felt like *she* was the one dying.

After an hour, she pulled off to the side of the road and covered her face with her hands, unable to stop herself from crying. Everything was shattering inside her. The man she'd come to care about, the man who made her feel alive whenever she was with him, would never forgive her. *I'm trying to save him, but he'll never understand.*

When her sobs gave way to shaky sniffles, she pulled out Mikhail's cell phone and called Mr. Thorne at the auction house. The phone rang three times before someone answered.

"Hello?" a familiar voice answered.

"Mr. Thorne, please, whatever you do, hear me out before you call Scotland Yard."

"Ms. Linwood?" Mr. Thorne spoke softly now. "Do you have any idea how serious this business is? I have professed your innocence, as has your colleague, but those fools don't believe you were coerced. I watched the footage from the alley myself. It's clear you were pushed into the car, but these idiots are convinced you are involved. It isn't safe for you to return, not unless we can prove your innocence. I can hire excellent barristers to defend you, but I don't want you locked up for the next six months while court proceedings are held."

His concern for her and his belief that she was innocent in all this touched her. He really was a wonderful, sweet man.

"I might have a way to prove my innocence, but I have to bring it to you." She rushed on before he could stop her. "I can prove that the man who stole the jewels is the rightful owner of them by right of his family's lineage. His family was given these jewels by the Belishaw family. You remember Mr. Belishaw from the reception?"

"Er, yes, I do. Go on."

She licked her lips nervously. "I have letters dating from the year 1559 that prove Queen Elizabeth stole those jewels from a family by the name of Barinov, who owned the jewels because of a treaty between the Barinovs and the Belishaws. These letters can prove that the thief believed he had a right to the jewels. I believe Mr. Randolph Belishaw will corroborate the evidence. Tell me you understand."

She hoped that if Mr. Thorne agreed, she could have Belishaw meet with the Elwes-Bush family, the people who owned the property where the jewels had been found. Belishaw could mesmerize them to convince them not to press charges against Mikhail and herself, accept the letters as proof of ownership, give up the trove to Mikhail's family, and take what had been left behind as a finder's fee.

Mr. Thorne pondered the idea. "Hmmm...I don't know..."

She hoped her hasty ramblings had made some kind of sense. She knew it would be outing the Barinov and Belishaw families, but she wasn't exposing them as dragons. The story still worked with both of them being descendants, and with Belishaw's family's connections. If she could just get so far as having Mr. Thorne agree to set up a meeting, she was sure the matter could be dropped.

Mikhail should have just come forward in the beginning with the letters and demanded the jewels be returned to him, but the stupid, stubborn man hadn't thought that through. No, he'd just acted on his emotions, stolen his treasure back, and kidnapped her.

There was a pregnant pause before Thorne finally spoke. "This is highly unusual, but since it is a private sale, there might be some room for negotiation. Do you have original letters, not copies? The museum will need to verify their authenticity."

She exhaled in relief. "Yes. I know you are a man of honor, Mr. Thorne, and this is a matter of the highest honor. He was wrongly branded a traitor and only officially exonerated upon Elizabeth's death forty-four years later. But the jewels were never returned to him. By then they were already lost. We must see justice done for his family."

Mr. Thorne sighed. "As much as I wish to have the rest of the jewels back, I believe you're telling me the truth. Or, at least, what you believe is the truth. It sounds like the ownership of the jewels is more complicated than we realized. I'm glad you called me, Ms. Linwood. The police have Ms. Harkness under heavy surveillance. They expect you to make contact with her."

"Yeah, I thought they might expect me to call her, but—"

"Ms. Linwood, we shouldn't talk here. It isn't safe. Why don't I come to you? They'll be waiting for you in London."

"Okay. Where should we meet? I'm just leaving Tintagel in Cornwall."

He took a moment to think before answering. "Go to Boscastle. It's not too far from where you are. They have a small museum about the origins of witchcraft. Across the street from it is a small pub. You can wait for me there and have some dinner. It should take me about four hours. Once I arrive, I'll meet you in the pub, and we'll head over to the museum. I'm acquainted with the owner, and she won't mind us using the shop to meet. We won't have to worry about surveillance that way."

"A museum of witchcraft," she repeated. What an odd place to meet. Then again, these small English villages had a wealth of interesting historical locales, and she did love history. It would be a nice distraction to see a museum; it might help her stop thinking about Mikhail for just a few minutes. "Okay, I'll wait for your call."

"See you soon." Mr. Thorne hung up.

Piper let out a slow, deep breath that she hadn't realized she'd been holding. Thorne believed her, at least enough for her needs. That had been one of the biggest hurdles she faced. If she could get him on her side, things might work out after all.

As she drove down the winding road, she tried to remain calm. She knew Mikhail would be mad that she'd left and taken his private letters. She would have given anything to be back in his bed, nuzzling him and counting his heartbeats until she fell asleep. The sense of peace she felt with him had been unlike anything she'd ever experienced before. She couldn't quite explain it, and in a way it seemed like madness.

She didn't believe in love at first sight and certainly frowned upon the idea of loving someone so fast. It had to be lust, basic physical instinct, not real emotion. Love was built over months and years. Yet even knowing that, it didn't explain the shattering feeling she had in her heart the farther away she got from Mikhail.

I can't stay with him. We don't have a future. She hadn't forgotten what she'd learned about dragons mating humans. It didn't end well. She didn't want to grow older each day while he stayed young forever. *No. Not forever.* Until she died. Then he would soon follow her. It wasn't fair to him, to either of them. She deserved to grow old with a man she loved, and he deserved someone who would spend centuries making him happy, not stripping those years away.

A fish may love a bird, but where would they live?

The reality of her departure left her hollow inside. But

she'd done what she had to do. *He'll go home to Russia, be with his brothers, and someday find a dragoness.*

A bittersweet smile twisted her lips as she remembered how he'd described drakelings. They were born human with a dormant dragon inside them, and for a time aged like normal humans, but at thirteen years the bond to their dragon began to strengthen, and they started to learn to transform. He'd told her how he'd felt the first time he'd learned to fly and how the thought of watching his own children someday having to learn made him both nervous and excited. She'd listened with tears in her eyes as she'd imagined for one shining moment that those children he spoke of would be hers.

But humans and dragons couldn't have children.

Piper rubbed away the tears in her eyes when she saw there was an exit coming up on the road, along with a sign for Boscastle, but she slowed when she saw a car with its hazard lights flashing.

A man stood beside his car which had a flat tire, and he held a tire lever. A rosy-cheeked boy who looked about five leaned out of the window of the SUV, watching the man. The grim expression on the man's face almost made her laugh. Many people didn't know how to change a tire, but she did. She had plenty of time to kill before she reached Boscastle, and right now she needed to feel useful. She drove up beside the man and rolled down her passenger window.

"Hey, I saw your hazards flashing. Do you need help?"

The man straightened and set his lever down. "Actually, yes. My son and I were trying to reach Boscastle when my tire blew. I can't get any bloody mobile service up here for a tow."

Piper pulled out Mikhail's phone. Two bars, better than nothing. "I have service. You want me to call someone?" She smiled at the little boy, who waved at her shyly.

"If you don't mind, it might be easier for me to make the call." The man sighed and set the tire lever down.

"Sure. I'll have a look at your tire while you wait." She handed the phone to him, and he began to dial. Piper got out and walked over to his vehicle, examining the tire.

That was odd. It wasn't just flat—the rubber had been slashed.

She turned halfway to speak to the man. "Hey, I think—"

Piper's last sensation was that of falling to the ground before she was consumed in darkness.

When she came around, her head was pounding. She moaned as she reached up to touch the back of her head with her left hand. It came away sticky. She blinked in the dim light and saw dark blood coating her fingers. Her right wrist ached. She lifted her hand to see what was wrong, but it jerked to a stop with a loud *clunk*.

She gasped at the sight of the thick iron manacle there. A heavy chain connected her right wrist to a bedpost. She sat up and realized she was on a bed in a dark room. A window was partially open, and the strong scent of the sea came through it.

Where was she? What had happened? The man with a flat tire... He'd knocked her out. Why?

"Oh God..." Had she been picked up by some serial killer or—

The door to the room opened. A man flicked a small light switch by the door, and two lamps beside the bed came on. She got a better look at where she was now. It seemed to be the upstairs room of a small cottage.

"Where are we?"

"Boscastle," the man said as he approached the bed. There was something familiar about him, she realized.

"Where's your son?" She had no idea how she'd ended up here, and if he wasn't afraid to kidnap her and tie her up, what would he do to his own child?

The man chuckled. His dark hair fell over his eyes as he stared at her. "That was an illusion. A simple trick. I doubt you would have stopped for a single man on the road, but I knew that if you saw a child, you'd be more likely to trust me."

An illusion? She stared at his eyes, feeling an almost hypnotic pull in his gaze. She'd only ever experienced that before with Mikhail. "Wait...you're a dragon?"

"Very good!" His praise was sardonic, and it made rage stir beneath her skin.

"Then..." Piper struggled to figure something out. "Why knock me out? Why not just hypnotize me?"

"Unlike Barinov, I like to cause pain."

Piper flinched as he caught her chin in his hand. He leaned down until their faces were mere inches apart. Then he closed his eyes and inhaled deeply.

"Blood and fear. Two scents that heat a dragon's blood. But not...not a virgin, not any longer. Pity," he murmured as he opened his eyes.

Piper peered at his face. She was sure she'd seen him before, but she couldn't figure out where.

"I waited two hours for you to come around, so forgive my lack of patience now. It's time we had a little chat, Ms. Linwood."

Piper tried to ignore the stabbing pain in her head. "How do you know my name?"

"How I know doesn't matter. What matters is what you tell me in the next ten minutes." He leaned back against the door.

"What do you want to know?" she asked. Her voice was surprisingly steady, despite the fact that she was shaking on the inside.

"I had expected to find Mikhail Barinov with you. I was on my way to see him, in fact. But my connections at Scotland Yard told me he made a call to Thorne. I realized he—or rather, whoever had his phone—was on the move, possibly with the jewels. Imagine my surprise when I then learned that Mr. Thorne was headed this way too."

The pieces began to connect. "Is he... Did you..." She

was too afraid to ask if something had happened to the older man.

"He's driving back to London, unharmed, but befuddled. He no longer remembers that he was coming here to meet you. We need to be alone, you and I, so I decided to take care of everyone in the village."

She could barely breathe. "Take care of?"

The man laughed. "Dragons have other talents besides transforming. The village is in a deep sleep, which will leave us undisturbed while I conduct my business."

Asleep? That didn't sound bad. Piper let out a breath, but the man chuckled. "Don't relax just yet. I still need my questions answered, and I have means at my disposal to make sure you answer if you choose to hold your tongue."

She said nothing, but held still on the bed, her wrists aching from the heavy iron manacles.

"Now, as I've been told from a reliable source, Mikhail Barinov stole the jewels. And you." The man didn't seem to require an answer from her yet, so she didn't reply.

"I had every intention of taking both you and the jewels, but now I understand who I'm up against. We've crossed paths before, though he doesn't know it, and once again he has put a wrinkle in my plans. So when you came along, it was almost too perfect an opportunity. I plan to trade you for the jewels."

Piper shook her head. "He won't trade me for the jewels." She knew in her heart it was a lie—Mikhail would do that, assuming he forgave her for leaving him, but she didn't want him to have to face that choice.

The man gave an almost feline grin. "It's charming that you think you can fool me. But I can smell lies. It's like a stale scent of fear. Barinov will come for you."

"He won't. I left him a note telling him it was over between us. He has no reason to come after me. I *betrayed* him." She emphasized the word, hoping that this dragon would believe her, and she also hoped more than ever that it was true. She could only pray that Mikhail had read her note and was so angered by it that he would not come after her. At least then he'd be safe and have the jewels, and whoever this asshole was could go to hell.

"Interesting. Now *that* you do believe, but I know something you do not, it seems." The man's curved smile was cold and serpentine.

"And what's that?"

"Barinov has mated with you. It doesn't matter what you do or say to him—he chose you and cemented the bond. It's unbreakable except by death."

Piper's lips parted. *Mated?* How could she be mated to a man and not know it?

Then she remembered when she'd felt what it had been like to be *him*, to fly, to fall, to be imprisoned...to both suffer and know the exquisite joy of being one with him. It had been so much more intense than the other times they had kissed. It had felt...*permanent*, but she hadn't wanted to face that, not when she'd been planning to leave while he slept.

"He would never let anything happen to you now," the man said. "But if I killed you, it would make him dangerous. Too dangerous. A dragon can be a terrible force after his mate's death, especially to those who caused it. I don't wish to fight him and am far too impatient to wait him out. A trade of the jewels for his mate will suffice, unless, of course, I have to kill him."

"Kill him?" she gasped.

"It doesn't have to come to that...*if* you help me in getting him to cooperate. As I said, I have no interest in facing a mateless male dragon. You love him, don't you? You want to save his life, don't you?"

Piper nodded, her heart racing wildly. She would do anything to save Mikhail, because it was true. She did love him. She'd been so blind, telling herself that what she felt was lust when it had always been something more. She could only pray her love was enough.

"Good." The man came toward her with an evil glint in his eyes. "I'm afraid you won't enjoy this next part, my dear, but it's all part of the show." He lunged for her, and she had only a moment to scream.

$\maltese$ 15 $\maltese$

They say dragons never truly die. No matter how many times you kill them.
—Suzanne G. Rogers, *Jon Hansen and the Dragon Clan of Yden*

Randolph Belishaw stumbled down the alleyway, falling against a trash bin. His cold body shook. He couldn't think. Couldn't speak. Blood trailed down his cheeks as he clawed the sides of the metal dumpster and tried to stand.

Must get to Jodie. Must warn Mikhail.

The thoughts were a shining glow in the darkness that consumed him. Conrad Sinclair's poison still filled his veins like black sludge, preventing the dragon from coming to his aid. He was just a mortal man—no, *weaker* than a mortal man—and for the first time in his life, he felt true fear.

Fear was something a dragon almost never experienced in its life. Being mortal had never been a possibility until tonight. And now it hung over his head like the sword of Damocles.

"Bloody...fucking...hell." He stumbled like a piss-poor drunk down the alley until he finally reached the street.

He squinted at the street signs. It was evening now, the sun a soft pale glow behind the townhouses. The streets were deserted, and a fine layer of fresh snow covered the road and the cars parked along the street. How long had he been with Conrad?

He squinted at the light glowing from the streetlamps. He'd lost too much time. He cradled a wrist against his chest. Blood dripped down his fingertips. He'd ripped himself out of the iron cuffs. It hadn't been easy. One of his thumbs was still dislocated, judging by the way it ached. Whatever was in the drug Conrad had given him had numbed him to most of the pain.

Lucky me...

Belishaw took several faltering steps into the street as he got his bearings. The clouds were pale, the growing moonlight behind them making them glow like luminescent pearls.

Pearls. He sighed at the thought. He did so love pearls. If he survived this, he was going to retrieve a cask of fresh-water pearls from his private vault and cover Jodie's naked body with them. The thought warmed him, and he kept walking. As he reached the next street, he realized that he was only half a kilometer away from where Jodie was staying.

"Sir? Are you all right?" A woman ahead of him had paused by her parked car. She was bundled for the cold weather, her breath coming out in gray clouds as she stared at him, keys in hand. He moved closer, and the light of the streetlamp behind her illuminated him. She gasped and stepped back in horror. He knew how he must look, bloody, beaten, and cut up.

The woman took another step back. "Oh my God."

"I'm...fine..." The words were slow to come out, but he couldn't get his tongue to cooperate to say anything more.

"You're bleeding. I should call an ambulance." The woman reached into her purse, but he got to her first, clasping his good hand around her wrist.

"I need a ride, please. It's not far from here."

The woman continued to stare at him for a long second. "Are you sure? I can take you to the hospital."

"No." He cursed Conrad for numbing his dragon. Otherwise, he would've been able to make this woman do his bidding. Right now all he had were his human instincts to get him through this.

"All right, but I really think you need a hospital." The woman unlocked her car. He climbed into the passenger side and didn't bother buckling himself in. The woman didn't say another word until she started to pull out onto the street.

"Where am I headed?" she asked.

Belishaw gave her the address and then rested his forehead on the window, briefly closing his eyes. Everything was fucked up. Conrad was after the jewels, and he would kill Mikhail to get to them.

And I'm the bastard who gave him up.

He opened his eyes again, the lights outside blurring into white and yellow lines. He recognized Jodie's townhouse and pointed. "There. Stop there."

The woman pulled over, and he fumbled for the door handle. The woman got out and helped him to the sidewalk. Uncertainty shadowed her eyes.

"I really don't think I should leave you like this," she said.

"No...I'll be fine. Thank you...for the ride." He cradled his left hand and walked up the steps. He gave her as much of an English stiff upper lip as he could manage, and she nodded. He heard the car drive off once he started to knock on Jodie's door.

A few seconds later the door opened. He fell heavily against Jodie.

"Randolph!" She braced him with her arms. "Oh my God, what happened? You're bleeding."

"I need a phone, quick..." he panted.

Jodie stared at him. "Phone?" He moved in slow, shuffling steps to the stairs that led to the upper rooms, collapsing on the second-to-last step.

"The phone, love, please." His ragged whisper sent her running. She came back with her phone, and he dialed Mikhail's cell. It rang for a long time, but there was no answer.

"Fuck!" he growled. Then he tried Mikhail's landline. When he got the answering machine, he spoke quickly. "Mikhail. Conrad Sinclair is coming for you and the jewels. He knows where you are. Watch your back—he is one of us. I'll be there as soon as I can, and I'll bring help."

He hung up and realized the room was silent. Jodie was watching him, barely breathing.

He rubbed a hand across his cheeks, wiping off smears of blood along his palm. "Jodie..."

"What's going on, Randolph? You're scaring me." Her beautiful dark eyes were wide with terror.

Belishaw rubbed his good hand over his eyes and exhaled. "It's a very long story."

She moved to sit down beside him on the narrow stairs. Jodie took his hand in hers, ignoring the blood, and held it tight. The connection gave him much-needed strength.

"I'm listening." The soft, warm pools of her eyes drew him in.

"I'm not exactly...human." It was the first time he'd ever told a mortal woman what he was, and he prayed she wouldn't run away screaming.

"Okay..." There was confusion in her eyes, but she hadn't run and hadn't let go of his hand.

"I'm only half-man. I'm...a dragon shifter. I've walked this earth for more than two thousand years."

MEG STRATFORD PARKED HER CAR HALF A BLOCK AWAY and watched the injured man disappear inside the townhouse. Her mind raced as she tried to puzzle out what she'd just seen. Eventually, when she felt she had no other choice, she pulled out her cell and dialed a number.

A woman's voice came on the line. "HQ. Please provide your identification."

"Stratford, Meg. 3592BFHS," Meg said.

"Voice print verified," the woman said. "What is your status?"

"Surveillance," Meg answered. "I need to file a code orange."

The woman on the line paused. "Code orange?" she clarified. Orange wasn't the highest level, but it signified that the hunter deemed an incident to be significant and required further instructions.

"Yes." Meg stared at the house, knowing that everyone at headquarters in Detroit would be scrambling. As a supernatural hunter for the Brotherhood of the Blood Moon, she was always on guard against creatures who posed a threat to humans. The dragons in England had been her latest assignment. And it was clear after tailing Randolph Belishaw that something was very wrong. Whatever this was, it went beyond inter-clan squabbling.

"Please stand by. I'm connecting you to MacQueen," the woman replied.

A few minutes later her boss, Damien MacQueen, was on the line.

"Meg, everything okay?"

"I'm fine, but there's something crazy going down in London. I don't like it."

"What are you seeing?" Damien asked.

"I had eyes on one of the Belishaws yesterday, and he was attacked by...well, you're not going to believe it."

"I think you forget what line of work we're in, Stratford. Tell me."

"It was a member of Parliament. Not his security detail, but the Right Honorable Conrad Sinclair himself. Alone. He shoved Belishaw into a car and drove off. I followed them to an unregistered location, a townhouse with no ties to the government that I could find. I waited twenty-four hours outside. Sinclair left twelve hours ago, but Belishaw only emerged from a side door in an alley half an hour ago. He was in rough shape, Damien. Sir, I don't have Sinclair down on any of my records as an SLF. And whatever happened in there, it didn't happen over a polite cup of tea." SLF was code for supernatural life form.

"But a dragon's healing ability should have kept him unharmed."

"*Should* have. But he wasn't healing. He'd been tortured, from the look of it. I know we aren't supposed to interfere unless humans are in danger, but—"

Her boss's usually laid-back tone turned gruff. "Meg, what did you do?"

"I had to help him. He saw me. It might have been suspicious if I didn't react to him stumbling and bleeding everywhere, right? I gave him a ride."

"To where?"

"A townhouse nearby, rented by an American woman named Jodie Harkness. She has no SLF connections that I know of. But then, neither did Sinclair. Belishaw went inside her place and hasn't come back out," she said.

"And Mr. Sinclair just *took* him?" Damien's disbelief was evident, but Meg was positive about who she'd seen shove Belishaw into the car.

"Yeah, that's the most messed up part of this. I mean, politicians have made alliances with shifters before, but how did he subdue and torture one on his own?"

"Fuck," Damien cursed. "I've had my suspicions about him for a while. Looks like I was right."

"Suspicions?" She didn't like where this was headed. If her boss was worried, then she was too. Very few things upset Damien MacQueen.

"I have reason to believe Conrad Sinclair might be a dragon shifter."

"We don't have any intel on a Sinclair line. Why wasn't I informed?" Meg was positive. Before she'd taken on her current assignment, she had studied all the noble lines of dragon shifters in England and mainland Europe. She knew almost as much about Randolph Belishaw as he did about himself.

"The last Sinclair dragon we know of vanished five hundred years ago. He was a close confidant of Queen Elizabeth," Damien said. "But then one day he just disappeared."

"Any idea what happened?"

"A hunch. We have records of Elizabeth imprisoning a dragon of the Barinov line several years earlier, though how she did it was a mystery. Then around the time Sinclair disappeared, Barinov was moved to more comfortable quarters, and an unnamed man took his place. I suspected that was Sinclair, but there was no record of him ever being released."

"Wow," Meg muttered. "A human queen stuck it to two dragons. Pretty impressive. Wonder how she did it?"

Damien's laugh lacked mirth this time. "That's something we'd like to know as well. Conrad Sinclair has all the right papers proving his birth and citizenship, yet we could find nothing about him from his youth, not even a yearbook photo. Word is he has eyes on becoming the next prime minister. Perhaps that's what this meeting was about, to try to ensure the Belishaws' support."

"Sounds like a piss-poor way to drum up campaign donations."

"True. It doesn't track. Which means it's something else. Something far more serious."

Meg bit her lip. "You think it might mean a war?"

"That's what I'm afraid of," Damien said with a sigh. "And we really don't need a war on our hands. Something in the dragon world is off. A month ago, our office in Saint Petersburg told me that two families, the Barinovs and the Drakors, had a massive battle. All but one of the Drakors died. We're lucky it happened in a rural part of Russia. If it had gone down in Moscow or Saint Petersburg, we'd have been up to our eyeballs in damage control. But here's the thing—what really got me looking into Sinclair was his recent diplomatic trips to Russia, where he met..."

"...the Drakors."

"Bingo. So I've got to ask myself, what does he have planned? And none of the answers I come up with are good."

A shiver racked Meg's body. She couldn't help but picture London burning, smoke filling the skies and people dying.

"What do you want me to do?" she asked.

"Continue observation of Randolph for now. I'll have the London office bug Sinclair's phones. If the dragons make a move toward war, we'll need to be ready. I'll reach out to every department that can send hunters at a moment's notice, just in case we have to intervene."

Meg stared at the dark windows of the townhouse where Randolph had gone.

"Be careful, Meg. If a war starts, bug out. We'll send in support. I don't want you anywhere near ground zero."

"But—"

"I mean it, Meg. You're too valuable." Damien's voice gentled. "Stay on Randolph and report if anything else happens."

"Understood." Meg ended the call and continued to observe the street. Above her the clouds thickened, and when she glanced up, snow began to fall. It was going to be a long night.

❧ 16 ❧

My task is set before me, girl,
My mission clear and true.
There'll be black knights and dragons, girl
But I will always come for you.
—Emme Rollins

Mikhail stretched in his bed, seeking the warm feminine form of his mate.

Mate. He had mated Piper. The thought of it made him grin, even half-awake.

"Little dove?" He rolled onto his back, opening his eyes. But she wasn't there. His bed was empty except for him. He sat up and let the sheets slip from his body.

"Piper?" he called out as he slid out of bed and

retrieved his clothes. He listened to the sounds in the house as he dressed, ears straining to catch any sign of her.

Nothing. A small knot of tension grew in his stomach.

"Piper?" he called again and left his bedroom. He searched every room, his anxiety spiking each time he came up empty. Where could she have gone?

He reached the kitchen and froze when he saw a small piece of paper, folded up, his name scrawled across it.

His stomach pitched south to his feet. "No..."

Mikhail opened the note, his hand shaking as he started to read.

MIKHAIL,

I never thought I would ever fall in love with a man like you, or that I'd have to give up a dream come true. But I had to. Please believe me when I say I never wanted to do this. Belishaw told me about dragons and human mates. You have hundreds, maybe thousands of years ahead of you. I don't. I refuse to be the reason that you will die before your time. I care about you too much.

I hope that when I'm old and gray, I'll still have the dreams that I flew with you and how we would watch the sun rise and set together. Maybe you won't forget me, even if humanity has crumbled to dust and all that's left are the gems we once shared, but I hope you'll look back on me fondly and not hate me for leaving.

My life is in shambles, and I have to fix things, or at least try. I have your letters, the ones between you and the Belishaw family.

I have a plan that will hopefully clear my name and yours. With luck, you'll be free to go home and be with your brothers, and the jewels will finally be yours. If I can set you free of the past, maybe you will someday find a way to forgive me.

Piper

THERE WAS A BLOTCH ON THE PAPER. A TEARSTAIN. She'd been crying when she wrote the note.

Mikhail tried to catch his breath. The knowledge that his mate had abandoned him burned through his chest. She didn't know they were already mated. His life was bound to hers, his heart, body, and soul. She could not undo the bond. Only death could separate them, and even then only for a little while.

He had to find her, explain to her. He had no regrets. This life was his choice to make, and he'd made it with open eyes. He would win his little dove back somehow. He had to. Mikhail started for the stairs, but the phone rang. The landline.

He froze. Only a handful of people had that number. He rushed back to the kitchen and answered it.

"Hello?"

"Mikhail Barinov."

"Yes. Who is this?"

"My name is Conrad Sinclair. You have something that belongs to me."

He knew of that name...he'd seen him on TV. A politician. He couldn't fathom why a member of Parliament would be calling him.

"What are you talking about?"

"Come now, Barinov. There's no need for secrecy. We are past that now. I know you have the jewels, the Cheapside trove. In exchange, I have something you want."

"How could you have anything I want?" Mikhail asked, his voice turning cold.

"Because I know what happens when you take a mate, *dragon*," Conrad said with a chuckle. The sound grated on Mikhail's ears.

"My mate?" Mikhail choked on the words. He couldn't have Piper. She was on her way to London. Conrad had to be bluffing.

"Yes. Ms. Linwood. You see, I was looking for you when your little dove fell right into my lap. That is what you call her, isn't it? Your little dove? She told me that was your nickname for her." Conrad's voice was velvet-covered steel.

There was only one way Conrad would know that he called Piper his little dove. Piper had told him. What had he done to her to make her give up that information? Mikhail's throat constricted, but he had to keep his dragon calm. The beast was already snarling inside his head.

"You want the jewels? Very well." He would give them away without hesitation. Piper was the only thing that mattered.

"You plan to give them up without a fight?" Conrad sounded surprised.

"She's my mate. I don't care about the jewels," Mikhail snapped. His hand tightened on the phone so much that the plastic creaked. He forced himself to relax.

"Very good. We won't have any trouble getting things sorted out, then, will we?" Conrad's voice was so damned businesslike that Mikhail wanted to roar.

"No. We won't have any trouble. As long as you leave her unharmed."

"She's quite safe, I assure you," Conrad said. "Now, I'm going to give you an address. Come here one hour before the sun sets. You will give me the jewels, and I shall return your mate to you."

"Fine." Mikhail listened as Conrad gave him an address in Boscastle, and then he went upstairs to pack a set of clothes, just in case. Piper must have taken one of his cars. His dragon paced restlessly, wanting to fly. Belishaw's words came back to haunt him. Had his dragon tried to kill him? Would it try again, or would it fight for Piper?

She isn't Elizabeth. He sent thoughts of Piper to his dragon, reminding the creature that not all mortals had betrayed him. Piper had been trying to free him from his past. She thought she'd betrayed him, but she hadn't. She had left him to protect him; it's what a true mate would do.

The dragon stilled inside him. He could feel the beast's

heart matching his own as it communicated with him through a wild array of images. *Protect Piper. Save Piper.*

He returned to the house and began to carry the boxes of jewels out to his car and load them in the trunk, wondering how a member of Parliament knew about him. He knew of dragons, so could he be a dragon himself? Or perhaps a different creature of the ancient lines? But he'd desired the gems for the trade, and that said *dragon* to Mikhail more than anything else.

After the last one he paused as he recognized a red bag that contained one piece that hadn't been featured in the museum. He slipped the Dragon Heart Stone out of its velvet bag. A fist-size ruby. He remembered all those centuries ago when Belishaw had placed it into his hand, warning him to be careful. Even then he'd sensed it was not just a normal gem, but filled with a kind of magic.

Keep me... The ruby seemed to whisper to him. He slipped it into his coat pocket. Then he got into the driver's seat and began the drive to Boscastle.

The small fishing village was on the edge of the coast, not as far away as he'd thought. He drove down the winding, narrow road into town. The sun was setting on the edge of the water along the horizon.

Mikhail found the little museum of witchcraft. A Closed sign hung in the window, but there was a light in the back of the store. He thought he saw someone move across the source of light. He parked out front and tested the door handle. Finding it unlocked, he eased the door open.

The museum was quiet, and the air was thick with the scents of old magic. He inhaled deeply and caught the light, natural aroma of Piper and the heavy, dark, cloying smell of another male dragon. *Conrad.* Mikhail curled his lip in a silent snarl as he prowled toward the back room.

He passed a glass display containing old bowls carved with ancient runes. A faint whisper seemed to echo from the bowls, and a shudder rippled through his body. These bowls had once been for human sacrifice. The runes trapped souls within the bowls, imbuing them with power. He'd seen it done once, long ago when he'd been a drakeling. There was so much magic in this room, it seemed to hum with life. As he got closer, he swore he could hear his mother's voice.

"Magic calls to magic."

His dragon froze within him, as though the beast was holding its breath. Mikhail reached the back door, which was slightly ajar. He leaned in and tried to peer inside, but he couldn't see anything. There was a soft shuffling sound within. A sound he recognized as Piper's. He kicked the door open.

Piper was tied to a chair, a cloth wrapped around her mouth. Conrad stood behind her, a silver blade pressed against her throat. Piper's eyes were bright with fear. He stared at her, willing her to calm, hoping she would trust him.

"Remember, Barinov, you play by my rules, and she is unharmed." Conrad pressed the knife a little deeper into Piper's neck. She flinched, shoving her head back, but she was unable to escape the blade.

"I'm here. The jewels are in my car." He held out the keys, not missing how Conrad's gaze fixed on them.

"Toss me the keys," Conrad demanded.

"Step away from my mate first," Mikhail countered.

Piper's eyes softened when he said *mate*. He wanted to smile at her, to reassure her that everything would be okay, but he couldn't allow himself to be distracted when facing another dragon. It could get them both killed.

Conrad slowly stepped away from Piper, but there was a dangerous glint in his eyes that Mikhail didn't trust.

"There's just one more thing." Conrad removed a slender black case from his coat pocket. He opened it up while still holding the knife. Mikhail saw a syringe inside the case, filled with green liquid.

"What is that?" he asked.

Conrad set the case down and kicked it over to Mikhail. The case bumped the toe of his boot. "My insurance policy."

"You want me to inject whatever this is into me? Do you think I'm a fool?"

Conrad sighed and lowered the long knife back to Piper's neck. She winced as a tiny bit of blood dewed on the blade's edge. Mikhail and his dragon both tensed. He curled his fingers into fists.

"This isn't negotiable, and its effects are temporary. It subdues your dragon for a day or so. You won't be able to transform. I need that time to secure the jewels. You might come after them once your mate is safe."

"I wouldn't," Mikhail vowed.

The other dragon gave a hollow laugh. "Forgive me if I don't blindly trust you. We are dragons, after all. So use it, and then we make the trade."

Mikhail looked at the vial, then to Piper. She tried to say something, but he couldn't understand the words. Conrad pushed the blade deeper, and she whimpered as another drop of blood trickled down the silver face of the blade.

"Time is running out, Barinov," Conrad said.

Mikhail retrieved the case and then took off his jacket. He rolled up the sleeve of his sweater and pulled the syringe out of its straps. The case dropped to the ground.

He pressed the tip of the needle into his flesh and depressed the plunger. A burning began to flow through his limbs. He moaned, helpless as he fell to his knees. The dragon inside him seemed to flicker, and then suddenly it vanished. The gaping hole it left inside him was almost too much to bear. It was a familiar feeling, one that he'd felt once five hundred years before, only more intense.

"What..." he groaned. "This can't be..." He struggled for words as he collapsed against the wooden beam closest to him, digging his fingers into the wood to stay on his feet.

"Feel familiar? You and I have both tasted its effects before."

Mikhail looked to the man, remembering the day he'd been transferred to better quarters and the ragged person who had taken his place in his old cell. "You..."

That recognition made the man smile. He let the knife drop to his side and started walking around the room while his rival was immobilized. "You have no idea how long I've waited for a moment like this. Do you realize what a thorn in my side you've been? The very moment you landed on our shores to make your alliance with the Belishaws, you've been interfering with my plans. And now, five hundred years later, you're doing it again, and just as oblivious to how you keep getting in my way."

Mikhail remembered what Elizabeth had told him about this man and his schemes. "You wanted to destroy the Belishaws."

"Destroy, exile, whatever. Only their removal was important. But I knew that Elizabeth would never listen to my words against them if she were mated to you. I had to remove you instead."

"She didn't listen to your words even after you removed me."

The man nodded. "A failure on my part. I should have waited another decade before moving against them. I underestimated your Elizabeth, and for that I paid the price. More than forty years bound in a dark cell barred with iron."

Mikhail noted the length of time. "You were released the same time as I was?"

"A fortunate clerical error. I should have rotted in there for the next century, being fed the very potion I'd helped her magician John Dee create." Conrad left Piper now and walked toward Mikhail. "Never thought I'd get a chance to use it on you again."

He stopped in front of Mikhail, taking the keys to the car and dangling them in front of his face in victory. Then, with a slow grin, he swung a fist at Mikhail's face and struck him to the ground.

✣ 17 ✣

***It simply isn't an adventure worth telling if there
aren't any dragons.***
—J. R. R. Tolkien

Piper screamed as Mikhail grunted and fell back, but Conrad was not through with him, not by a long shot. Mikhail tried to fight back, but it was clear he had been weakened from whatever Conrad had put in the syringe. Blow after blow struck Mikhail, in the ribs, in the head, in the back, until he finally had no energy left to defend himself. Only then did Conrad finally stop. Piper was hoarse from screaming. Conrad pocketed the car keys and stared at Mikhail's body, his face filled with loathing.

"It's nothing personal, Barinov. Oh, who am I kidding? It's become *very* personal. But it's more than that. You became too human. Mating for love? Mating with a human? Didn't you learn anything from Elizabeth? She played us both for fools, but unlike you, I learned my lesson. Humans are not meant to survive, not like *us*. And dragons who weaken our lines and destroy our race by settling for humans, don't deserve to survive."

Piper thrashed in her chair, finally getting the gag around her mouth loosened until it fell around her neck.

"You said you wouldn't kill him!"

Conrad turned to her, and the chilling stillness in his eyes seemed almost dead. "I'm a politician—what did you expect?"

"Please, untie me," she begged. "You have what you want—just let me go. Let me see if he's okay."

"I suppose it would be amusing to kill him while you watched." Conrad ran a finger along the edge of his blade and then walked back to her, slicing the ropes on her wrist.

Piper rushed from the chair and fell to her knees by Mikhail, cradling his face and wiping blood from his mouth.

"I'm here," she whispered, choking back a sob. *"I'm here."*

She helped him get to his feet. He was unsteady and weak, leaning on her and a nearby wooden support beam that stretched from floor to ceiling.

She realized Conrad was watching them. There was a hatred building in his eyes as he stared at them. A hatred born of jealousy, perhaps? It replaced the deadness that had been there moments before.

"You truly love him," Conrad said. His black eyes seemed to flash with fire.

Mikhail's breathing was labored, and the sound sent violent shivers of fear through her. What if the drug didn't wear off? What if he never got his dragon back? Would he die?

"I do," she replied. "Not that you even know what that is, you monster. You got what you came for. Just leave us alone!"

"I'm afraid it's not that simple. There can be no loose ends." Conrad lunged and thrust his blade toward Mikhail's chest. Only it never hit its mark.

Piper almost didn't feel the blade sink into her stomach. She had hoped to wrestle the blade away, but he had been so fast...so fast. It had cut so smoothly that it left only a deep ache behind as Conrad pulled the blade out.

"No!" The roar she heard was human, but it carried all the force of the dragon Mikhail had once been. Clutching her stomach as she dropped to her knees, Piper watched in horror as Conrad rammed the blade into Mikhail's side twice, then twisted the blade. Conrad stood, wiping the blade and putting it away as he dusted himself off.

"*Now* I've got what I came for." Conrad's words barely

registered with Piper. Already the world was beginning to feel distant to her.

"You...bastard!" Mikhail snarled, clutching his side as blood oozed between his fingers.

We're both...lost...

Piper fell to her side. Sounds started to become slightly muted, as though she had covered her ears. Mikhail dragged himself over, turning her head toward him. She glimpsed Conrad slipping out of the room, a cold smile on his lips and eyes black with evil.

"Mikhail, I can't...can't catch my breath," she whispered. She felt weak, too weak. Her hands, still covering her abdomen, were warm and sticky.

"No, no..." Mikhail whispered as he cradled her in his arms. His face was etched with pain, but he didn't let her go.

The world began to get hazy around the edges of her vision, but she could see his beautiful face soaked with tears. She used what strength she had left to lift a hand to cup his cheek.

"Don't cry...*please*..." she begged. "I just wanted to... save you."

"You did. More than you know. I was lost before you found me," he rasped. "We were supposed to be together. You can't leave me now. I love you."

She brushed her fingertips over his lips, trying to imprint them upon her memory, how soft they felt. "We are together." His dark lashes glinted with tears like diamonds. So beautiful, and for a short time he had been hers.

A chill crept along her limbs and a heaviness filled her chest, one that was slowly suffocating her. She wanted to remember him and take that memory with her into the next world.

She tried to catch pieces of memories, shattered shards of a life she could have had with him, but they were moving like leaves in a fall wind. She knew that wind, recognized it deep inside as the thing that would soon carry her away.

"Piper..." He pressed his forehead to hers, and a tear fell from his cheek onto her skin. "I never deserved you. You are a treasure beyond my reach."

"Keep me warm," she whispered, her hand dropping from his face. Her strength was fading now, and it took everything she had left just to breathe.

"I will." His words broke as more tears fell.

"You belong...to me," she said, mouthing the words.

He nodded. "My heart is yours. Will *always* be yours," he promised. He kissed her. It was the last thing she would feel. The gentle burning kiss and the beat of her dragon's heart. And then she felt herself slip away on the cold wind.

MIKHAIL FELT THE MOMENT HER LIFE SLIPPED AWAY. The last bit of breath in her body vanished, and the silence where her heartbeat should have been was deafening.

There was nothing there now. Nothing. Nothing at all.

He threw back his head and roared. The rafters of the small museum quaked around them as his dragon surged to the surface. It forced itself through the thick, deadening weight of whatever Conrad's drug had done to it, but not even that could stop the dragon now. Mate-grief was too strong—*love* was too strong. Already his wounds were mending. Flames filled his vision as he vowed to destroy the man who had taken his love from him. It would be the last thing he would do before his broken heart killed him.

His mother's voice seemed to whisper from all around him. *Magic calls to magic.*

Magic. He was in a museum full of magical artifacts. But he knew of no spells that could bring back the dead. *You can't be gone. You belong to me.*

The memory of Piper's voice teased his ears. *Yes, I gave you my heart.*

He stared down at Piper's still form. A faint hue of red lingered in her cheeks, a hint of the life that had deserted her.

His mother's voice seemed to fill his head, almost as though she were shouting. *The heart of a dragon, which beats ruby red...*

An image of the Dragon Heart Stone flashed across his eyes. He reached for his coat and pulled out the fist-size ruby and held it out. The light cast flickering shadows over the stone's depths. There, in the shadows of the ruby, he saw what he must do.

He laid the stone upon her breast, then lifted Piper's blood-covered hands and pressed them to the surface of the gemstone. He closed his eyes and spoke words that did not come from his own mind, but somewhere beyond.

"I bind this soul to yours, this dragon to yours. By the gods which gave me breath, I return yours to you." Then he leaned down and kissed his love's lifeless lips.

Come back to me, little dove. Let me show you how to fly.

A spark leaped between their lips, and he pulled back in shock. Piper's body was glowing. The Dragon Heart Stone gleamed, a bright light shining like a flame in the depths of the heart of the gem. Then the stone shattered into a thousand glittering red shards before those shards turned to dust. The stone was gone.

Heat rolled off Piper's body. Her temperature rose higher than that of a human's. He reacted instinctively because he knew what that heat meant. He scooped his mate up and ran from the museum out into the deserted streets. Conrad was in the car with the jewels and was already driving away. Mikhail placed Piper on the ground in the small square, and then he stumbled back. Her clothes tore at the seams as her body transformed.

A white dragon, pale as the first snow of winter, now

lay hunched on the ground, its tail curled protectively around its body. It was new to this world, new to existing as a dragon within a human body. Its soul had slept for untold millennia inside the stone, waiting for a home.

Mikhail held up a hand and brushed his palm down her nose, smiling as the female dragon huffed softly. Her eyes were like quicksilver as she gazed at him. The wild beast gentled at his touch because she recognized her mate. She nudged his chest with her snout. Fine-boned, yet strong. She was exquisite. His dragon rumbled in pleasure.

"My beauty," he said, and meant it. She was glorious, and she was his. His heart swelled with an intensity he'd never thought possible. There was no desperation, no fear that this would end because she was human. Piper was one of his kind now.

Piper gave another snort, then lifted her head to stare at something over his shoulder. He turned to follow her gaze. The distant sight of a retreating SUV made him suddenly grin as he looked back at Piper.

"What do you say? Are you ready to fly?" He stepped back and stripped out of his clothes, his dragon rushing to the surface as he transformed.

PIPER STARED AT THE DARK GREEN DRAGON. HE WAS beautiful, and she knew him. He was hers. Her dragon wanted to dance and nuzzle against him. But the sight of the car—Mikhail's car—driving away grabbed her attention. That car needed to be stopped.

Her mate nudged her shoulder with his snout, urging her to follow. He took a running start and leaped skyward, his wings flapping hard enough to create a small windstorm. Piper ignored the flutter of nerves at thinking this was her first flight; even her dragon was nervous. It had been asleep for so long. But she did exactly what she'd seen Mikhail do. There was a second of gut-wrenching panic when she lifted into the air, and then she was shooting even higher, her wings catching the wind, and she was flying.

Their wings pulled them forward through the night air like twin bolts of lightning, until they were alongside the retreating vehicle. Mikhail angled his wings, making a sharp turn back toward land, and she copied him. They flew toward the car, and Piper flew ahead of her mate, drawing her mouth open. Fire exploded from her jaws as she swooped in front of the SUV. The car skidded to a halt, dust mixing with the flames she released. The pair landed on either side of the vehicle and watched closely as the man in the car stumbled out.

"No!" Conrad shouted, his arms already beginning to bulge. "It's not possible! I killed you!"

Piper sensed the coming transformation. Fury took over. Her tail lashed out like a whip and slashed him across the chest, sending him crashing into a large rock fifty feet away. He didn't move. The scent of blood reached her nostrils, and she hissed, satisfied by it.

Piper prowled up to Conrad, nudging his body with one clawed front foot. The wound to his abdomen was deep. He still didn't stir, and there was no heartbeat. His neck lay at an impossible angle, limp as a ragdoll. She turned to look at her mate and froze.

On the horizon, silhouetted against the setting sun, were more dragons. She tensed and made a low growl. Mikhail also noticed them and put his body in front of hers as they waited for the others to land. There were six of them, all deep red in color.

There was a long moment of silence. The new dragons stared hard at Mikhail and Piper. Then they started to shift. Piper cocked her head, amused at the parade of naked men who now bent over to open small duffel bags of clothes that had been roped to their back legs. She saw no threat from these men, especially not while they were in human form.

Next, Mikhail transformed back to his human form, and she grew nervous. Wanting to protect him should the others try to harm him, she started to push him back with her front foot, but he shushed her and patted her neck. Then he caught something one of the men tossed to him, and he started to dress.

"We were afraid we wouldn't reach you in time. My father knew Sinclair from the old days and said he was one nasty dragon to battle with. We thought you may need additional assistance," one of the men said. "But it seems you handled the situation on your own."

The dragon part of her didn't recognize the man, but the human certainly did. Randolph Belishaw. Had he brought the others?

"We're fine. How did you even know we needed help?" Mikhail replied, embracing the other man.

"I was afraid you didn't get my message. It's my fault Conrad found you. The bastard drugged me and got it out of me. He had some serum that kept me from—"

"Transforming? He used that on me too," Mikhail growled.

"But...you were in dragon form just now. How?"

"It's a long story."

Belishaw looked at Conrad's corpse with a scowl. "It seems we missed out on the pleasure of ripping him to pieces."

"I'm afraid my mate was quite upset with him. The bastard didn't stand a chance." Rather than showing horror at her actions, Mikhail sounded proud.

"*This* is Piper?" Belishaw stared at her, eyes wide. "How is that possible?"

"I promise to explain it all to you over drinks."

"And I look forward to hearing it. You've found quite a mate, Mikhail. I envy you." Belishaw approached Piper, but she sensed he was teasing her by the way his eyes glinted. He knew who she was, but she couldn't get her dragon to calm down, not after her first transformation.

Not after her first kill. The beast was edgy and still full of energy.

Mikhail chuckled and stroked her frill, which lay flat back against her neck. She shivered in pleasure at the tickling sensation.

"Come now, little dove. It's safe. Come back to me." He continued to run his hands down the edges of the sensitive frill. Her nerves and fears evaporated. Before she could stop herself, her body was changing. Suddenly she was being held in Mikhail's arms.

"Anyone have a spare set of clothes?" he asked.

The men around them chuckled, and Piper flinched. She was completely naked.

"Here." Belishaw threw a long black peacoat to them, and Mikhail helped her into it. She shivered, but she wasn't as cold as she expected to be.

"I'm not that cold," she whispered to him, completely mystified. She should have been freezing.

"It's your dragon blood," Mikhail said before he pressed a lingering kiss to her lips. "You'll run hotter from now on."

She realized Belishaw was eyeing her with a mix of awe and concern. "I cannot believe she's a dragoness. There hasn't been a transformation like that for our kind in centuries."

Mikhail hugged her close. "She's nothing short of a miracle."

Belishaw nodded at the five dragons behind him.

"They'll take care of the body. My family will smooth over the situation with his disappearance. A tragic accident I think, perhaps on a fishing boat near Cornwall." He shot a dark glance at the cold corpse. "He had dark designs for this country, and being a braggart he couldn't help but boast about them."

"Who is he really?" Mikhail asked. "I've been this man's bane for centuries, yet I don't even know him. Just a vague sense of having seen him before in Elizabeth's prison."

"His name was Conrad Sinclair. He was a member of the House of Parliament, very influential. He planned to run for prime minister next. He'd have won, too. Both because of his dragon charms and the alliance he wished to strike up with what is left of the Drakor family."

"And then?"

Belishaw huffed. "As Prime Minister he planned to treat this country as his personal plaything and ultimately destroy it. It is good he was dealt with now."

"Agreed." Mikhail walked over to his car, his arm still around Piper's shoulders. "Why don't we meet at my house? Come as soon as you finish here."

"See you soon." Belishaw waved at them before Piper climbed into the car and Mikhail began the drive back to Cornwall.

Piper didn't speak the entire way. When Mikhail parked the car outside his home and came over to her door, she was still staring off into space, her mind stuck on all that had happened.

She had turned into a dragon. *A dragon.*

"Piper, love, are you all right?" Mikhail reached into the car and helped her out.

"Yes. I'm just... It's a lot to take in," she said in a dreamlike state. She'd died in his arms, then came back to life as a dragon. And she'd killed someone. How did one process all this?

Concern shadowed his eyes. "I know you didn't ask for this. I know I bonded with you without asking permission, and that's why you didn't want to stay. I've royally screwed things up." She saw pain deep in his lovely green eyes.

"You're wrong," she said.

He raised his brows but remained silent.

"I didn't know we'd bonded. I wanted to stay, so much that it hurt me to leave. But I didn't want to shorten your life...to effectively kill you because I had a short human lifespan. I would have given *anything* to stay with you."

He was speechless, and before she could react, he lifted her up in the air, holding her tight as he spun her around.

"Mikhail?" She laughed, unsure what he was doing. When he set her back down, she was biting her lip because it hurt too much to keep smiling.

"You'll stay? I won't lose you?"

"No. I'm yours," she vowed.

She didn't want to think about the details, where they would live, what they'd tell her parents, let alone her job or the police. Right now she had him in her arms, and that was the only thing that mattered.

"Let's get you inside," Mikhail said, seeing her shiver. "You'll freeze. You may be a dragon, but you can still get cold." He tugged her back to the house and set her on the couch. She giggled as he removed the coat and kissed her naked body before wrapping her up in warm blankets.

"I'll put some tea on, and then we can talk." He vanished from view. She watched the snow begin to fall. Snow? She thought the weather forecast had called for rain. She was too busy staring at the landscape along the coast to notice the car coming until it was almost in the driveway.

"Mikhail, there's a car headed this way," she called out.

He reappeared with two mugs of hot tea. Mikhail frowned as he stared at the car.

"That's not Belishaw," Mikhail said, setting the mugs on the table. "Why don't you go upstairs and change into some clothes. I'm afraid our talk will have to come later, after we deal with these visitors."

"Is it trouble?" she asked.

"Hopefully not."

She slipped upstairs to get dressed, trusting Mikhail had the situation under control. By the time she returned, she heard voices—both male and female.

"Piper, we're in the kitchen," Mikhail called when she

reached the bottom stair. Once in the kitchen, she found a handsome blond man and a pretty woman with dark brown hair standing close to Mikhail.

"Piper, this is my brother Grigori and his mate, Madelyn."

Piper stared at Mikhail and the man beside him. The family resemblance was there, the proud features, the beautiful eyes, only Grigori's were blue rather than green.

"Hi," Madelyn said, her eyes bright and her smile warm. She was American like Piper, something that made Piper relax instantly. Madelyn held out a hand, and Piper shook it.

"Belishaw mentioned you might come," was all she could think to say. She'd learned much about Grigori from the sketches with the small notes, and yet she still felt shy around him, afraid to make eye contact.

"Belishaw, eh?" Grigori said with a chuckle and shared a smile with Mikhail. "Good man...for an English dragon." Grigori spoke in the same soft, slightly rough, and yet irresistible Russian accent as Mikhail.

Madelyn spoke up. "Why don't you guys go out to the living room? Us girls will have some tea and see what's in the kitchen to make for dinner." She shooed the two men out of the kitchen and turned to Piper. "I can't cook to save my life. I just needed a way to let them have a private talk. It's been almost two hundred years since they last spoke. Besides, I'm dying to hear all about you."

"Me?" Piper swallowed. "Well, you probably heard about the jewel heist..."

Madelyn grinned. "Not *that*. Don't you realize you are the first human in a thousand years to turn into a dragon? At least, that's what Grigori says. This is *huge*."

Piper sighed. "It really hasn't sunk in. I just... I mean, my old life is over, isn't it? I'm still thinking about... I mean, I don't know how to..." She couldn't finish, and she suddenly felt like crying. Madelyn was there in an instant, hugging her.

"Hey. It's going to be okay. I've been exactly where you are. I spent my life thinking I was human, but then I met Grigori and learned I was a Thunderbird. My whole life got turned on its head."

"What's a Thunderbird?" Piper wiped her eyes, curiosity outweighing her confusion.

"Sort of like a phoenix," Madelyn explained. "A mythical bird that can kill dragons. It summons storms and can create sonic booms with its wings."

"Wait, you kill dragons?"

Madelyn bit her lip and nodded. "They're supposed to be my mortal enemy. It's a long story, but being with Grigori changed the way I saw things. And being a part of the Barinov family... It's amazing. You won't regret being mated to Mikhail. Change this big is always scary, but it's going to be okay. You're meant to be one of us. We'll help you get through this." Madelyn gave her another warm hug. "Now, let's find something to cook. Surely between the two of us we can make something edible. Dragons have big appetites. So do Thunderbirds, for that matter."

Piper chuckled as she touched her stomach. She was definitely hungry.

She followed Madelyn to the fridge and realized she could actually hear Mikhail talking in the other room. Her sense of hearing had improved. How cool was that? She was dying to know just what other abilities she'd picked up now that she was a dragon shifter.

Hopefully she'd have the next several millennia to find out.

❧ 18 ❧

It is time to end a story that began in sorrow and ordeal and has ended in a deep and lasting happiness. May it be so for others.
-Anne McCaffrey

"It's been a long time, brother," Grigori said.

"It has indeed," Mikhail replied. A hundred things he'd longed to say simply faded. He pulled his elder brother into a fierce hug. Two hundred years had passed since he'd seen Grigori, and in that embrace he felt every single day fade away.

"Now that you have the jewels back, tell me you will stop this exile nonsense and come home. Rurik and I miss you. Besides, now that you shall be an uncle soon..."

Mikhail's lips parted in shock. "You mean you..."

"Madelyn and I are expecting a drakeling. Should be

here in eight months. Can you believe it? I'm going to be a father." Grigori's blue eyes sparkled like diamonds. He'd never looked happier.

Mikhail slapped his brother's back. "Congratulations." But then he sobered. "But how? Madelyn isn't a dragoness." Belishaw was sure Mikhail's brother had mated a mortal. He'd thought that Grigori wouldn't want to have to watch his mate die, and children wouldn't be possible.

Grigori's expression sobered. "No. Madelyn isn't a dragon, but she's not mortal either."

Mikhail was confused now. "Then what is she?"

"She's a Thunderbird. I think that dragons can mate with other supernatural creatures because of the way our ancestors bonded to spirits in the same way."

That wasn't possible. The Thunderbirds were extinct, weren't they? Their father had made it his life's mission to kill them to avenge the loss of his own father. But if there were still Thunderbirds alive, and one was here...

"Piper." Mikhail's gasp sounded more like a hiss than he meant it to. His brother tensed as he barred the path to the kitchen.

"Easy, brother, she's not going to hurt you."

Mikhail curled his hands into fists. "She's in the kitchen with my *mate*."

"And Piper is perfectly safe," Grigori promised. "Sit, and let me tell you all that's happened since you left."

Mikhail reluctantly sat down and listened as his brother shared an almost unbelievable tale of how he'd met Madelyn when she'd discovered James Barrow's old journal in a library in Russia. Then he explained what had happened that fateful night when their parents had died. Only Mikhail's mother had survived the battle, and she'd lived long enough to tell Grigori and Rurik what had happened. Mikhail had known their father wasn't perfect, but to learn that he had tracked down and killed the last mated Thunderbirds on earth, when they hadn't even wanted to fight, left him feeling cold.

"It was Mother. She found Madelyn, who was just an infant at the time. Mother took her to safety before she died. It's all connected. Don't you see?" Grigori asked, his voice full of awe. "It was *fate* that bound our lives together. First as enemies, and now as mates."

"How did Rurik take the news?" Mikhail knew how hotheaded their younger brother could be. It was a trait in battle dragons to act rashly and without thought. It usually kept them alive.

"He was hesitant at first, but when we had to face the Drakors, Madelyn killed all of them. You should have seen it. They were all circling around this high mountain and coming out of these caves. Madelyn came screaming down from the heavens in her bird form and created a sonic boom that crushed the mountain down on them. I'm just glad that battle was in rural Russia or else the damned Brotherhood of the Blood Moon would be knocking on our door." Grigori chuckled as though recalling some memory. "After that, Rurik became a fan." It pained

Mikhail to know he'd missed out on so much of his brothers' lives.

"So," Grigori said, focusing on him again. "Will you come home, brother?"

It was what he'd hoped to hear from his father, but he never would. Forgiveness from a dead man was not something he could ever get.

"I still need to talk to Piper. She's only just become a dragon. This is all new to her. She'll need time to reorganize her life. She might not want to move to Russia. So until she decides, I'll go where she goes."

Grigori nodded. "Wise answer. A good dragon puts his mate's needs above his own." It was something their father had said over and over again, a code he'd lived by, except the night he'd gotten himself killed, dooming their mother in the process.

"I'm sorry I didn't reach out," Mikhail said, his voice a little rough as long-buried emotions began to claw back to the surface.

"I know," Grigori replied. "I'm sorry too. Father put so much emphasis on duty, you never had a chance to learn that life was also about love and joy." Mikhail had never seen his brother like this before. Grigori's eyes were soft as he spoke. He had always been hard and strong, like their father, but now he seemed strong in a different way. More like their mother.

"You've changed." Mikhail smiled.

"We both have." Grigori glanced over his shoulder

toward the kitchen. "Finding one's mate is like learning to fly for the first time. Excitement, fear, joy, love, and exquisite pleasure."

His brother had summarized it perfectly. Finding Piper, loving her, and almost losing her had shown him just what he'd missed out on by hiding away. He'd lost Elizabeth, and that had almost destroyed him. But Piper had saved him.

"How did you do it?" Grigori asked quietly. "How did you turn her into a dragon?"

"I'm not sure. It all happened so fast. Piper leaped in front of Sinclair's blade and..." The words died on his lips. It took a moment to compose himself. "She was dying in my arms, and I heard a voice that told me I needed to give her a dragon's heart."

Grigori frowned. "A dragon's heart?"

"Yes, but not an actual heart. The Dragon Heart Stone. A fist-sized ruby that was imbued with magic." He curled his fingers into a fist, remembering how it had felt to hold the ruby and feel the power surging through it into Piper. "I held her as she breathed her last, and then the stone exploded with power and turned to dust. There must have been a dragon's soul sleeping in there, one that bound itself to Piper. I can't think of any other explanation, but I've never heard of such a thing before, have you?"

"The Dragon Heart Stone," Grigori mused, his blue eyes serious. "I remember Father telling us about it, how even the Belishaw clan feared to keep it in their possession. Yet none knew what power it held. But if this is true, if it did hold a sleeping dragon's soul, then it might not be the only stone out there with such powers. You remember our uncle, Vasili? He was searching for the Heart of Sorrows, a sapphire the size of an apple. What if it holds a similar power?"

"Did he find the stone?"

Grigori shook his head. "His mate died while they were exploring the Alps together, and he passed away shortly after her and failed to discover its location. We never found either of them. Father believed they were buried beneath snow after they perished."

For a long moment neither brother spoke as they thought of all the dragons long gone.

Then Mikhail smiled as a new thought occurred to him. "You and Rurik never got to see the hoard I was supposed to bring home all those years ago. Do you want to see it?"

Grigori shook his head. "Better not. I would end up spending all night counting pearls, and my lovely wife would be upset."

The brothers laughed, then paused when they heard their mates' laughter coming from the kitchen.

"It's nice, isn't it?" Grigori asked. Mikhail nodded. For so long it had been just the three of them against the world. Now with mates and a drakeling on the way, the

Barinovs would be a real family again. "All we need now is to find a nice dragoness for Rurik," Grigori said.

"Find Rurik a mate? I doubt that will ever happen." Mikhail snorted.

Grigori grinned. "Never say never, brother."

PIPER SAT ON THE EDGE OF MIKHAIL'S BED, WATCHING him undress. It was close to midnight. They'd had a wonderful dinner with Grigori and Madelyn, who at this moment were settling in for the night in a bedroom down the hall.

"It's time for our little talk." Mikhail came over to stand in front of her, wearing only his jeans with the top button undone. He did that on purpose, she supposed. Something about him in just jeans made her a little crazy. She stared at his chest until he cupped her chin and tilted her head to look up at him.

"Hmmm?"

"We need to talk," he repeated. His green eyes were warm. Piper couldn't help but smile, even though there was a sudden flutter of nerves in her belly. She held her breath as she tried to stay calm.

"Is it a good talk or a bad talk?"

"A good talk...I hope." He brushed the pad of his thumb over her lips and flashed her a smile. Then he knelt down in front of her and took her hands in his.

"So much has happened this last week. I know you still need time to adjust to being one of...my kind." His face turned ruddy, as though he was embarrassed.

"A dragon," she said with a giggle. "You can say it, you know. It's not so scary anymore. I talked to Madelyn, and she faced the same thing, becoming something she didn't know how to be. Knowing that I'm not alone—" She paused a moment. "That makes it easier."

Mikhail raised her hands to his lips, pressing a kiss to her knuckles. "And you have me." The kiss singed her skin deliciously. She wanted those lips all over the rest of her body.

"I do," she agreed, pulling them up so he towered over her. "Why don't we talk later?" She trailed a finger down his chest toward his jeans.

Mikhail's eyes went from green to molten gold as he groaned. "If I have to tie you down to talk, little dove, I will."

She held out her wrists. "Yes, please."

"Fuck, you are driving me wild, love." He captured her wrists and closed his eyes. "Just let me say what I need to say first. Then we can play." He opened his eyes again. "I love you."

Piper held her breath, her heart racing like it had the first time she'd leaped into the air as a dragon.

His face turned red. "You must understand, for me to say this might seem rushed to you, but it is different with our kind. We know, deep down, about those we choose to love. There is no doubt, because the bond couldn't happen without it."

"I know," Piper said, both confused and understanding. "I feel it too. I just...*know*. It's not something I think I could have ever felt as a human. Like I can actually sense a piece of me that's missing, and you fit it perfectly." She said the words softly, a little afraid to admit something so intimate, so vulnerable. She'd never loved anyone before, not like this. It was terrifying, exciting, and overwhelming. But he felt the same way about her, and that made it so much better.

"You feel the same?" Mikhail's eyes widened.

Her eyes stung with tears. "Of course I do." She climbed onto her knees on the bed, putting their faces level. She curled her arms around his neck and pressed her forehead to his. "It's insane to love someone so soon, I know, but I do. It's like a part of me was missing all these years, and being with you... It's that missing piece settling into place. I am *whole*." She feathered her lips over his, and their breathing matched the steady beating of their hearts.

"Let's go home. To Russia," she said before kissing him again.

"You want to?" he asked.

Piper nodded. "Once we get the treasure situation sorted out, I want you to take me home."

Mikhail smiled. "We'll be the first dragon family to

have our own private gemologist." He kissed the tip of her nose. "The others will be jealous."

Piper laughed. "Just promise me I get to look at the jewels from time to time." She was teasing, but a mischievous glint filled Mikhail's eyes.

"Oh, little dove, I plan to strip you naked and cover you with pearls, drape you with diamonds, torture and tease you with topaz, entice you with emeralds, show my love with lapis lazuli—"

This time she did giggle, unable to stop. "That sounds like a wonderful dream."

"Which I promise to make come true." He nudged her back on the bed and covered her with kisses, each one more tender than the last. As she and Mikhail made love, she swore she heard a faint whisper of sound sighing against the windows.

For whoever owns a dragon's heart will know love unending.

EPILOGUE

__But it is one thing to read about dragons and another to meet them.__
__—Ursula K. Le Guin__

Charlotte MacQueen sat in the elegantly designed lounge of the Brotherhood of the Blood Moon. The front desk was a dark matte gray, where a young woman with metallic-framed glasses stared at a computer screen. Charlotte pivoted the black leather armchair around to watch the water feature across the lounge. It was a wall of crystal with water running endlessly down its surface, and she could just make out the shadows of people through it.

This was a world she was never supposed to be a part

of. It was the world of the paranormal, full of danger and excitement. Her two older brothers—Damien, who headed the organization, and Jason—monitored those creatures that posed a threat to humans and, if need be, hunted them down. Charlotte had never been allowed to follow in their footsteps. She'd had to live a normal life and had almost finished earning her PhD in chemical engineering.

If her brothers knew she was here right now, they would be upset. She wasn't supposed to come here, but she'd gotten a call from her friend Meg Stratford, one of the Brotherhood's best hunters.

"Charlotte!" A woman exited from a door close to the front desk, grinning.

Charlotte rushed over to embrace her friend. "Meg!"

Meg Stratford was one of her closest friends. But they hadn't always been friends. Meg had been a junior hunter for the Brotherhood and assigned, covertly of course, to follow Charlotte around on her dates when she was in high school. Her brothers had been real jerks when it came to trusting her to date nice guys. Meg had seen how timid Charlotte had been and given her a lot of great advice on how to deal with guys and especially how to deal with her brothers. They'd been fast friends ever since.

"I'm so glad to see you. I just got back from London, and I swear I'm still jetlagged. But this is important." Meg tucked Charlotte's arm in hers and led her out of the waiting room.

"What were you doing in London?" Charlotte asked. She and Meg walked down a hall and entered a small private conference room. It was clear Meg had been working here for several hours. A stack of Diet Coke cans lined one side of the table, and a few containers of Chinese takeout littered another part of the table. There were files everywhere and a clear plastic bag that contained a syringe, and another bag that contained ancient leather journals.

"I was dealing with dragons, if you can believe it. Scary things. Sexy...but scary."

"Dragons?" Charlotte whispered the word in awe. It was one thing to know they existed, but it was another thing entirely to think of her friend being around them. "Do they really breathe fire?"

"Umm." Meg tilted her head. "I've heard so, yes. But I've only ever seen them in human form. They just dress in expensive suits and go about London bedding women—who, by the way, just fall at their feet, begging for it. I think it's something to do with dragon pheromones. I'm not really sure on the science there. I try not to get too close to those guys." Meg chuckled. "There's nothing worse than a dominating man, right?"

Charlotte blushed, not wanting to admit she'd give anything for a boyfriend with a bit of a dominant streak. "Right..." It had been ages since she'd even had a date, and thanks to her overprotective brothers, who saw threats around every corner, she was still a virgin. It was not a good thing.

"So here's the thing. I need your help. I know how Damien wants you kept in the dark when it comes to this stuff, but you're the only one I can trust with this." Meg picked up the bag with the syringe in it.

"What's that?" Charlotte leaned forward, nudging her chair closer to the table.

"This is a drug that I believe subdues the dragon part of a shifter. I've been poring over these journals written by a man named John Dee. He was Queen Elizabeth's court magician and advisor way back. It seems that he researched dragons for some time and came to some interesting conclusions about their physiology. He came up with a means to affect the shifting ability of a dragon, and another drug which *both loosens their tongue and makes them stay on the path of truth*,' as he put it. We found this sample, or what's left of it, and these books at Conrad Sinclair's house, a member of British Parliament, who it turns out was a dragon himself. He refined Dee's formulas and seemed to be using them against his enemies. Unfortunately, his notes aren't completely readable, and some of the ingredients we can't identify. We believe Sinclair had firsthand knowledge of the formulas and was able to fill in the gaps, but we're lacking that advantage. I want you to analyze the sample I recovered from his residence and see if you can replicate it. Do you think you can do that?"

"Sure, but..." Charlotte bit her lip before continuing.

"Doesn't the Brotherhood have top-notch labs that can handle this?"

Meg nodded, but her expression made Charlotte's stomach churn. That was her "bad news" face.

"I'm worried that in the wrong hands, this could be used poorly. It might even be weaponized. This version seems to dampen a dragon for only about a day. The oath of the Brotherhood is to watch first and hunt only if we must, but not everyone sees that oath the same way. Some believe in a more 'proactive' approach. Remember what happened with Serena? A large minority of the Brotherhood voted for an all-out war against all vamps after she was killed."

Charlotte closed her eyes. God, she wished Meg hadn't brought her up.

Serena had been eighteen, fearless and beautiful, and more importantly, the love of Charlotte's oldest brother's life. Damien hadn't voted for war on the vampires, but the vote by the hunters had come dangerously close. If the majority had voted death, then the Brotherhood would have been obligated to kill all vampires they encountered, and Charlotte knew Damien couldn't stand for that. He knew many vampires who were good men and women who never killed or hurt humans.

"I want to make sure we know what this is before anyone starts using it."

The syringe's tip was covered in a green liquid that almost seemed to glow.

"Okay, I'll check it out," said Charlotte. "But Damien and Jason can't know."

"That's the plan." Meg handed the bagged syringe to Charlotte, who tucked it into her purse.

"I want to know everything about that drug," Meg said. "It might help us stop a dragon war from breaking out."

Charlotte nodded. A dragon war? That sounded like a really bad thing, but it almost faded from her mind in importance. The only thing that mattered right now was that she finally had a chance to make a real difference alongside her brothers—even if they couldn't know about it.

Wait! Don't close this book! Thank you for reading Mikhail and Piper's story! Did you know that Rurik and Grigori both have their own stories too? You don't want to miss Grigori fall in love with a woman who discovers dragons, or Rurik falling for the sister of some supernatural dragon hunters!
Grab Grigori's book!
Grab Rurik's book now!

Sign up for my newsletter to get 3 FREE romance novels, new release alerts, exclusive bonus materials and more:
http://laurensmithbooks.com/free-books-and-newsletter/

Join my Facebook group:
Lauren Smith's League for exclusive giveaways and
sneak peeks of future books.

NEVER MISS A NEW BOOK OR A
DISCOUNTED BOOK! FOLLOW ME HERE
FOR ALERTS:
Amazon
Bookbub

Turn the page to read 3 chapters from *Rurik: A Royal Dragon Romance* now!

Brothers
of
Ash & Fire
A ROYAL DRAGON ROMANCE
RURIK
USA TODAY BESTSELLING AUTHOR
LAUREN SMITH

RURIK: A ROYAL DRAGON ROMANCE
PROLOGUE

"**G**reat heroes need great sorrows and burdens, or half their greatness goes unnoticed. It is all part of the fairy tale."
- Peter S. Beagle, *The Last Unicorn*

RURIK BARINOV WATCHED THE MEN AND WOMEN dancing in his nightclub *Logovo*—The Lair. The dark interior was lit by flashing strobe lights and fog from the machines at the opposite ends of the dance floor. The entire club looked like a mix between a cave and a dungeon. The walls were rough stone and there were iron barred cages where dancers could show off their moves.

While Rurik's older brother ran a sensible business, one that was built on technology in commerce, Rurik traded in pleasure: dancing, drinking and sex. He was not so buttoned up and proper like Grigori. He enjoyed wild nights with wicked women, bodies straining and yearning for that headlong rush of mutual satisfaction. It never ceased to amaze him that Grigori had walked away from sex. But he'd heard that after a thousand years a dragon tended to lose his wildness, at least in part. Only when they found their mate did he have a resurgence of that frenzied lust.

Rurik chuckled. He could not picture Grigori doing *anything* with a frenzy except slaughtering the competition in a boardroom. He was damned good at that. Scary as fuck too. He was always cool and controlled, yet when Rurik had shown interest in the little mortal professor, Madelyn Haynes, Grigori's eyes had blazed and he'd growled a dark and dangerous warning that sent warning shivers to Rurik's entire body. It was the first time he'd ever been afraid of his own brother. Dragons were possessive by nature, and as Russian Imperial dragon shifters they were more covetous than other breeds when it came to jewels and women.

Thinking about jewels always made Rurik think of his other brother Mikhail. The brother that was lost to them because he'd failed to secure a hoard of jewels from a treaty they'd made with English dragons. Mikhail had sent word that the treasure had been stolen and their father had exiled him for his failure. For one brief year their father and mother had traveled the world. While they were gone Grigori had called Mikhail home. For four brief seasons, Mikhail had been part of the family again. That was two centuries ago.

He wished Mikhail was here now. Mikhail knew Grigori better in some ways, even though he'd been exiled since the sixteenth century. Mikhail would have known how to warn Grigori against the temptations mortal females presented.

"Rurik?" A sweet voice caught his attention and dragged him out of ancient thoughts. A beautiful woman with dark hair and green eyes watched him from across the bar. His bartender, Nikita, wore silver sequined dress and killer black heels that made every man in the room assume she was a customer and not the bartender. Whenever he looked at her, the hardness in his heart always softened. But she was human and he couldn't never be with a human.

"How are the numbers tonight?" he asked as he joined her, leaning on the bar toward her. He couldn't help it, she pulled him in like the glint of a diamond just within reach. It made him practice his self-restraint.

She smiled warmly, a smile meant only for him, and he knew why. She was in love with him, but she was too much like him, a free spirit, unchained even by the forces of love. Any other woman he would have slept with and moved on, but he didn't do that with Nikita. She had the potential to be a possible true mate and if he dared to even kiss her, it could destroy his family. Battle dragons couldn't risk love, their lives were dangerous. If they dared to mate a human, the human could be used against them. A fragile mortal life would be easy for their enemies to snuff out and that would kill the battle dragon.

"Good. We are at maximum capacity, but—" her voice trailed off, her eyes widened as she stared at something over his shoulder.

"Niki?" he queried.

Her green eyes cut to his and she whispered one word. *"Drakor."*

He spun, battle instincts kicking in. Ruslan Drakor stood only a few feet away, grinning like the devil he was. As the eldest son of Dimitri Drakor, the head of the Drakor family, Ruslan was an arrogant bastard who believed he didn't have to abide by the terms of the treaty between the Barinov and Drakor families.

"Ruslan. What the fuck do you want?" He made a grand show of leaning casually against the bar, even though every muscle in his body was tense.

He prayed that Ruslan wouldn't be so stupid as to attack them in a club full of humans. There was a treaty in place for a reason. The Drakor family ran the eastern half of Russia while the Barinovs controlled the west. The Yenisey River acted as the formal boundary between their territories because it split Russia almost cleanly in half.

The Barinovs, having control of both Moscow and St.

Petersburg had, under Rurik's father in 1750, made a treaty which allowed the Drakors to enter and leave those two cities without incident, so long as they did not interfere with Barinov business or cause trouble.

"I've come for a drink and women." Ruslan laughed, but there was a feral gleam in his eyes.

Rurik remained still, the picture of casual ease. They both knew that Rurik could knock Ruslan on his ass in three seconds.

"Good for you, Ruslan, but find another club. *Not mine*." Had they been outside the city, Rurik would have attacked, but the damned treaty was keeping them on his best behavior.

Ruslan brushed his dark hair out of his eyes and walked to the other end of the bar, his expression changed to one of hunger as he spied Nikita.

"You, female, bring me the best vodka in the house." He slapped his palm on the counter hard enough that the expensive glass layer over the wood fractured, tiny cracks in the glass fanned out around his hand like spider webs.

Son of a dog ... Rurik growled softly, the dragon inside him stirring. He could feel the tattoo move on his back. He'd never been very good at restraining the beast within him. His father had said it was because he was built for battle.

"Ruslan, leave now," he warned.

The other man made a show of getting comfortable.

Then he looked over at Nikita and licked his lips. That was it.

"Nikita, the alarm if you please." Rurik tried to stay calm, but he could feel the dragon surging to the surface.

His bartender ducked beneath the bar and slapped a red button. An alarm siren blared, cutting the music off. Dancers scrambled out of the cages and off the dance floors, rushing toward the exit in varying degrees of panic.

It was a shame to lose a good night of business, but better to have an empty club than risk human casualties. There was nothing like a spike in mortality rates to draw the Brotherhood of the Blood Moon into their business. They had no offices in Moscow that he knew of, but there were always agents about, and they could mobilize more from St. Petersburg in short order. The last thing either he or the Drakor family needed were supernatural hunters swarming the city looking to take down dragon shifters.

"One last chance, Ruslan. Walk away and I leave your pretty face intact."

The other man laughed. "I was about to tell you the same thing."

Rurik sensed Nikita close behind him. Not everyone had left when the alarm went off. "Nikita, get out of here."

"But—"

"Go!" he roared. The sound reached a low pitch as his vocal cords started to transform to that of a dragon's.

Nikita tried to flee, but Ruslan threw up a hand. Fire shot out of his palm and a blazing beam, cutting off her escape. Ruslan's eyes morphed into red irises with slitted pupils. A hint of smoke puffed from his nostrils. Both Rurik and Ruslan were fighting to stay in control and not fully transform. The club wouldn't be able to hold two full-grown dragons, let alone one.

"You would break your father's treaty?" Rurik bellowed, raising his own palm. He unleashed a spray of fiery sparks toward the other dragon. It was the closest thing to a warning shot he could manage without starting a fire in his club.

"I am not bound by *his* word!" Ruslan balled his other fist and slammed it down on the bar. The glass counter shattered, thousands of pieces in the wood beneath exploded in a burst of massive splinters.

A six-inch piece of wood buried itself in Rurik's lower belly. *Fuck!* Pain set in like a dull ache and he knew that was bad...

"Rurik!" Nikita screamed and ran toward him. He gripped the splinter and ripped it out. Hot blood streamed down his shirt and his wound throbbed. He would heal fine, but the sight of it must have scared her. When Nikita reached him, he waved her away.

"You have to get out." He panted. "I can't fight him and worry about you."

She bit her lip and nodded. "Be safe," she said. She kissed his forehead and fled, but never reached the door. Ruslan raised his hand aimed a jet of fire straight at Nikita. She was knocked into the wall against a massive mirror just feet from the exit. The mirror shattered and her limp body fell to the ground. Blood dripped from Nikita's lips and the light in her green eyes faded like the light of a dying star a thousand miles away. Something inside him broke, a piece of his heart fractured.

A cold, harsh laugh escaped Ruslan's lips. "What's one more human, more or less?"

Shock and grief raged inside Rurik. His Nikita, *his Niki* was gone. A red mist descended over his vision. He didn't care about the club, the treaty, or the Brotherhood right now. He cared only of vengeance.

With a deafening roar, Rurik's clothes shredded to the floor as his body transformed into a fifteen-foot-tall black scaled dragon. His frill fanned out around his neck as he opened his jaws and a stream of fire shot out that was so hot it was nearly blue.

Ruslan tried to morph into his own beast but. Rurik's jaws caught Ruslan's elongated neck mid-change and snapped shut. The heavy crack echoed in the room as Ruslan went limp beneath him. Rurik released him, and the body transformed back fully into a man, laying broken and bleeding at Rurik's feet. Rurik's eyes darted around the room, seeking out more threats, then he saw Nikita's body. The beast recognized the loss of a woman he cared about and he let out a mournful sound.

Rurik let go of the dragon side of him and his body shrank back to its mortal shell. Rurik fell to his knees.

Nikita was dead, Ruslan was dead, and a three-century old treaty was broken.

He dug his hands through his hair, trying to stop them from shaking as emotions rolled through them like violent riptides. How was he going to tell Grigori that he killed Dimitri Drakor's eldest son?

I've just started a war...

CHAPTER 1

mong all the kinds of serpents, there is none comparable to the dragon.
— Edward Topsell, 1658

MOSCOW, RUSSIA – THREE MONTHS LATER

Charlotte MacQueen tugged the sweetheart neckline of her red satin cocktail dress up a few more centimeters. Despite the fancy but thick winter coat she wore, her exposed skin had drawn the cabdriver's eyes and made her shift restlessly until he'd had to focus back on his driving. But then, she'd know her dress would have this effect. She was practically falling out of the damn thing, but she had a hunch this would be one of the few times having full breasts would be an advantage instead of a hindrance.

She'd spent most of her life hiding her curvy figure

behind draping sweaters and lab coats. It was silly, but she'd never felt comfortable in sexy clothes.

Charlotte wasn't sure if it was how the slide of satin felt on her skin or the way every masculine eye fixed on the high cut of her dress or the lowered neckline, but tonight she was trying hard to ignore how exposed she felt because she was pulling a Mata Hari. She was going behind enemy lines—or rather, into dragon territory—to seduce a seriously dangerous dragon shifter.

Before tonight, she would have thought the idea of her chasing down a man who could shift into a dragon was impossible. Not because she didn't think they were real, mind you. She'd grown up her entire life knowing the truth about things that went bump in the night. Vampires, dragons, werewolves, shifters—all of it. Until now, she'd been kept safe by her overprotective older brothers, but she was done with that. She wanted to do something meaningful with her life, and tonight that meant quite literally walking into the mouth of the dragon's den.

If my brothers figure out I'm here, they'd probably try to send me to some convent like it was the middle ages. The thought almost made Charlotte smile, despite the dangerous situation. Her brothers, Damien and Jason, were the experts at this sort of thing—well, not the seduction part, but the infiltration. They would know exactly how to handle something like a dragon shifter. But she'd never been a part of that secret supernatural hunter lifestyle. Until tonight.

If I bring home a Russian dragon, they'll have to admit I'm not just their kid sister anymore. Maybe then they'll let me join the Brotherhood instead of shutting me out.

But if she were being honest with herself, coming all the way to Moscow hadn't just been about proving her brothers wrong. It had been about seeing the man from the files she'd gotten from the Brotherhood of the Blood Moon's headquarters. The man she couldn't get out of her head. The man she planned to capture.

Her target was Rurik Barinov, youngest of the three remaining dragons in the Russian Imperial bloodline who controlled the western half of Russia. Pulling out her cell phone, she scanned the pictures she had of him, probably for the hundredth time. She'd been lucky enough to snap some shots of the surveillance photos they had of him on file.

He was gorgeous in a dangerous sort of way, with a strong jaw, bright green eyes, and wavy dark hair that was a little too long, making him look a bit like a pirate from those swoon-worthy romance novels she'd devoured as a teenager. Charlotte hadn't known men could look like that in real life, and she'd already had some seriously dirty thoughts about what he was like in bed. He'd been her first choice out of the three brothers to try to capture.

Rurik tended to wear leather jackets, jeans, and biker boots, and there was a long scar down one side of his face, which only made him look that much more dangerous. Her sexy biker dragon was too much of *everything*, and she had to admit getting close to him tonight was going to be one heck of a thrill. *God, there has to be something wrong with me. He's not my sexy biker. He's my target.* But she couldn't deny the fact that the idea of getting up close and personal with Rurik turned her on.

Keep your cool and focus on the mission. It was the tenth time she had to remind herself of that tonight.

This mission was strictly recon, though. She needed to get into Rurik's club, survey the scene, locate and observe him. Nothing more. She'd read the notes on the Brotherhood's dragon monitoring. They really just tried to keep an eye on the dragons' activities and not interfere but a few months ago two dragons had fought in a nightclub and a mortal woman had died. There were rumors of a coming dragon war between two families in Moscow and Damien and the other hunters were desperate to figure out how to stop the war. And it all came down to Rurik.

He'd been the dragon at the nightclub who'd survived by killing the other dragon from the rival family which had brought the dragon shifters in Russia to the brink of war. Damien had made a note in the file that if they could bring in Rurik, they could question him, determine whether the Brotherhood would have to intervene or not to prevent human casualties.

So far no one had been able to get close to Rurik, he never let any female agents get close enough to lure him to a location where he could be trapped, like a room with pure iron bars hidden in the walls. And bringing him by force would only result in danger to the agents and possibly innocent humans.

That's why I'm here alone. Rurik won't see me coming.

She grinned a little. She wore a light perfume she'd concocted that contained a bit of enhanced human pheromones. If it worked, she could catch his interest and then she'd go with him, rather than try to lure him off somewhere. And once she had him alone, she'd use her secret weapon to incapacitate him long enough to call in the Brotherhood to help her transport him to secure facility where he could be questioned safely.

The cabdriver hit the brakes as a car ahead of them swerved into their lane. Charlotte winced as she jerked forward and collided with the back seat of the cab.

"Sorry!" the driver muttered in heavily accented English. Then he flashed an obscene gesture at the driver ahead of them. At this rate, it would take them forever to reach the club where Rurik was supposed to be tonight.

Charlotte slid back in her seat and tried to still her jittery nerves. She would have been back in her little lab in Detroit, safe and sound, instead of here dragon hunting if it hadn't been for her friend Meg.

Meg Stratford, a hunter for the Brotherhood, had called her secretly to analyze a serum Meg had found in London. Charlotte had unraveled the chemical composition in a matter of days. The product she'd synthesized based off the sample Meg had given her should be able to mute a dragon's shifting abilities. It essentially made them human for a period of time depending on the dose, but it wasn't permanent. She'd made samples that would last around twenty-four hours on an average sized shifter.

But the drug was potentially dangerous. Not in terms of directly harming the shifters, but because of how easily it could be misused. In the wrong hands it would threaten the balance that existed between the various supernatural factions. Even certain members of the Brotherhood, known for their overzealous nature, couldn't be trusted with it. Meg had sworn her to secrecy, even from her own brothers.

A stab of guilt cut through Charlotte. She'd told Meg she needed more information on dragons to help her solve the mystery of the serum, but that wasn't true. The real reason she needed to know everything about dragons was because she planned to catch one to prove she was a worthy hunter just like her brothers, but didn't want to get herself killed in the process.

She'd created a batch of the dragon-dampening serum for herself, and had the vials tucked away safely in her hotel mini-fridge to use when she was ready. She went over the list of what she knew about dragons in her head as the taxi drove toward Rurik's nightclub, The Lair.

1. Dragons could grow old—really old, like thousands of years—but for most of their lives they resembled men and women in their mid-thirties.

2. There were more than a dozen breeds, including

Russian Imperials and Nordic ice dragons. Rivalries were common between many of them.

3. Dragons could breathe fire as well as control it.

4. They had protective thick hides with scales, and those scales were often used in magical spells.

5. Dragons could shift between their human and dragon forms in seconds.

6. They were completely obsessed with jewels.

7. They were sensitive to pure iron and could be contained and unable to shift if trapped in iron cells. They could also be injured while in dragon form while weapons of iron. In human form any weapon could hurt them but their healing rates were fast enough that only iron weapons could do lasting damage.

Charlotte studied the Moscow nightlife nervously as the taxicab came to a stop in front of The Lair nightclub. Being out of America for the first time in her life, she definitely wasn't used to the cultural differences. On the flight over she'd listened to some Russian language podcasts, trying to learn some phrases, but it gave her a headache. It didn't help that Russian was a notoriously difficult language, requiring a greater range of vocabulary just to reach a basic understanding. Luckily, the majority of the hotel staff and taxi drivers spoke English, something she was incredibly grateful for. However, once she stepped foot into that nightclub, she was positive it was going to be all Russian. The driver had warned her that this was a

Russian-only nightclub, off the beaten path from where tourists would go.

"Here is okay?" the driver asked.

"Yes, thank you." She slipped him a few hundred rubles and then got out of the cab. There were several men lingering at the entrance of the club, one of whom whistled when he caught sight of her.

She clutched her cell, which contained emergency number for the Brotherhood office in Saint Petersburg, hoping she wouldn't have to use it. *Please don't let this be a bad idea.* If things went poorly, she'd have to face her brothers and listen to them tell her "I told you so" about staying in Michigan, where life was safe but boring.

One of the men by the door said something to her in Russian, but she didn't understand him. She smiled but kept her head down as she brushed past them. One of the men slapped her ass as she passed by. She tensed and almost tripped.

Just stay cool, her inner voice warned her. She might not be a hunter like her brothers, but she'd taken enough self-defense classes to know how to take care of herself. If this guy wasn't careful, she'd kick in the balls so hard they'd snap up into his throat. But she couldn't afford to make a scene. She needed to stay calm and not call attention to herself.

Ignoring the harsh laughter of the men outside, she slipped into the dark club interior. The energetic techno dance music enveloped her, and the bass pounded so hard against the walls that she could feel it shake as she skirted the club's interior. It took a moment for her eyes to adjust, even with the flashing white lights and pulsing strobes. Fog filled the bottom of the club, hiding a clear view of the dance floor. Everywhere people were dancing, drinking, and laughing. It was a hedonistic gathering where pleasures ruled the night.

Charlotte clutched her slender purse and headed for the bar. A dark-haired man with an intricate neck tattoo of a wolf howling was flipping bottles and pouring drinks. He took one look at her and retrieved a large rounded glass, then poured a dark red wine in it. He slid it across the slick wood surface of the bar to her. He chuckled when she caught the glass, which glided smoothly into her waiting hand. Then she took a sip.

Wow. The red was soft and dark with a hint of oak and...cherry? Yes, cherry. She smiled at the man, who gave a roguish wink before he turned to see to his other customers. A bartender who guessed your style of drink... that was certainly interesting. A guy like that would kill in tips in America. She studied his wolf tattoo more closely. Was he a shifter? She'd heard from Meg over the years all sorts of things about shifters. Tribal tattoos were pretty popular among the wolves and the odds that a wolf shifter was working in a dragon shifter owned bar? Pretty high odds.

She watched the dancers on the floor for a while, scanning the room until she found what she was looking for. A back door. It probably led to some offices. That might be where she could find Rurik. But she had no plans to barge in there and look. She would stay here and wait. Hopefully, he would come out soon so she could start her reconnaissance.

The files she'd studied assured her that he always stuck close to Moscow and rarely went to his second residence, which was somewhere south in the country. She took another sip of her wine and looked back to the dancers. She froze. Three of the men from outside the club stood in front of her, watching her with wicked grins. The man who had slapped her ass was talking to her again in Russian.

"I'm sorry—I don't speak very much Russian," she told him in the best Russian she could manage and tried to turn back to the bar. One of them grabbed her from behind and dragged away from her seat.

"Let go of me!" She swung her purse, smacking him in the face. The heavy gold clasps thunked as they made contact with the man's nose. He cursed, clutching his face as he waved his other hand at his friends, who rushed her.

Oh shit! She dropped into a fighting stance, praying she wouldn't break an ankle in her low heels when she tried to roundhouse whoever made the first move on her. A man swung a meaty balled fist at her head, and she pulled herself back an instant before he would have clocked her. She countered, the man was too close for a roundhouse, but not a solid knee to the breadbasket. He dropped with a gasp, and Charlotte backed away, waiting for the next. But there were too many of them, and she doubted they'd oblige her by coming one at a time after that.

A deep bellowing shout thundered through the room, and sent the men scrambling away like rats.

Panting, she held her purse, which dangled on its chain from one of her hands. She then felt someone's eyes upon her, a gaze as tangible as a caress along her skin, making her shiver. She looked around for whoever had scared the men off. Her heart thumped in a panicked beat against her ribs when she saw who had rescued her, standing behind her.

Rurik Barinov. He looked dangerous and sexy in jeans and a black T-shirt and especially those biker boots. If she was being honest with herself, those boots played quite a role in her fantasies whenever she thought of him. Which was a really bad thing considering he was supposed to be her target, not the star of her most sensual daydreams.

"Are you all right?" he asked. His accent, a deep, rumbling, slightly growling tone, did funny things to her insides. For a second she couldn't speak—her brain had short-circuited.

"I..."

Rurik gently grasped her by the elbow. That got a reaction from her, as her first instinct was to pull back. But his response to this surprised her; he looked at her and said, "Please," while holding out his hand. Something about his voice disarmed her, and she allowed herself to be led away.

He took her into a dark, quiet alcove where the acoustics of the room couldn't reach them. He pressed her back against the wall and cupped her chin, lifting her face. His eyes, a beautiful green, swept over her from head to toe. She shivered as his thumb caressed her bottom lip.

"You're not hurt?" he asked.

She managed a nod.

He tilted his head, still studying her in that intense manner. "American?"

"Y—yes."

"You shouldn't come to a club like this alone. It is too dangerous for a flower such as you." He let go of her face, but he leaned in a few inches, inhaling deeply before he murmured something to himself in Russian.

"I'm not that delicate," she replied stiffly. Sure, she wasn't a kick-ass supernatural hunter like her brothers, but she wasn't *totally* helpless.

His lips curved into a crooked grin that made a storm of butterflies come to life in her stomach. "It is true. Some flowers have thorns, and you certainly showed yours." The dim lights and the way he stood half in shadow exposed the thin scar that swept down his face across his cheek. It had a distinctive slashing shape to it. Was it from another dragon's claw? She had to admit she was fascinated. The Brotherhood files on the Barinov dragons were slim. She wished she knew more about him, and she had a feeling she was about to.

"Yet I think you are more delicate than you realize,

little one." He reached up to brush the back of his fingers over her cheek. She shivered as a wave of arousal buzzed through her at his touch. She opened her mouth, even though she had no idea what she was going to say, but he placed a finger over her lips.

"Why don't you leave your purse with my bartender and come dance with me?" He was already tugging her away from the wall before she could argue. He slid her purse off her shoulder and tossed it at the tattooed man, who caught it in one hand and tucked it beneath the bar.

"Hey—"

"Shhh." Rurik pulled her against him as music wrapped around them, pulsing and thumping. His hands curled around her hips, the tips of his fingers just riding the edge of her ass as they began to dance. He moved smoothly with a rolling gait and the slide of his feet. She'd always been a terrible dancer, but with his hands and body guiding hers, he made it seem so easy. It was almost surreal, to be here with him, the lights of the club spinning around them and music pouring into her soul.

Is this real? Maybe I'm just dreaming about him again.

It wouldn't have been the first time since she'd seen his face in those files that she'd woken up in the dead of night, her heart racing and her body hungry for the touch of this man...this dragon.

Her plan to capture him was still on track. If anything, this could work to her advantage. But she could relax, enjoy herself for a few songs, couldn't she? Dancing was one of the few ways a man and a woman could speak to each other without words. Well, that and kissing. But she couldn't let him kiss her, not after she'd heard Meg's lecture about dragon pheromones. As a biochemist, she was well aware of the drugging influences of pheromones in some animals. She did not want to come under the influence of anything she couldn't control, biological or chemical. Part of her worried that he might have already exerted some kind of subtle influence over her. There were rumors that dragons could compel humans with a form of hypnotism.

"You are enjoying yourself?" he asked in her ear.

His hands drifted lower, cupping her ass. A new flash of arousal hit her, and she couldn't help but moan when he pressed closer to her. She was too aware of him, of his undeniable sexuality. At times like this it sucked being a virgin. She felt like a live volcano ready to blow whenever she got too close to someone with raw sexual chemistry like Rurik.

"Yes, this is fun!" she shouted over the music.

What the hell, right? Life is too short not to enjoy this....

She spun in his arms, grinding her backside against him. She watched the dancers around them. The club was modeled to resemble a cave, but it also had a hint of a dungeon about it. There were even cages with women dancing inside them. Iron-barred honest-to-God cages. For a second she pictured herself in one of those cages, Rurik outside of the bars, hungry to reach her, and yet knowing he had caught her. It was... Holy hell, it was so hot just to think about it.

"Want to give it a try?" Rurik's hand slid up her body from behind, not quite cupping her breast, but coming close.

"Try what?"

"The dancing cages. I can see that you're tempted."

She tried to shake her head, not wanting him to know she'd been way too turned on at the idea of him putting her in a cage. "No..."

He chuckled, his lips feathering against her ear. "Yes, you are."

She ducked her head, hair falling in front of her face, trying to hide from him. But he brushed it back, tucking it behind her ear and over her shoulder.

"Come." He led her toward one of the cages where a blonde girl was shaking to a type of dance rhythm that Charlotte would never be able to copy. He opened the cage door and jerked his head. The girl left immediately.

Rurik pushed her toward the cage. "Get in, little one." She stumbled, caught herself on the bars, and turned to face him as he closed the cage door. Then he leaned against the bar doors, his arm muscles flexing. He had *trapped* her in the cage.

"Now, dance for me, sweetheart." Rurik's green eyes met hers, and she seemed to spiral into them. Every worry, every self-conscious thought she'd ever had seemed to fade into the back of her mind.

"Dance for me. Show me your heart's desire." The words were his, but he hadn't spoken. It was as though she'd heard the words in her head. An irresistible compulsion to do exactly what he said came over her, almost as though she was drunk—only on words instead of alcohol.

Charlotte rolled her hips, feeling the beat of the music and letting it run through her blood like a current. She moved, spun, leaned against the bars and threw her head back, sending her hair in a cascade as she gave in to the wild part of herself. A part she'd always denied, ignored, or repressed.

All the while he watched, satisfied, the dragon with dark brown hair and emerald eyes. The green of his eyes was pure like uncut gemstones. His lips were parted, and his hands were white-knuckled on the bars. Was he restraining himself? Holding himself back? That only made Charlotte bolder, wilder. Dimly, she was aware that she was being very reckless, but she couldn't seem to stop.

I'm playing with fire. She just prayed she wouldn't get burned.

CHAPTER 2

Stars would fall to their knees at his compelling vision.
– Rainer Maria Rilke

"COME IN WITH ME," SHE SAID, KNOWING HE WOULD hear her despite the pounding music. A dragon's hearing was keener than any human's.

They stared at each other, the bass of the music making her heart thud fast and heavy against her ribs. His gaze was one that could pull a woman in and drown her with its promise of dark, delicious things. Charlotte could feel every cell in her body hum with sexual tension. Would he join her? Would he touch her again in a way that made her forget her very name?

Please...please make me forget everything but you. It was

dangerous, but she wanted it, wanted to lose herself in this moment, lose herself in him.

Rurik flung the cage door open and entered, clanging it shut behind him. She swallowed hard as the reality of what she'd just asked came true. She was trapped in a cage with a dragon—ancient, powerful, accountable to none but themselves—and this one was making her legs shake as he kept looking at her as though he wanted to eat her.

He spun her around to face away from him, and she gripped the bars, bracing herself. He pressed his body against hers from behind and nuzzled her neck. She moaned when he began to kiss her throat and bare shoulder. It was as though he knew just where the sensitive spots were on her skin that electrified her entire body. Their bodies still swayed to the music, but everything had changed. She wasn't focused on capturing him, not now—she could barely think straight. All she wanted was to stay close to him, to keep touching him wherever she could. She needed to feel his body caging hers and his mouth and hands on her body. She'd heard people talk about animal magnetism, but *holy shit*, this was beyond that.

They weren't dancing anymore—they were slowly grinding against each other, the sensual movements almost too much to bear. She was so close to danger, so close to the one thing she knew she couldn't let happen.

I don't care. I should...but I don't. I want him...

His right hand touched her right knee, sliding up her leg beneath her skirt. When he reached her panties, he brushed a fingertip along her satin-covered slit. She whimpered at the explosive reaction her body had at that single caress. Rurik bit her earlobe, and a zing of pleasure shot down her body straight to her clit. She knew people were all around them, probably watching them and she couldn't find it in here to care, not when he was making her feel so wild, so out of control in the best way.

"Tell me your name," he whispered in her ear.

She struggled to focus. "Charlotte..." She wouldn't tell him her last name. She wasn't stupid enough to use her brothers' last name. Even through the fog of her desire, she was able to remember that.

"Charlotte." Her name rolled off his tongue in that decadent accent, and she shivered. "My name is Rurik." He flicked his tongue into the shell of her ear. She jerked at a new bolt of arousal shot through her.

"I'm going to kiss you now, little one," he warned, and she nodded, wanting, *needing* his mouth on hers. It didn't matter that it was breaking her promise or that she knew her brothers would kill her for kissing a dragon. She had to kiss him. Something inside her demanded it with a force that she couldn't stop. He turned her around to face him, chest to chest, their bodies still pressed tight together. The bars of the cage dug into her back, but she didn't care. All that mattered was this slow, delicious burning moment leading up to his kiss.

He lowered his head and their lips brushed, and then he kissed her. *Hard.* It was the kind of kiss that made a rational, sensible person like Charlotte lose her mind and forget her name. It was a kiss out of her darkest fantasies, one that she would have died to experience. He moved his lips over hers with a hint of roughness that kept her on her toes, as though at any moment he could take things to the next level. It left her dancing on a razor's edge of fear and excitement. He curled her hair in his hand, fisting the strands while he held her captive. His other hand gripped her hip, his firm hand keeping her right where she was. *A dragon's prisoner.*

The music around them changed from one song to another, and then another, and yet neither she nor Rurik wanted to come up for air.

It was strange, but the more he kissed her, the more she had this funny feeling that she could hear whispers— soft, dark growling sounds deep inside her head. Like a man murmuring dirty, erotic words to her, but she couldn't explain how she was hearing it. It must have been her imagination. Were all kisses supposed to be like this? Her previous boyfriends had never made her feel like she was on the verge of such sweet madness.

When he finally broke their mouths apart and pressed his forehead to hers, she closed her eyes, hands gripping his shoulders as she tried to slow her racing heart. His muscles were taut beneath her palms, and she could feel the heat radiating off him. It didn't soothe the aching need her body now had for him. For the first time in her life, she understood what her friends had joked about when they'd talked about wanting a man so much they were ready to beg for it. She was *ready* to beg.

"Club's going to close soon," he said, his voice a low rumble.

"What?" she asked, distracted by his intimate embrace and how much she didn't want this moment to end. His body was warm, and the leather of his jacket smelled so good. She wanted to bury herself against him, rub her cheek against his chest like a cat in heat. Her lips felt bruised, swollen from his kisses, and she licked them.

"We've been at this for over an hour, little one. I would like to continue, but I must close down the club." A surprisingly rueful smile twisted his lips.

Reality crashed down around her. An hour? She had spent an *hour* making out with a dragon shifter in a club. A dragon she knew was dangerous. The dragon she'd come to capture... God, no wonder her brothers wouldn't let her become a hunter. She'd walked right into the lion's den—er...dragon's lair—and had all but jumped his bones. Mortification heated her face as she tried to shake the lingering flames of desire that his kisses had left burning within her.

"I should go." She released his shoulders and looked away, but his green eyes kept drawing her focus back to them. She raised a hand to her kiss-swollen lips and almost smiled but had to shake herself to remember that this was dangerous to have gone this far.

He cupped her chin and forced her to meet his gaze.

"Will you wait for me? I will close the club. Then we

can go to dinner." The earnest desire in his words made her hesitate. Could she stay near him and not lose her head again?

"Please, my little rose, do not make me beg." He winked at her, and the harsh lines of his scarred face seemed to fade into boyish playfulness as he teased her.

"Eat? It's after midnight!" she said, half laughing.

"An early breakfast then."

She knew the logical thing to do was to thank him for the amazing evening and leave—but she couldn't.

If I can keep control over my hormones, maybe I can learn more about him. That's what a smart hunter would do, right?

She needed to know more about him, learn his weaknesses if she was going to figure out a safe way to inject him with the serum and call the Brotherhood to come and get him. It was incredibly important that they find out how close the dragons were to war with each other and Rurik was the key. He feathered another kiss over her lips, and the last ounce of her resistance crumbled.

"An early breakfast it is." She grinned up at him foolishly. Maybe it was okay to play the bad girl and do something wild and reckless. Just once.

"Excellent. Come with me." He led her to the back of the bar and sat her down on a stool, then waved over the bartender. "Victor, please keep this lovely woman company while I close up."

The bartender spoke to Rurik in Russian, and Rurik responded with a chuckle and nodded. Victor handed

Charlotte a fresh glass of wine. Rurik leaned in close and playfully tugged a lock of her hair before he walked through the club's dwindling crowd and disappeared through the back door she'd spied earlier.

"My boss really likes you," the bartender said. His accent was heavy, but his English was decent.

She took a deep sip of her wine. "You think so?"

The bartender chuckled. "He danced in a cage with you. He never does that with other girls."

Charlotte wasn't sure why that mattered, but God, it had been so hot, so *fucking hot*. She was wet just thinking about it. Clamping her thighs together, she tried not to think about what it said about her that a simple make out session had gotten to her like that. But then, there had been nothing simple about that make out.

She finished her wine and watched the club close down, the bouncers escorting the last of the partiers out and locking up. The lights dimmed, and the fog cleared from the floors. Only then did the back door open and Rurik come out. He still wore his black-and-red motorcycle jacket, but he held two helmets and came over to her.

"Ready?"

"We're not taking a car?" she asked as she took one of the black helmets from him.

"I do not take my car to the club, I only have my motorcycle." He held out a hand. She didn't have to go with him—she could see it in his eyes—but there was a longing there, a need that matched her own. She took a deep breath and placed her hand in his.

The bartender handed Charlotte her purse, and she let Rurik lead her out onto the street. A sleek black motorcycle with dark green trim was parked on the curb. He stopped and turned to her.

"The helmet is for you." He helped her put it on, then straddled the bike and started the engine. Rain began to fall around them, misting the streets that were still warm from traffic. Charlotte shivered, glad she'd brought a coat. She pulled it on and slid onto the back seat behind Rurik and wrapped her arms around his waist.

"Hold on tight, little one. I'll see you are dry and warm as soon as I can." He patted her hands and then gunned the engine. The motorcycle shot forward as they sped into the brightly lit Moscow streets. Rain made the lights from the cars seem like foggy halos. She watched the world around her blur as Rurik guided his bike into the traffic. He was fearless, flawless, and sexy as hell. She never thought she'd have a thing for motorcycles, but tonight she totally did.

There was something magical about the way they had to work together, their bodies leaning in the same direction as he took sweeping curves for turns. She felt connected to him in a way she hadn't expected. They were one being while they rode together, a single blur on the streets of Moscow. For the first time in her life she felt bonded to another person. A person who was a danger to humans, a person she had every intention of betraying when she used the serum on him and called in the Brotherhood for a containment team. Charlotte swallowed down the uncomfortable burn in her throat at just thinking about what had to be done. But not right now. Not yet.

Rurik finally stopped in front of an expensive-looking glass building and helped her off.

A young man in a valet's uniform rushed out, and Rurik tossed him the keys before he took off his helmet. Charlotte removed her helmet, and the young man collected both hers and Rurik's.

She gazed up at the bright lights of the beautiful glass exterior. It looked more like a high end apartment building. "This doesn't look like a restaurant."

"That's because it isn't. Nothing good is open this time of the morning. This is where I live."

"Here?" She quelled the flutter of nerves at the thought of going up to his apartment and focused instead on the fact that the building was classy, refined, and didn't match the gritty biker vibe Rurik put off. Yet this was exactly the opportunity she needed. He would feel safe at his own home and lower his guard.

He laughed and took her hand, the moment so natural that she didn't pull away. "Of course. Did you think I would live somewhere else?"

Blushing, she shrugged. "I don't honestly know. This building is beautiful." She marveled at how well their hands fit together and how warm his palm was. They walked through the lobby and Rurik took her to a set of gold-painted elevator doors. Inside, he removed a black keycard from his wallet and swiped it through a scanner next to the buttons.

"I thought we were getting breakfast?" she asked.

"We are. In my apartment." He thumbed the button for the tenth floor, and the elevator doors closed.

"But—" she started to object. She'd agreed to food, nothing else.

"Don't tell me you are afraid? You are safe enough with me." A mischievous twinkle in his eyes sent her pulse racing.

"I'm not afraid, but you changed things. You can't do that." She protested a little, letting him feel that he was the one who was safe, the one in charge. So far so good...

He curled an arm around her waist and tugged her close. "Of course I can. I'm the one in control." She pressed her palms on his chest in an effort to either push him away or touch him. She wasn't really sure.

"Rurik..."

He grinned. "I love it when you say my name." He leaned in and nuzzled her neck. "And you will say my name many times before the night is over."

That should have scared her, but it didn't. From the moment she'd met, she wasn't afraid of the dragon side of him—she was more afraid of the man, of how much he affected her. Yet she wasn't able to turn away. The pull between them, at least for her, was so strong that she stared at him, mesmerized, unable to speak. He didn't seem to want to say anything either. He held her close, their bodies touching, their faces inches apart.

Would it be so bad to lean in for a kiss? Just one more? Her resistance wavered, and she was giving in—

Ding! The elevator doors slid open with a chime.

"This is my floor," he announced, the words simple, yet she heard the offer in his voice, the choice of getting off with him or staying inside the safety of the elevator.

"For the record," she began, blushing, "I do not go home with guys...like *ever*." She bit her lip when he smiled at her.

"Then I'm honored to be the first, little rose." He towered over her and stole a quick, hard kiss. There was only one door in the hallway on the floor, and Rurik led her to it. He turned the knob without using a key or keycard.

"You don't lock it?"

Rurik gave a shrug of one shoulder. "It's unnecessary. I own the whole floor."

As they stepped inside, Charlotte gaped. It was a huge set of rooms with high ceilings and modern furnishings. This place was a lot like a hotel, though a pricey one. There were glass chandeliers and dark leather couches. It was a mixture of various forms masculine luxury, right down to the blue diamond fireplace against the interior wall of the living room. The windows were floor to ceiling, giving the impression that she could take a leap out of the building and fly. Which was not a good thing. They got closer to the windows as he took her to the kitchen, and Charlotte's breathing kicked up.

Rurik turned to face her. "What's wrong?" he asked, reading her panic.

"I have a thing about heights." She nodded at the windows.

His dark chuckle momentarily distracted her from her fear. "Afraid of heights? Whatever will I do with you?" He winked and then picked up a slim black remote from the granite countertop of the kitchen, aiming it at the nearest windows. Black screens came down, turning the windows into walls. Charlotte relaxed, and her muscles, which had tensed, began to relax.

"Better?" Rurik asked.

"Much."

"Have a seat. I'll order some food." He nodded to the table. She sat down, kicking off her heels. She rubbed her sore feet and watched him pull his cell phone out of his back pocket. He dialed a number and spoke rapidly, then hung up and turned to her.

"Food will be here soon. Would you like another drink?"

Why not? She was still feeling a bit buzzed from the club, and she didn't want that relaxed feeling to go away just yet.

"Sure." She pointed and flexed her toes and blushed

when she realized he was watching her. "I'm not used to wearing heels." In the lab, she'd always worn sneakers.

"I never understand how you females squeeze into those dresses or stand in those shoes, but I certainly won't complain because the end result is..." He waved a hand at her body, his eyes heating with open appreciation.

She raised one brow, wondering if he'd finish that sentence. He didn't, but the heat in his eyes assured her that he was more than pleased with how she looked. Rather than be embarrassed, she felt emboldened and sexy. Was this how a woman was supposed to feel around a man she liked? He made her feel beautiful and attractive, and she loved it.

"So, if you do not go home with men like this, why me?" Rurik poured a glass of wine for her and a glass of bourbon for himself. He watched her take a sip before he raised his own glass to his lips. Charlotte swallowed, unsure what to say. The truth was more complicated than she cared to admit.

Because you're sexy as hell and I can't think rationally around you? Because I want to know if you make love as dirty and sinfully as you kiss? Because I'm here to capture you and bring you to my brothers because you might be the key to stopping a dragon war?

None of those were safe answers, and she had to try to play it safe—at least enough to keep him from discovering her true purpose.

"I guess there's something about the way you kiss," she finally admitted.

He laughed, the sound dark and forbidden in the best possible way. He removed his leather jacket and tossed it on the counter. He walked over to the table, but didn't sit. Instead, he cocked his hip and took another slow drink as he watched her. Charlotte fixated on his throat as he swallowed and how he licked his lips when he set the glass down. She missed those lips already, wanted them against her own, her skin, her...*everything*.

"What are you doing here in Russia? It's a very long way from home, is it not?"

"It is." She had practiced her story, knowing it was best to stay vague but at the same time keep as much truth as possible. "I'm a biochemist from Michigan. I came here for a vacation." She smiled a little. In a way it was a vacation. A vacation from her controlling brothers.

"A biochemist?" He finished his bourbon and took a seat next to her at the table. "You don't look like a biochemist."

"Yeah. Everybody expects me to be constantly wearing the lab coat and glasses and be stuck in a lab." And that's exactly what she had been until Meg had called to consult her about the shift-repressing drug. She tried to turn the focus back on him. "So, you own a nightclub?"

"I do." He reached across the table and stroked a fingertip along her arm as he spoke. "My older brother is a respectable businessman. My other brother, well, he's a..."

Rurik snorted as though whatever he was thinking was amusing.

"He's a what?" she asked.

His green eyes burned into hers with mischief. "An international jewel thief."

"What?" Her heart jolted. "A jewel thief?" Was he kidding? There hadn't been anything in the files on that. All she knew of the brother Mikhail was that he'd lived in England for a few centuries and had recently gotten into a deadly fight with an English dragon. It was part of the reason the serum had come into the Brotherhood's possession. But international jewel thief? Rurik had to be kidding...right? She started to pull away, but he curled his fingers around her arm, possessive but gentle.

"Afraid of me again? I never promised that I was a good man. My family, well, we are quite the opposite, especially me." His words rolled along her skin, giving her goosebumps. They scared her, but not enough to make her run. She couldn't let him know she knew what he really was. She had to pretend that she didn't know what he was talking about.

"Are you in the Mafia, the Russian Bratva or something?" Yeah, *that* sounded like a proper question to ask. No way that could get her in trouble. Sheesh.

The hard smile he flashed her sent a wave of heat through her. *Apparently, I have a thing for really bad boys.* It was not a comfort to learn this about herself, certainly not right now. No wonder her brothers kept a close eye on her.

"The Bratva? Those fools have nothing on my family."

That was the truth. She'd spent the last few weeks reviewing everything she could about the Barinov family, and they had survived countless numbers of attempts by the Bratva to rub them out or marginalize their power. The smart ones quickly learned to leave the Barinovs alone. The dumb ones didn't last very long.

I really shouldn't be here doing this. But she had to prove that she wasn't a helpless little girl anymore, and the best way to do that was by bringing them the one creature that scared even her brothers. More importantly, she would be bringing them the one creature that could stop a war between dragon clans and save innocent human lives.

"So you're a Russian club-owning badass," she said.

His lips twisted into a crooked grin. "Something like that."

"Does that mean you're dangerous?" She was teasing, but she also wanted to see if he would argue he wasn't. He'd already admitted he wasn't a good guy, but she was curious to see how far he'd open up about himself to a "mere mortal" who wasn't supposed to know what he was.

"I—" The apartment door chimed.

Rurik growled to himself but left her to answer the door. A man in a wait staff uniform rolled in a cart with covered serving trays. He paid the man, who set the dishes on the table and promptly rolled the cart out.

"What kind of apartment building has room service?" she asked right before he lifted the lid to reveal two steaks with asparagus and mashed potatoes. She'd always loved a good steak.

"I own this building, and I like the convenience, so I had a skilled kitchen built in. My tenants are wealthy, and happily pay for room service when they want it. I hope this is all right. I assume it's a more American fare?" He passed her a white napkin rolled over silverware.

"Yes, this is perfect, thank you," she said. "So, if you own the building, I take it the nightclub business pays well?"

"Well enough, but my family has always had money, and my oldest brother is quite good at investing."

Now that made sense. The Brotherhood's files on dragons indicated that they seemed to have a good source of wealth from collecting jewels over the centuries. They were obviously shrewd investors too. She opened her mouth to ask another question, but he cut her off gently.

"Enough about me. I'm more curious about *you*." Rurik took a bite of his steak before continuing. "Why visit Russia? Surely Russia in the middle of winter is not a good vacation spot. I could picture you on a tropical island in a teeny red bikini." He winked.

Charlotte blushed. "I'm not really the bikini type." Being curvy, she'd always felt too self-conscious to wear something so revealing. The tight-fitting dress she wore now was bad enough, but there was no way she would wear a bikini in public.

"Then why Russia?" he persisted.

Charlotte tried to share part of the truth. "I've always loved history, even though I didn't get a degree in it. I wanted to see the Winter Palace while it snowed, but the forecast for the trip seems to indicate only rain, so I decided not to travel to Saint Petersburg." She'd loved learning about the czars and the whole Anastasia mystery when she was younger.

Rurik's rakish grin faded, and his eyes softened with shadows of sorrow.

"The Winter Palace is quite beautiful when it snows. We used to have the most wonderful winter balls there. Outside, the windows would glow with gold light, and you could hear music drifting across the ice and snow. In a world of white and heavy winter silence, the palace was brimming with colorful life."

His gaze turned distant. He seemed to be seeing something past her, many years ago. He probably didn't even realize the slip he'd made by admitting he'd been there, when the palace had hosted balls. Charlotte couldn't imagine what it must be like to live as long they did. She wanted to ask him. She had so many questions about his life as a dragon, but she couldn't reveal herself. Not yet. It might get her killed.

Rurik focused on her again. "I think I know someone powerful enough to summon snow if that is what you wish." He reached into his pocket and pulled out a cell phone. He dialed a number and waited. A few seconds later he spoke.

"Grigori..." He grinned at her. "Make it snow in Saint Petersburg tomorrow, say around noon? I'm taking a lovely young woman to the Winter Palace." He listened to Grigori, the oldest brother, Charlotte knew from the files. "Thank you." They hung up. "Grigori will make it snow for you."

Charlotte laughed, pretending to assume he was only teasing her. But she couldn't help but wonder if what he was saying was possible. Nordic ice dragons were able to manipulate precipitation. But Grigori, Rurik, and their third brother, Mikhail, were Russian Imperials. Perhaps Grigori would call in a favor?

It occurred to her that while she was here she wanted to gather as much data as she could from Rurik. She would have to collect blood samples from him both before and after the serum was administered because she wanted to see if he shared anything in common with the latest research coming from studies on Komodo dragons.

Researchers at George Mason University had created a synthetic version of a peptide found in the blood of Komodo dragons. They had dubbed it DRGN-1. DRGN-1 had proved to be tough against microbes. Bacteria stuck together to create biofilms that attached to surfaces and help to protect themselves during an infection. Even infected wounds healed faster with DRGN-1, and the layers of skin were rehabilitated. If Rurik and other shifters had similar peptide structures in their blood, it might explain how their bodies aged so slowly and healed so quickly.

I could change the world, make it a better place. It eased the guilt of what she was planning to do, but only just. She was lucky that Rurik distracted her with his company.

They ate the rest of their dinner, conversation flowing easily between them. She was surprised how much he seemed at ease with her and she with him. He was charming, more so than she ever expected of a nightclub owner who rode a motorcycle, but then, he was more than a thousand years old and had been born into an age of chivalry.

"So, your two brothers..." She pushed her empty plate away and waited to see if he would talk more about them.

"Grigori and Mikhail." A glint of humor made his eyes sparkle. "Both are my elders. Grigori is the head of the family. He only recently married. He and his wife are already expecting a dr—a child, I mean." He corrected himself, but Charlotte suspected he'd almost said *drakeling,* the dragon shifter term for children.

"That's wonderful." She leaned back in her chair, relaxing. His responding grin took over his features.

"It is. I cannot wait to see that child run circles around my uptight brother."

"And Mikhail...the international jewel thief and man of mystery?" She tried to sound teasing. Most women wouldn't stay for a midnight snack in a man's apartment when he told her that his brother was a criminal.

His expression was suddenly shadowed with sadness. He played with his empty bourbon glass, rolling it between his palms. "Mikhail was gone for a long time. Our father made a rash decision by disowning Mikhail and preventing him from returning to Russia, but my father is gone now. Mikhail is finally home. He too has settled down and married. He kidnapped a gemologist when he stole his jewels." A flash of humor was in his eyes again. "It worked out in the end."

She laughed, playing along with his comments as though he was still telling tall tales.

"And you? Any siblings? Any overprotective brothers I should know about?" he asked.

Charlotte was caught off guard by the alarmingly accurate query. A nervous giggle escaped her.

"Yeah, actually, I do have two very protective brothers. Neither of them know I'm here." Now that was certainly the truth.

"They wouldn't approve of you being here?"

"Not in Russia. Not anywhere, really. I've never even left the United States before, if you can believe it. They would flip out if they knew I'd come here alone."

His brows rose. "You're alone in Moscow? No friends? No one?"

She shook her head very slowly. "No one."

A dark scowl stole over his features. "That is very

dangerous. Moscow is a dangerous place. You had a taste of it tonight at the club. I love my country, but it has a heart of darkness beneath the glittering surface. You aren't safe here alone." He rose from the table and towered over her again, his eyes darkening. She backed up even more as he invaded her space.

"Do you understand? A man like me could take you, little rose. He could make you his, possess you in every way, and you would have no chance of escape. No way to get home. No recourse. No salvation. A man like me would be very tempted by an innocent young creature like you." His words softened into a deep, threatening purr.

She peered up at him from beneath her lashes, trying to still her shivering. "But you won't... right?"

He curled his fingers under her chin, lifting her face up to his. "Are you quite sure about that?"

Take home Rurik today! Grab this sexy Russian here!

TURN THE PAGE TO READ ABOUT THE CHEAPSIDE Hoard Jewels which inspired Mikhail's heist and Piper's obsession!

THE CHEAPSIDE HOARD JEWELS
A BRIEF AND HOPEFULLY INTERESTING HISTORICAL NOTE

Often my stories are born in ordinary places, like the back of a crowded coffee shop or nestled in a midst of a busy library by my house. But every now and then a story is born in a place of magic. For me, Mikhail's story was born and written in a wintry castle in Southern France in November 2016.

I was staying in the castle with a group of fellow writers. As we shivered by the fireside and watched a family of feral cats play upon the stone terrace in the winter sunlight I was struck by the light glinting over the window panes and how it made me think of diamonds...the kind of diamonds a dragon would hunger to steal and hide in his cave. Thus Mikhail's story was born. My dragon jewel thief then would need to steal a hoard of impressive jewels and as luck would have it, history had already shown me the way.

Some months before I'd seen a book that discussed the history of the Cheapside Hoard and I immediately knew this cache of rare jewels would be my inspiration. Every single jewel mentioned in the book (with the exception of the Dragon Heart Stone) are completely real and modeled off the hoard's actual jewels.

Now for a bit of history...

The Cheapside Hoard dated back to the late 16th and early 17th centuries, discovered in 1912 by workmen using a pickaxe to excavate in a cellar at 30–32 Cheapside in London, on the corner with Friday Street. They found a buried wooden box containing more than 400 pieces of Elizabethan and Jacobean jewelry, including rings, brooches and chains, with bright colored gemstones and enameled gold settings, together with toadstones, cameos, scent bottles, fan holders, crystal tankards and a salt cellar.

Most of the hoard is now in the Museum of London, with some items held by the British Museum and the Victoria and Albert Museum.

The hoard demonstrates the international trade in luxury goods in the period, including gemstones from sources across South America, Asia and Europe: emerald from Colombia, topaz and amazonite from Brazil; spinel, iolite, and chrysoberyl from Sri Lanka, Indian diamond, Burmese ruby, Afghan lapis lazuli, Persian turquoise, pearls from Bahrain, peridot from the Red Sea; Bohemian and Hungarian opal, garnet, and amethyst.

Relatively few pearls have survived in good condition after being buried for approximately 350 years.

Large stones were frequently set in box-bezels on enamelled rings. Most of the gemstones are cabochon cut, but there are a few with more modern faceted cuts, including rose cut and star cut. A particularly large Colombian emerald, originally the size of an apple, had been hollowed out to accommodate a Swiss watch movement dated to around 1600, signed by G. Ferlite.

The items include a Byzantine gemstone cameo, a cameo of Queen Elizabeth I, an emerald parrot, and some fake gemstones made of carved and dyed quartz. A small red intaglio stone seal bears the arms of William Howard, 1st Viscount Stafford, dating the burial of the hoard between his ennoblement in November 1640 and the Great Fire of London in September 1666, which destroyed the buildings above. Most of the gold is the "Paris touch" standard of 19.2 carats (80 per cent pure).

Each piece of the hoard is fascinating and unique. Like this emerald salamander brooch below.

It's exactly the kind of hoard a dragon like Mikhail would want to steal. *wink

OTHER TITLES BY LAUREN SMITH

Historical

The League of Rogues Series

Wicked Designs

His Wicked Seduction

Her Wicked Proposal

Wicked Rivals

Her Wicked Longing

His Wicked Embrace (coming March 2018)

The Earl of Pembroke (coming March 2018)

His Wicked Secret (coming soon)

The Seduction Series

The Duelist's Seduction

The Rakehell's Seduction

The Rogue's Seduction (coming March 2018)

Standalone Stories

Tempted by A Rogue
Sins and Scandals
An Earl By Any Other Name
A Gentleman Never Surrenders
A Scottish Lord for Christmas

Contemporary
The Surrender Series
The Gilded Cuff
The Gilded Cage
The Gilded Chain
Her British Stepbrother
Forbidden: Her British Stepbrother
Seduction: Her British Stepbrother
Climax: Her British Stepbrother

Paranormal
Dark Seductions Series
The Shadows of Stormclyffe Hall
The Love Bites Series
The Bite of Winter
Brotherhood of the Blood Moon Series
Blood Moon on the Rise (coming soon)
Brothers of Ash and Fire
Grigori: A Royal Dragon Romance
Mikhail: A Royal Dragon Romance
Rurik: A Royal Dragon Romance

Sci-Fi Romance

Cyborg Genesis Series

Across the Stars (coming soon)

329

ABOUT THE AUTHOR

Lauren Smith is an Oklahoma attorney by day, author by night who pens adventurous and edgy romance stories by the light of her smart phone flashlight app. She knew she was destined to be a romance writer when she attempted to re-write the entire *Titanic* movie just to save Jack from drowning. Connecting with readers by writing emotionally moving, realistic and sexy romances no matter what time period is her passion. She's won multiple awards in several romance subgenres including: New England Reader's Choice Awards, Greater

Detroit BookSeller's Best Awards, and a Semi-Finalist award for the Mary Wollstonecraft Shelley Award.

To Connect with Lauren, visit her at:
www.laurensmithbooks.com
lauren@laurensmithbooks.com